Tempt Me

BOOK II OPERATION SERIES

Christina James

Operation: Tempt Me

Published by Valerie Harris

Cover by Angela Anderson, Angela Anderson Design
Interior layout by www.formatting4U.com

ISBN: 978-1-938799-01-3

Previously published by The Wild Rose Press under *Operation: Tempt Me by Christina James.*

To contact see www.christinajamesauthor.com

Dedication

To Courtney and Scott, my wonderful children
who amaze me more each day.
To Angelo who helped me find true love.
And to the men and women who serve
in the military…thank you for all you do.

Prologue

If he didn't touch her, Miller would die.

The vision of the woman that haunted his dreams nightly wouldn't fade away tonight. Instead, she hovered above him, only visible from the waist up. Long, dark hair flowed around her in a wild, sensual halo. Lush, pink lips beckoned for his kisses. The sexy smile she tossed him aroused him more. Her breasts filled the tight blouse, her cleavage spilling over the satin material.

His cock hardened, constrained inside his pants, begging to plunge into that pretty mouth of hers.

Miller fought the urge to burst through the dream and capture the temptress. Did she know she played with fire? Driving him wild with desire was a sure way to get bent over and fucked until she exploded with his name on her tongue. His hands reached for her, but like always, she faded away, disappearing into blackness.

Fuck!

Pain tore through Miller's chest as he woke and shook the grogginess from his head. Losing her beauty was akin to having his heart ripped from his chest and stomped on. Each time she visited him on this mission, she stayed a little longer than the last. Tonight there was something different about her, her features taking a more definite form, but still he couldn't see her face clear enough to determine if he could recognize her.

Sitting up on his cot, he rubbed sleep from his eyes and slowly opened them. Darkness surrounded him in the tent he shared with four fellow Navy SEALs. Their mission in the middle of a fucking Middle Eastern desert had deprived him of comfort for too long. A decent night's sleep in a real bed instead of on the rickety cot would do wonders for him.

He stood, attempting to be as quiet as possible so he wouldn't have to take any shit from the others for waking them. With a big gulp of the bottled water he kept on the side of his sleeping area, Miller quenched his dry throat, but his head still spun. Images of the sexy woman floated in and out of his vision until he shook his head to lose them. He couldn't risk seeing anything but the real thing, not when his enemies surrounded the area, probably watching him even now in the dark of night.

Miller cupped his hand, poured water in it to splash onto his face before setting the bottle back down. Who was this woman who shared his nights but never his bed? Oh, he knew for a fact that he had never bedded the beauty. Hell, he'd remember that mouth, those lips, her touch. Never had a woman kept his attention long enough to dream of her. So where the hell did she come from? Talk about aggravating the shit out of a man, edging him closer to insanity.

Miller needed to take a piss. Grabbing his rifle, he stalked to the entrance of the tent without a sound. A brief perimeter scan showed no obvious enemies in the dark of night, but they lurked somewhere in the shadows and the surrounding volatile land. He stepped out from the place he'd called home for the past five weeks and whistled.

Cade Granville stepped from the darkness into the slit of moonlight, suited in full body armor and helmet, his rifle held firmly, and greeted him with a smirk. “Daly, you looking to relieve me?”

“Fuck no. Dream on,” Miller said, walking toward the giant cactus that had been elected as their outhouse.

“Asshole. I hate doing surveillance rounds. Bored stiff.”

“Better than getting a bullet in your ass, Granville,” he said, stopping behind the prickly desert bush, his dream induced hard-on making completion almost impossible, his thoughts still consumed with the mystery woman from his dreams. What he wouldn’t give right now for the privacy to stroke his cock to thoughts of her and relieve the pressure within his balls.

Goddamn fucking mission! Man can’t even jerk off in peace. Irritated with himself for being so obsessed with his mystery dream woman, Miller zipped his pants.

Maybe it was the extreme boredom of this mission that his mind kept wandering to the gorgeous woman. Normally, his team was entrenched in fighting and pursuit of the enemy but not this time. All they could do for this stint was sit back and observe…and wait. Wait to be attacked or wait to find their man. Too much quiet time meant too much thinking for Miller. Damn, if he could get some decent sleep then he wouldn’t mind so much.

Striding back toward Cade, he grumbled, “Gonna take in some air. Be over there a few minutes. Don’t shoot me, fool.”

“What air?” Cade said with a laugh. “Haven’t

felt a breeze at night since we've been here. Only blessing is less heat than the hundred thirty degrees in the day."

Miller didn't reply, just walked to the tent and stood on the side, staring up at the black sky dotted with bright stars and a half moon. Cade was a great guy. All his team members were. They were more like brothers than fellow soldiers. Hell, they had to be if Miller trusted them with his life every day of their active tour.

He rubbed the mermaid tattoo on his arm, replicated from his nightly dreams over the past year. "I know you're out there somewhere, darlin'. I'm damn sure gonna find you some day," he whispered into the night.

Imagining all of the hot sex he would have when he found the woman who lived in his imagination, Miller smiled, his cock aching with need. "Gonna spank your ass for haunting my sleep."

Oh, hell yeah. He owed her big time for torturing his dick.

Chapter One

Cambrie Brasher sat across from her boss. The scrawny older man, dressed in plaid pants and yellow dress shirt, waved a fistful of papers. Who the hell wore plaid pants any more? Cambrie cringed, the ugly outfit gave her a headache.

"You're not good for this library's needs, Miss Brasher." Mr. Hackler's harsh tone made her jump in her seat.

"Excuse me?" Her cheeks warmed with her embarrassment. What was his problem now?

"We need someone who can win us that hundred thousand dollar federal grant offered by the Veterans Affairs Department. If we don't get that then they'll be nothing or no one to keep these doors open. Maddyville will lose the only library left around these parts for fifty miles," Mr. Hackler complained, his voice quivering with nervousness.

The old man had always been eccentric, but this was over the top even for him.

Cambrie cleared her throat and kept her gaze on his. "Mr. Hackler, I'm sure if you explain what you need, then I will do what is required. I have a masters in English and know this library inside and out. I can write a very decent proposal on why Maddyville should receive the grant."

He sighed. "It's not about writing proposals. I can do that, Miss Brasher."

Now he confused her. "Then I'm not sure I understand what you need me to do."

"Get this library the recognition it needs with the Veterans Affairs Department. We have to show the town's support for our soldiers and not just by hanging yellow ribbons and singing patriotic songs. A member of our staff must lead by example and it cannot be me as the director. It has to be a librarian who can prove this foundation supports our troops in other ways than what I just mentioned. That's the requirements for the grant. And you happen to be our only librarian."

How this man ever became Director of Library Services was beyond her. He didn't make a lick of sense and she'd already wasted twenty minutes in here when she wanted to get back to her cataloging project. Computerizing the library's antiquated files had taken her six months already. With autumn approaching and the busy holiday season around the corner, Cambrie wanted to complete the improvements and add it to her list of accomplishments before she started planning the holiday events the library hosted.

Cambrie leaned forward in her chair. "Well, sir, I can certainly lead by example. Is there a website where I can review their information?" She absolutely couldn't lose her job. Not when Aunt Annabelle depended on her.

The cranky old man pushed a paper toward her and wiggled it until she took it. "That's their online information. You have until 5pm tomorrow, Miss Brasher, to share with me your plan to win the grant, or I'm afraid I will need to post your position and hire someone who can do the job."

Her mouth dropped open. "You're planning to fire me?"

"Don't be dramatic. I need to do what's in the best interest of this library. I won't fire you if you can do the job."

She counted mentally to ten. "But I have done my job and done it very well. I've collected all back revenues of books not returned, began the Teen Readers Group, and I'm almost done cataloging the books online."

"Wonderful accomplishments, Miss Brasher, but none that will keep Highland Library's doors open. This hundred thousand dollar grant is our only hope. I wouldn't place our chances in your hands if I thought you weren't capable." He raised his palm when she went to speak. "Now, I know you have been an exemplary employee so that's why I'm not firing you now. And I know you are the sole caregiver to your sweet aunt, one of the last true Southern Belles if I may add. That's why you have today and tomorrow to come up with a plan. Now you can continue to sit here and debate this matter or get cracking on the project. Huh, Miss Brasher?"

His menacing stare made her want to poke his eyes out. "I won't be fired. I'll get this done, Mr. Hackler," Cambrie said, standing and waltzing to the door. She resisted slamming it on her way out. The old geezer would just add to his list of why she should be terminated.

Back at the front desk, she smiled at the volunteer. "Mrs. Ginnity, thank you for watching the desk for me. I hope it wasn't too busy."

The elderly woman, dressed in an impeccable pink business suit, stood straight and spoke with a clear voice. "Not at all, Miss Brasher. I did tidy up the mess you left behind though."

Cambrie's heart sank. She what? Twisting her head to view the entire desk, all her carefully divided piles had been placed into one. "Um, Mrs.

Ginnity, I was working with those piles. Reorganizing our filing system."

"You mean, that was the project for that computer thing?"

Did the woman purposely sabotage her work? After all, she had been very vocal in her opposition to computers. Cambrie wanted to scream. "Yes, for the new computer cataloging which, even though some people may not like computers, the current generation lives for technology. I've worked very hard to make the improvements. Please check with me next time before you move my work around."

The other woman squared her shoulders, her chin angling up in that aristocratic way she had inherited. "I assure you, I am very sorry for trying to make the desk look presentable for the customers. Just remember this library has run well for over seventy-five years without the aid of computers and such. I only volunteer here because, as you know, my kinfolk have sat on the Board of Directors for generations. I have an interest in seeing that Highland Library is properly operated."

Of course she did. Just like she thought she had a right to meddle in Cambrie's work, or the way she dressed, or who she associated with. "I do appreciate all that you and your family have done, and continue to do, for the library. Mrs. Ginnity, I don't mean to be rude, but I'm afraid I have to get right to work on an urgent project for Mr. Hackler."

"Oh," Mrs. Ginnity said, perking up. "Anything I may assist with? You know I have been part of many projects concerning this place, and I do have a lot of time on my hands now that my dear Charles, God rest his soul, has left me alone."

Oh, no. Cambrie just didn't have time for one of her crying jags. Wrapping an arm around the petite woman's shoulders, Cambrie walked her from behind the front desk toward the backroom that served as an office for the volunteers. "Actually, there is something that you can do for me if it wouldn't be too much of an imposition."

She pulled from Cambrie's grasp and faced her with eyes filled with curiosity. "Just spit it out, child."

Cambrie wrung her hands and plastered her sweetest smile on her face. "Well, I had planned to visit Aunt Annabelle this evening, but I'm afraid this project won't allow me to do so. I had wanted to bake a batch of blueberry muffins with cream cheese frosting and bring them to her and sit with her a bit to give her some company."

Mrs. Ginnity jumped into Cambrie's words. "Say no more. It'd be my pleasure to visit dear Annabelle. Why I should be ashamed of myself," she stated, walked into the back room and returned in seconds holding her purse. She put on a pair of dainty white gloves as she spoke. "I haven't been to see my dear friend in weeks. I'll bake her my special muffins and spend the evening with her. Why we'll have so much to catch up on. I bet she has yet to hear about Mrs. Lolly's dog, Chipper, attacking the poor woman's ankles the other day."

Cambrie wasted no time. If she didn't move along Mrs. Ginnity then she'd end up hearing about a story that would put her to sleep. "Oh, Aunt Annabelle will so enjoy seeing you. I can't thank you enough for your graciousness, Mrs. Ginnity. I'll let you get going now. Please give Auntie a hug for me and tell her I'll make it up to her."

Mrs. Ginnity patted her arm. "You take such good care of her, Cambrie. You're young. You should be raising a family of your own instead of being burdened with the care of an elderly loved one."

The familiar tears tickled Cambrie's eyes. "I owe my aunt my life. It's no trouble for me at all."

"Yes, well, the Good Lord remembers our sacrifices and when He deems fit He rewards us. Good night, my dear. And I am terribly sorry about your papers." Mrs. Ginnity disappeared down the stairs.

Cambrie sighed and stomped back to the front desk. An hour until closing time. Today had been a slow day. Maybe there'd be few customers for the remainder of the day and she could at least have the time to research the Veterans Affairs Department's requirements. This just warned of an impossible feat.

But since when did a Brasher go down without a fight? After all, she was born and bred Southerner and there wasn't a losing cause a Southerner wouldn't fight for if they thought they should. It just so happened that Cambrie needed to fight for her job or risk losing everything that she had barely held onto this past year.

An hour later, Cambrie locked the library doors behind Mr. Hackler as he left for the evening. After reviewing the requirements to qualify for the veteran's grant, Cambrie had three pages of notes but no solid ideas on how she could lead by example in honoring a member of the military. In desperation, she had emailed the person in charge of the program asking for specific ideas on how she could prove her military support.

Her inbox showed a new message. Opening

it, Cambrie read the email.

Thank you, Miss Brasher, for your interest in the Military-Friendly Library Grant Program. I will get right to the point as you stated you needed the info immediately. Adopt a soldier, Miss Brasher. It's as simple as that. Then we will ask that person how well you supported them over the next few months. This will involve how much you kept in contact with them (should be no less than once a week).

We understand that the economy is tough right now, but care packages from home boost our soldiers' morale more than anything else. Helps them know they are on our minds. While we don't expect one person to shoulder this expense, you can prove your worthiness for the grant by organizing efforts to solicit donations of items from your customers, friends, and family.

This grant has been established by the Veterans Affairs Department to highlight the need to have individual participation in the U.S. military's missions. Not everyone can serve in the military, Miss Brasher, but everyone can support those who do. That's what we aim to emphasize to the American people.

You all can make a difference in the lives of our military personnel deployed around the world. They sacrifice their time and sometimes their lives to bring us all the freedom we enjoy every day without a question or a fear it could be taken away.

Now I implore you, Miss Brasher, to adopt a soldier and support him or her in the best way you can. How do you find this soldier? Well, I'm afraid that's up to you as part of the program's initiative.

But it must not be a family member or someone you already know. We expect that you'd already be supporting such members.

With this program our goal is to make sure every military member has someone they know is thinking of them. So ask family and friends who they know in the military and adopt that person.

Then keep a detailed log of communications sent to him or her and of other efforts, such as soliciting donations from customers. I will contact you soon for a detailed report and will follow-up with your adopted soldier for his or her input.

Remember, this is about them. Yes, the grant money is certainly important to libraries, but we need to keep focused on the project's theme. Boosting our military's morale is a job for all Americans. Helping a special library, one that goes above and beyond all others to do so, with financial support will benefit all our citizens as books are immensely important to the military-aside from letters from home they are what military members read to pass the time before returning to loved ones.

I thank you for your time and appreciate your interest in the Veterans Affairs Department's Military-Friendly Library Grant Program. I look forward to your report. Sincerely, General Sherwald

Cambrie sat back in her chair with tears in her eyes. Wasn't that the most touching email she had ever read? Wow. When she had set out on this quest, she only had visions of saving her job. Now she could actually make an impact on someone's life halfway across the world.

With a new enthusiasm for the project,

Cambrie kicked off her shoes, wiggled her sore, cramped toes and sat down to make a list of what to do next. She didn't know anyone in the military.

Correction. Her good friend from college, Emma Shields now Emma Coleman, did. Emma had recently married a Navy SEAL, Finn Coleman, who retired to live with his new wife on her farm in Vermont. Cambrie would just have to look up Emma and beg for her assistance. Finn should be able to refer her to a military member who could help her win the grant. If there was one thing Cambrie could do well, it was write. Holding a masters degree in English would help her win this money and maybe make a new friend with her adopted soldier.

Cambrie began a new email.

Hi Emma, How are you? Hope married life is treating you well. Aunt Annabelle is still doing well in the nursing home. I wish I could write more, but I'm pressed for time and need a HUGE favor please.

Will you ask Finn if he could refer a soldier to me to "adopt." Yes, that's right. My boss will fire me by tomorrow night if I can't prove that I can win a grant that will financially benefit the library. The requirement to participate in the grant is adopting a soldier and writing him or her once a week, sending care packages, etc. I really need someone. I don't know anyone except Finn that has served in the military. If you would please get back to me ASAP, girlfriend. I'd owe you big time. Lots of hugz, Cam

Cambrie logged off the Internet. She needed to head home, change into comfortable jeans, and snuggle on her couch to brainstorm more ideas. She could solicit the Southern Ladies League for donations. She'd make giant posters listing donations needed and hang them in the library. She'd have the Teen Readers Group write letters to her adopted soldier, too.

Oh, there was so much she had thought of since the general's email. Now she had a purpose other than taking care of Aunt Annabelle, which she never minded, but this was important too. She'd bring a smile to a soldier's face somewhere in a distant land. Her job no longer needed to just be about paying the bills. She could finally make a difference.

Slipping her shoes back on her sore feet, Cambrie squished her notes into her briefcase and headed for home.

Chapter Two

Walking into her empty apartment, Cambrie sighed at the silence. Wouldn't it be nice to actually walk in and be greeted by someone? Dumping her briefcase on the couch where she'd work, she turned on her laptop. Running into her bedroom, she changed and returned to the kitchen to start dinner. When she logged back online, she wanted to jump up and down. Emma had replied.

Hey, Cam. Wow, long time no talk to. Miss you! Finn's not home yet, he's been out with the horses all day. He started a stud program and I swear the horses are getting more action than me, LOL.

But, hun, not to worry. I'll make sure he gets you a contact tonight. I'm thrilled that you let me know about this. What a fantastic program!

You know that Finn and I met online...well, thanks to my friends and his men playing matchmaker. You never know what could happen with the right pen pal. Wink! And of course, you'd better share all the juicy details LOL. OK. Will email in a few. Hugs to you too. Em

Had Emma gone and lost her mind? Cambrie laughed and set her laptop on the coffee table and hurried to the microwave. Her frozen dinner was overcooked, but she was so hungry she didn't care. It was food and, at the moment, she had more important things, like her job, to worry about than nourishment.

If Emma thought that Cambrie had the time for a relationship then she didn't know her well enough. The last thing Cambrie needed was another person depending on her limited time when she needed to keep the bills paid for Aunt Annabelle to stay in the nursing home.

Taking a bite of the pasta, Cambrie sat at her tiny kitchen table glancing around her small apartment. It had been all she could afford after she sold Aunt Annabelle's beloved house once the doctors said the frail elderly woman needed to remain in the nursing home for round the clock care. The medical bills had eaten up Aunt Annabelle's small savings until only the house was left.

Cambrie didn't need much though. Some day she'd have her own big, southern house with floor to ceiling windows, fireplaces in the great room and bedrooms, and a large eat-in kitchen like Aunt Annabelle's house. Then Cambrie's maid would prepare the meals because Lord knew Cambrie's specialty wasn't cooking. She was one step away from the local fire department issuing her an order forbidding her to cook anymore. The old biddies in town had actually thought the constant calls for assistance from the firemen for burnt dinners had been a clever way for Cambrie to land herself a husband. She could think of better ways than smoke inhalation to attract a man.

The ding on her laptop indicated a new email. Cambrie jumped up from the kitchen table and dashed into the living room. Clicking on the email, she opened it.

Good news, Cam. My husband laughed hard

when I told him of your request. Then afterward, when Finn got this evil look to his handsome face, I knew the wheels were turning in that thick head of his and that someone was in trouble. Hahaha.

He's grateful to have the opportunity to refer one of his former men for your program. Lt. Miller Daly was one of the guys responsible for me and Finn getting together. So in my hubby's words, 'it's only fair that he repay the favor to all his men and he'd like to start with Miller.' But be warned, Cam, Miller's not very sociable and is probably the most opposite man from you. His email address is at the end of this one.

You better let me know what happens-LOL-this is so much fun. Wait until you see how hot Miller is. Write me soon, Em

Cambrie laughed. If Emma thought that she'd be part of her or her husband's matchmaking scheme then she was crazy. But Cambrie was a desperate woman and now had the first link to fulfilling the grant's requirements: a soldier to adopt. But she had to admit that she was intrigued by Emma's description of the man she needed to write. With any luck, maybe this pen pal thing wouldn't be boring. If she had someone who could at least have a decent conversation via letters, she'd be happy.

What would she say? She settled back on the couch and thought of some of her favorite romance books. As a librarian, she was well versed in all genres of books, but the romances had always held a special spot in her heart. They were the perfect solution to her lack of a love life. Cuddling with the characters on the couch or in her bed, had been one of her favorite past times when sleep didn't overcome her.

While Cambrie wasn't known as a flirt, she did have a great imagination and knew how to use it. She needed to write something to this guy Miller that would interest him so he wouldn't brush her off as spam or a pathetic lunatic. She remembered Emma's wedding and all the military guys there, how they had all been larger than life. Tall, muscular, dangerous. And very yummy. Cambrie sat straight up.

"Oh, my God! Had Miller been at Emma's wedding?" Talking out loud to herself had become a bad habit, one she would surely be committed for sooner or later.

Which man was he? They were all gorgeous and intimidating, caught up in their closed circle of friends, dressed in spiffy military uniforms. And they were loud. That she remembered, how they had howled and laughed all night. Still, they weren't obnoxious. It had been heartwarming to witness how close the men were, huddled together for the evening, throwing a punch to the arm or a slap on the back every so often. Emma and Finn had been their focus most of the time.

Cambrie sighed. Someday, with any luck, she'd have a wedding day too and wear Aunt Annabelle's wedding dress like she had promised. If she could hit the lottery then maybe she'd buy back Aunt Annabelle's house.

A fist tightened around her heart at the memories of growing up in the home that had been in Annabelle's family for generations. And because Cambrie didn't make enough money here in Maddyville, she had to give it up. Oh, well. The past couldn't be changed.

But the future she had a say in and, for now,

she needed to win the grant.

Sitting on the couch with her laptop, she typed.

Dear Lt. Daly, Finn Coleman referred me to you saying you'd help me with a very important project. I need to adopt you. Well, figurately speaking that is. You see, I am a librarian at Highland Library in Maddyville, Kentucky, a small town that hosts the only library for 50 miles. It's a vital part of the community. My boss has asked that I apply for the grant offered by the Veterans Affairs Department rewarding the employee in a library that proves their support of our troops.

That's why I wish to adopt you. I would write you weekly and send care packages. All you'd have to do in a few months is report how well I did. Please, Lt. Daly, email me back ASAP so I know you got this and then we can start. Sincerely, Cambrie Brasher

She logged off for the night. Sitting and pressing the refresh button every minute wasn't her idea of fun nor would it make him reply any faster. What if he didn't get it? Would he even be stationed some place that had the Internet?

She remembered Emma going crazy not having any contact with Finn when he was on his last mission and somewhere that had no phone or Internet service. Cambrie had always taken modern technology for granted. Whenever she read a book that highlighted the lack of technology in developing countries then she appreciated having it all that much more. But Miller was military…surely he'd have a means to communicate with loved ones, right? Maybe not every day, but most days, she hoped.

Setting her alarm for 5am, she snuggled under the covers not even bothering to undress. Her pillow beckoned her and sleep teased her. Giving in to both, Cambrie shut her eyes.

****

What the fuck was Finn up to now? Miller wondered re-reading the email from Cambrie Brasher. Did Finn think he was a charity case who needed his friends to find him female companionship? Hell, no. And no way in hell did Miller feel like being a guinea pig for some small town, snooty librarian and her silly ass program.

If she wanted to support the troops then she could donate blood or knit blankets or something. He sure didn't need some tight-assed broad writing him and preaching about the proper way to act or the ethics of war or how God could save him.

Miller was going to kick Finn's ass once he got back to the States. He'd be sure to swing by Vermont and visit his ex-commander.

Miller typed his brief reply to Cambrie and hit the send button. Then he sent an email to Finn.

So you think it's funny trying to match me up with a librarian, you ass? Just wait, buddy. You'll get yours. Gonna kick your sorry ass all over that fucking farm of yours. You're in deep shit, pal, and you know I ain't all talk. Give that pretty wife of yours my condolences for marrying a butt-head. You are such a fuck-nut. Miller

Miller smiled. Guess Finn's plan backfired on him. Thought he could get him back like he'd threatened countless times for signing Finn up for the military pen pal program that had won him Emma.

Miller leaned back and rested his head on the pillow on his cot. Finn should be shaking Miller's hand for helping him find Emma. If Miller hadn't taken the step for him, the poor bastard would still be a lonely fuck.

Now Miller, on the other hand, just wanted to get laid. Settling down might happen some day, but not any time soon. Missions were his life and getting laid was easy.

Closing his eyes, he waited for his dream lady to come. God, what he wouldn't do to be able to stroke his cock and come to the vision of the beauty who haunted his damn dreams. Bunking in close quarters with four guys wouldn't allow him that opportunity, so he settled for the throbbing in his cock.

She was out there. And he'd find her if it killed him.

****

"What does he mean, no?" Cambrie screeched.

She had awoken in the middle of the night unable to sleep, worried about losing her job. In her nervousness, she had checked her email.

Hi Miss Brasher, while I'm appreciative of your efforts to run your library, I'm afraid that I'm just not interested in being adopted. I apologize that Finn misled you. I wouldn't make a good pen pal for a librarian. Best wishes, ma'am. Lt. Miller Daly

"What the hell is that supposed to mean?" Cambrie said, pacing her living room. "Wouldn't be good for a librarian? What am I? The plague or something?"

Oh no, he didn't. Cambrie plopped on the couch and typed, her fingers moving so fast across the keyboard that the click clack echoed within the otherwise silent apartment.

Lt. Daly, thank you for your prompt reply, but please reconsider. It will take no effort on your part to assist me. You don't even need to write me back if you choose not to. All you will need to do after a few months is report how well I corresponded. I am desperate for this program to work, so please email me with good news. I am willing to do anything. Cambrie

Cambrie sighed, logged off and went back to bed. The comfort of her blankets did nothing to take her mind off her troubles.

What other options did she have if Lt. Daly refused to cooperate? Sure she could email Emma and maybe Finn could refer her to another guy, but there wasn't a whole lot of time to go back and forth via a hundred emails. If she didn't have a plan in place by tomorrow to present Mr. Hackler, then she could kiss her job goodbye.

There was no way in hell she'd give the cranky ol' bastard the chance to fire her if she could help it. She was a very smart woman, top of her class. Figuring out a solution to this problem should be easy enough. Maybe if she went online she could solicit someone off a chat site or something.

She buried her head into her pillow and let out a long scream, the stress pouring out of her.

What was so damn hard about being a pen pal? Weren't military men always thrilled to have someone from home write them? Hadn't the general's email implied that? Wasn't her letter supposed to boost Lt. Daly's morale?

Then why would he turn her down flat without even giving her a chance? The jerk! He held her life in his hands and didn't even know it. Well, Lt. Daly also didn't know that Cambrie Brasher was a fighter and she wasn't about to give up on him so easily. Not when Emma had been so sure he'd cooperate. And Finn wouldn't have wasted her time if he didn't think so, too.

Cambrie groaned, remembering the email she had sent out earlier asking the local news station for a press conference to announce her military support program. Hoping to use the press to gain support in the community and assist her in catching up on valuable lost time, it had been a great idea. But now with her plan backfiring and her adopted soldier bailing before she even got started, Cambrie just wanted to sink under the covers and fade into her dreams.

Or nightmares at this point.

Chapter Three

"Well done, Miss Brasher," Mr. Hackler said after the press conference held in the main lobby of the library.

"Thank you," Cambrie said, glancing around, still amazed at the outcome.

Every major news channel and newspaper in the area had attended the event highlighting the library's quest for the grant. After the noontime news aired, the library had been under siege with community members wanting to participate and support the efforts. Cambrie figured most thought they could get on TV if they had come to the library, but the news crews had since left and only a few reporters remained, mulling through the crowd and interviewing people.

"I'm very pleased, Mr. Hackler," Cambrie said, wanting to get away from her boss. She needed to send an email. Oh, God. Keeping a straight face while lying was damn hard.

"I can't wait to see the response you get from the community," Mr. Hackler said, interrupting her panic. "I think we have a great chance at winning that grant now that you've put on your thinking cap, Miss Brasher. Splendid ideas." He walked away to catch up to the mayor.

Cambrie ran in the opposite direction of the crowds. What the hell was she going to do now? She had just promised Maddyville an adopted soldier to support. Now she had to come up with one since the last time she had checked her email an hour ago showed no response from Lt. Daly on her second request to adopt him.

Why did she kid herself? The man wasn't about to reply. He had already said no, had declined politely. He didn't need to waste his valuable time with her.

But she couldn't go down without a fight…or at least one more try.

Slipping into her office, while customers mulled around the library hadn't been easy. She had to claim an important phone call to keep moving and avoid the clutches of the well-meaning but overbearing members of the Auxiliary Women's Club not to mention all the people who inquired about Aunt Annabelle.

Cambrie locked her office door to avoid prying eyes. Privacy is what she needed. Logging online, she pulled up her email, disappointed again to not find an email from Lt. Daly. But there was one from Emma. Oh, how would she tell her friend that she failed to gain Miller's support?

Hey Cam, Finn told me he got an email from Miller that sounded like he might've turned you down or blown you off. Now, the Cambrie I know would never take no for an answer when she set her mind to something. Don't let Miller scare you off, girlfriend. Go get him. Believe me, he will make your program win. Keep me updated. Hugs, Em

Oh, those words were the fuel she needed for the fire in her belly. Encouraged by Emma, and determined to win the grant, not just to save her job but to keep the library open for all the deserving customers, Cambrie typed.

Lt. Daly, while it's obvious from your lack of a reply that you're ignoring my requests for your participation with the adopt-a-soldier program, I must try one more time. I have made a commitment to the program and to the library, so there is no backing out now without losing everything—my job, the library, and my Aunt Annabelle.

I don't expect you to understand my predicament nor is it your problem. I just ask that, as a friend of Emma and Finn's, you help me out. I'd do anything if you'd just cooperate long enough for me to get my boss off my ass.

Listen, I'll be blunt since I gather you military types prefer it that way. I'm not ugly, boring, or dull. We can and will have decent conversations. I may work with books, but I also love adventure. I tend to be a bit clumsy, but that just leads to more fun with my escapades.

I read a lot but I love romances the most, especially the erotic ones, and I'm not ashamed to admit that. I believe sex is healthy and testing our sexual boundaries can only bring a heightened awareness of ourselves.

And don't even think about busting my balls because I read romances. I know men don't understand why women enjoy a good romantic story (and they are not all about lovey-dovey crap), but maybe if you guys read one then you'd understand what a woman is looking for. There's a lot of information in those books that may unravel some of the mysteries of the woman's heart, LOL—but that's a topic for another time.

I'm attaching a picture, not that I'm a beauty queen or anything but it's to dismiss any pre-determined perceptions you may have based on my occupation, and it'll be nice for you to see who you're talking to. I don't have gray hair twisted in a bun or act prim and proper. Whatever you may think about librarians, well, I'm the complete opposite. I have long, brown hair, light brown eyes, average height, slender build, and am not shy about having some fun.

Ask me anything you want to know and I'll respond truthfully. Be my pen pal for this program and I promise we'll have interesting conversations that will help pass any boring times wherever you may be. Hell, it'll give me some male companionship and adult conversation that I've been sorely lacking due to other commitments.

Come on-just do it. It'll be fun, I promise. I'm sure I met you at Emma and Finn's wedding, but I can't remember because I met so many people that day. Please reconsider, Lt. Daly, I really need you.
Cambrie

She hit the send key before she could think about what she just wrote-how bold she'd been.

She sat with her forehead resting in her palms. If she could find another job in Maddyville where she could stay close to Aunt Annabelle and one that paid like this one then she'd give her notice now instead of embarrassing herself anymore with Lt. Daly. What was she thinking writing all of that stuff to a complete stranger? Oh, if he didn't think she was a whack job before, he would now.

She sighed. How did life get so damn complicated? One minute she's in Nashville pursuing a great career as a magazine editor and then life threw her a curve ball, and sent Aunt Annabelle to nursing care after a heart attack and breast cancer.

Well, Cambrie had to be grateful for the heart attack or Aunt Annabelle's breast cancer would've been discovered too late.

Ding!

Cambrie's head shot up and she stared at her screen. Incoming mail from Miller Daly.

Oh. My. God.

Here it came. He more than likely sent her an email blasting her forwardness and demanding that she leave him alone. With a shaking finger, she clicked and opened the message.

Cambrie, please accept my apologies for not getting back to you sooner. The slow response was in no way to avoid you. I was on a mission that lasted longer than expected with no access to email until I returned to camp. Now that I see we have something in common-I too enjoy erotic stories-then I'd be more than happy to help you out but on one condition...

What? He had rules to play by? She could live with that. Hope consumed her.

Okay. Anything. The message disappeared from her screen as soon as she hit the send button.

Sitting at her desk, she wiggled her feet in a dance on the floor. Yes! Finally some progress. If this worked out and Miller helped her with getting the grant then she definitely owed Emma and Finn dinner.

Ding!

Clicking on his reply, she read it.

Ahh. Careful what you promise. I'm a guy of many ideas with lots of time between missions. We could be potent together.

Did she read that right? Did he just hit on her? Holy shit!

Ding!

Sorry. Forgot to attach my pic since you were kind enough to share yours, Cambrie. I couldn't attend Emma and Finn's wedding—if I had then I would've made sure to make your acquaintance…and more. Wink!

Cambrie swallowed hard, her throat dry. One look at the man in the picture on her screen had her pussy awakening with tiny aches, creating a throbbing that she'd never felt before.

The man was so amazing. Dressed in military pants and sleeveless white T-shirt, he had to be at least six-foot-three, maybe weighed two-twenty. Staring at the camera with his massive arms crossed, he was indeed the epitome of strength. She couldn't see his eyes behind the dark sunglasses, but his light brown hair was short.

A tattoo on his upper arm caught her attention. She squinted to see it better but couldn't make out what it was. The grin on his face had her imagining kissing the corners to nibble along his angular jaw.

Christ, what had come over her? Okay. If he wanted to play with fire, she was game.

I may be a librarian, but don't let the title fool you, Lt. Daly. I bet I could convince you to enjoy some books after a few sessions of…say…tutoring.

She slammed her finger on the send button and twirled in her seat, laughing. Wow, so this was what it was like to dabble in cyber sex. Holy shit, she was getting excited. She could feel her wetness gathering between her legs. She couldn't remember the last time she had creamed her panties. Looked like she had gone too long without a lot of things.

Still smiling, she focused on the computer when the alarm sounded of an incoming email.

OMG! Sign me up. But only with you. Now tell me more…I have a passion for details. Logging off now but I'd love to have an email when I get back on, Cambrie, baby. Start doing your troop duties and work for this grant, LOL. Miller

PS—luv the pic. You're a woman a man can dream about.

That gorgeous man could dream about her? Well, hell yeah! She could deal with that. What a great perk it would be if her job allowed her to enjoy cyber sex with a sexy-as-all-hell guy. A wickedness crept through her, naughty thoughts fighting for recognition. Her boss said she had to do whatever it took to get the grant. He never said she couldn't have fun doing it.

Cambrie laughed and began typing her reply, saddened that Miller had to leave for now but at least she'd send him a sexy email to keep his attention. Wow, the rush of adrenaline flowing through her compared to the arousal she felt in a man's arms. But never had she had a man as built as Miller or as dangerous. He looked like a one-man fighting machine with those muscles.

"Miss Brasher," a woman called from the other side of the door after a faint knock.

Cambrie immediately stood to move to the door, her body heated from head to toe, her head spinning with a giddiness she hadn't felt since her first kiss.

Opening the door, Cambrie found Mrs. Ginnity dressed meticulously in a peach suit and matching heels. "So sorry to bother you, but there's a reporter needing to speak with you. Shall I show him in?"

Cambrie glanced back at the computer knowing her email to Miller would have to be postponed. There was business at hand and Miller wasn't going anywhere. His interest in her was very much apparent. This day was turning out to be pretty damn good.

Chapter Four

Miller had finally found her after all of this time. The woman from his dreams now stared back from his laptop. The picture Cambrie Brasher had sent him could've been painted from his dreams.

Hell, yeah!

Sitting on his hard cot in the tent, he couldn't stop staring at Cambrie's picture. And what a name for the hot woman. *Cambrie.* It rolled off his tongue sweet as sugar with a hint of spice. Miller knew the minute he set eyes on his mystery lady there'd been no denying it was the right woman.

Fuck! He couldn't get leave for at least another month. After all this time, wondering where she was out there, she happened to find him instead of the other way around.

Now he was stuck in this remote desert. The tour had lasted a month longer than planned with still no end in sight. The goal hadn't been achieved and the team was fucked without reliable information from their local resources in the Afghan village.

Miller tossed his laptop onto the cot and grabbed his weapon to go seek out his commander. Walking out of the tent, Miller scanned the area to ensure no insurgents had snuck up on them. Caution could never be enough. His eyes caught sight of his boss.

Marching across the sand, Miller stopped a foot away from the man. "Lieutenant Commander Wallace, have we received the coordinates of our target yet?"

Chance Wallace faced Miller. The two had been best friends since boot camp. Now with Finn retired they each got turns running different ops. And Chance had been assigned this one.

"If I did, do you think I'd keep it a fucking secret, Daly?"

"Don't give me any shit. This sun's baking all of our brains. I think we need to review our mission and devise another plan since this one hasn't worked. It's like we're just sitting around with our thumbs up our asses."

Chance narrowed his eyes. "So now you want to run the show?"

Miller shook his head and stared at the ground before looking back up and losing formality. "Shit, it ain't that, Chance, and you know it. I just want to be doing something. We've trained for months and it'd be nice to finally get to put that shit to the test. Seems no end in sight."

"Never heard you complain before about a mission taking too long." Chance studied him. "What's her name?"

Miller grimaced. "Get fucked. This ain't about a woman. It's about progress and I don't see us making any."

"Then don't get antsy on me now. Granville has intercepted some static on the radio. May be talk of an attack. Gear up. Let's take a walk to the northern side, see if we can spot any movement and get you some exercise."

"Will do," Miller obeyed, turned and made quick strides to the tent. Chance could be a prick sometimes. Exercise his ass. What he really needed was Cambrie's naked hot body under his while he fucked them both into oblivion.

Dressing in his BDUs, Miller fitted the seventy-pound backpack loaded with ammo and water and headed back to Chance. Miller may be dying to meet Cambrie, but he'd never disobey orders. His missions always came first. No matter what. Cambrie wouldn't go anywhere in the next few hours until he could get back online. Sucks that the Internet here was so damn spotty. If they lost their connection, it could be days before they managed to get it back. He should've told her that so she wouldn't think he was ignoring her again. Then again, it may prompt her to send another hot email.

"Ready when you are," Miller said, stepping beside Chance.

"Lynch, Granville, hold camp. Harper, continue staking the coordinates for the village. Daly and I are headed to the northern post for patrol. Granville, I'll be looking for more info on that static, so keep on it."

"Yes, sir," Lynch, Granville, and Harper replied, without interrupting their duties. Lynch stayed on watch while Granville worked the radios and Harper wrote on a clipboard.

"Come on, Daly. Try and keep up," Chance said, marching away from camp not waiting for Miller to follow.

Miller ignored Chance's dig. He wasn't in the mood to be teased unless it was by Cambrie's sexy body. Walking behind Chance, Miller held his rifle steady, his eyes roaming the land for any combatants. Catching a bullet in the ass now would severely fuck with his plans to meet Cambrie and get laid.

"Tell me her name, bro," Chance said, his sharp words breaking the silence.

"Don't know what you're talking about," Miller responded without emotion, even though waves of electricity spiraled through him. He still couldn't believe he had found the woman from his dreams.

Chance laughed loud and Miller shot him a warning glare that was ignored because Chance continued without a flinch. "Shit, tell that to someone who don't know you as well as I do. Now we may be stuck out here in the middle of the goddamn desert, but that doesn't mean you haven't found a hottie to play around with. I know the Internet connections have been pretty steady, so spill it. Who'd you meet online?"

"Get fucked, would you?" Miller cringed knowing that Chance wasn't about to let his interrogation go any time soon. Not when they were surrounded by sand and no other forms of life. Miller was prime picking. Great.

"Now that I'd love to do, bro, but since I ain't got no hottie chasing me, suppose you dish on who you got? Does she got nice tits and ass?"

Something about the way Chance spoke about Cambrie, even if he didn't do anything out of the norm when it came to talking about women, had Miller's blood pressure rising and his hand tightening on the gun. No way in hell did he want his best friend to talk about the woman who had captivated his attention since her emails began. She deserved respect. There was something different about Cambrie that Miller had sensed immediately, well once he gave her a chance. He sure as hell didn't want to have a conversation about her with their typical gutter talk.

"You know, ignoring me won't shut me up," Chance said, interrupting Miller's thoughts. "Hell, we've got a couple of hours out here by ourselves on this patrol. I'm damn good at getting information that I want. You might as well fess up the juicy details now, Miller, or face my endless, mind numbing questions until you crack."

Miller smirked and pushed his sunglasses up onto his helmet, squinting in the bright sun. Chance was the biggest asshole when he wanted something. "She's different. Don't talk about her like a slut."

Chance whipped his head around to face Miller who only offered a grin and returned his focus back to the horizon in search of enemies. "Oh, Lordy. What the hell have you gone and done?"

"Don't know what the hell you're talking about. I swear, you talk in circles sometimes, Chance."

"I know how to talk. And you damn well know you're hiding a lot more than you're sharing. Fucking spill."

Was he that transparent? "Nothing you need to know. When I feel like telling you anything then I will. Until then…fuck off."

Chance grinned and slapped Miller on the back. "You, dawg, you. Getting action even out here in the middle of no man's land."

Before Miller could reply a bullet whizzed past his head. "Fuck!" He dropped to the ground with Chance and returned fire, stopping only to yell into the radio attached to his shoulder. "Taking fire. North ridge. Send goddamn backup."

"I've got your back, Miller," Chance yelled while firing. "Don't you fucking get shot or I'll kick your sorry ass."

Miller understood the danger and Chance's

underlying meaning. This would be one hell of a battle to get out of without being maimed let alone get out alive. More bullets whizzed by their heads and into the sand around them. "Looks like only a few assholes. Let's show them who the fuck they're messing with." Miller growled, removing his spent cartridge and replacing it with a fresh supply of bullets. "Don't you get shot either, Chance. I don't feel like carrying your ass out of here."

When a bullet landed in front of them, the sand kicked up into Miller's eyes blinding him. Son of a bitch! With his vision useless, Miller relied on his other senses and Chance. "Fuck. Can't see."

"Just aim forward so you don't shoot me," Chance replied, his voice edgier than he let on. "I've seen two fall. There's two more. You take eleven o'clock. I've got three o'clock for getting your eyes."

Miller aimed in the direction Chance instructed and emptied his gun. Now what?

Chapter Five

Cambrie had never been more grateful to cuddle on her couch with her laptop. She had been too busy after the press conference at the library to write Miller an email like he had requested. But now the night was hers and she tapped away on the keyboard.

Hi Miller. Sorry about taking so long to get back to you. Work was busy, but I'm all yours now. LOL.

She bit her bottom lip. Her inner friskiness warred with the businesswoman. Miller was a man who had said he had lots of time on his hands and there was a good chance he was really bored. Did he really want a dull email? Of course not. He wouldn't give a shit what she was up to. Cambrie had to use her vivid imagination to keep his attention or she'd never win the grant. He had to be thrilled with her. She may have begun this project to keep her job, but the woman in her wanted to play.

So, Miller, I'm a bit curious as to how you'd think we'd be potent together. You sound like a man who knows what he wants and doesn't hesitate to get it. My life has gotten a little predictable, so I'm looking forward to spicing it up with my new friendship with you.

I hope we can benefit each other. Hopefully,

I'm not being presumptuous in thinking there's a level of sexual attraction between us. It would be fascinating to see how that plays out. Maybe cyber sex is just what we both need. LOL. I look forward to your next email…and can't wait to personally thank you for agreeing to participate in this pen pal program. I promise not to disappoint. Wink! Hugz for now…Cambrie

Cambrie hit the send button before she could chicken out and hit delete instead. She shoved her laptop onto the coffee table and jumped up. Biting her nail, she stared at the screen.

Message sent.

Oh. My. Good. God.

She laughed. Wow. She had really done it. She had allowed her inner vixen to take control and seduce Miller. Now time would tell if it worked or if Miller thought she was a nutcase.

Waiting for a reply was silly since she couldn't be sure when he'd get the email or even what time it was wherever he was. Housework wasn't nearly as inviting as emailing Miller, but if she didn't keep herself busy the time would drag by.

Ding!

Cambrie froze and stared at the screen. She hadn't even moved from the living room yet. Sitting back on the couch, she opened her email.

Now that's the way I like to wake up. Getting a hot email from an even hotter woman. Had a bit of trouble sleeping last night. Thoughts of you wearing lingerie and high heels kept entering my mind. I'd wake up with a huge hard-on each time.

So, baby, I'm game for anything. I can tell

you one thing though, I can't wait to taste every inch of your hot body. Holding your hands over your head, my mouth sucking your breast until the nipple stands tight and hard. Yeah, baby. Now that's what I'm talking about.

What do you like sexually? What would you like to try? Any fantasies or fetishes? Don't worry about offending me, cuz you can't. I've got a very open mind and have learned that my sexual appetite is very hard to match. So when a beautiful, interesting woman like yourself comes along, I want to do everything in my power to satisfy her...make her yearn for me. Did you think about me today after our emails? Mmmm. Hope it was naughty thoughts. Write soon, Miller

Cambrie had to swallow hard. Now that was pretty straight forward and to the point. How did Miller manage to arouse her with just an email? Was she so pathetic that a few erotic words from a man she had never met could make her pussy throb to the point of aching for his cock? Closing her eyes, she could envision his naked body hovering over hers while he sucked her nipple. Her hand covered her T-shirt over her breast. Her fingers rubbed the nipple between them while she imagined it was Miller's mouth working her.

Realizing that she was about to masturbate in her living room, she opened her eyes and returned her hands to the keyboard to send a reply. She could at least wait to orgasm until she could lie in her bed.

Did I think of you? Of course I did. It's not every day I get a sexy, handsome pen pal to play with. And after reading your email, I believe I can match that sexual appetite you boasted of. You asked what I like sexually and if I have any fetishes. Well, I don't like the same boring position all the time. Would love to find new positions that would allow your cock to stroke my G-spot while you fuck me harder and harder.

Cambrie breathed deep and fanned her hot face. She wasn't sure if she'd complete writing the email before she burst into flames. For once in a very long time, she was enjoying herself and nothing would hold her back now. She loved feeling this aroused and sensual.

I've had fantasies about being spanked, but I'm guessing it would be painful and I don't like pain. I'll admit that envisioning you holding my hands in place made my throbbing pussy cream my panties. Would you like to tie me up, Miller, and have your way with me? I bet that would be very kinky and enjoyable. Being at your mercy would increase my pleasure, I'm sure.

I won't lie. I'm blushing profusely while I type. I have never spoken to anyone like this and really can't believe I'm being so open with you. Maybe it's because I don't expect that you'll judge me for having a vibrant and active sexual imagination.

Where I live, there are not many opportunities to meet someone like you who isn't afraid to speak his mind. The attention you've given me so far kinda makes my head swim-never really had a man take this kind of interest in me. So I guess in a way you're my fantasy, Miller. Having a guy like you interested in a girl like me is something I hadn't expected when I set out to do this project.

But please don't think I'm complaining because I'm not. Your openness and attention have been a major bonus and a breath of fresh air. I only hope we can both enjoy this time spent via email. Hugz, Cambrie

Waiting for his reply was torturous. Sitting on the couch, tapping her foot on the cushion and ringing her hands while she stared at the inbox would probably drive her insane. Switching on her television, she flipped through the channels without noticing the programs. Fifteen minutes later when the alarm alerted her that she had a message, she opened it and read with heightened interest.

Cambrie, honey, you're fine. Don't change a thing about you. I've enjoyed each email more than the last. Don't know when I'll be able to email again, but just wanted to say that once this mission is done, I'm coming to meet you. Then we will see if I can't prove to you how beautiful you are.

I'm glad other men have been stupid enough to not make you theirs because that means I can work on making you mine. While these sexy emails are very enjoyable, there is so much more I look forward to discovering about you. Like what's your favorite color? Your favorite flower? Your favorite food? What do you hope for the future? What's your past?

I want to learn all about you. Just now, I was imagining us sitting on the couch, naked and huddled under a blanket, just talking. Talking about anything that came to mind. That's something I'd enjoy as much as sex, having someone just to talk to about anything.

On missions, the loneliness can kill a man before a bullet. The thought of us spending time together will get me through this very boring mission. Cambrie Brasher, I've got to tell you that you've forever changed my perception of librarians. LOL. And for the better!

Reading your last email, I couldn't help but imagine pushing deep inside your hot pussy with my thick cock and hearing you scream my name. Oh God, baby, what I wouldn't do to be lying in your bed right now, discovering all of the secret erotic zones on that delectable body of yours.

But in time we will do all that and more. I want you, Cambrie. Very much. You can tell me no, but I'm afraid I will just have to seduce you until you melt in my arms and let me make love to you all night long...or all day long. My cock won't be satisfied with fucking you just once. Oh, no, baby. I want to pleasure you until my name is all you can scream. I want to see the pleasure wash over your beautiful face, watch as your cheeks flush and your eyes flutter.

Stay rested, baby. You'll need it for when I arrive which, God willing, will be any day now. Please send your address and I'll let you know when to expect me. Of course, you don't know me but Finn does. He'll vouch for me that I'm not a psychopath and that you can trust me. Mmmm. Can't wait to give you your first spanking. Mwah!
Miller

Oh. My. God.

Miller's coming here? To visit her? To make love to her? All night? All day?

He didn't waste any time. Wow. The air whooshed out of Cambrie's lungs while she stared at the words on the screen, words that now blurred as her thoughts jumbled and her heart pounded. She jumped up and paced the apartment. Biting her fingernail, she began a mental list in her head.

She'd need to clean the apartment. Do some food shopping, since a man built like a machine probably wouldn't survive on mac and cheese and frozen pizza. Get her hair done. Maybe a manicure and pedicure. Schedule a waxing session.

Oh, but when could she fit it all in between working and the extra hours needed to do fundraising for Miller's care packages? And she desperately needed to visit Aunt Annabelle. Even if the old woman sounded vibrant on the phone earlier and fully supportive of Cambrie's efforts at the library, Cambrie could hear the sadness in Aunt Annabelle's voice. A phone call never replaced a visit in person.

Cambrie sighed. There just weren't enough hours in the day and taking a day off from work when her job was on the line would be a sure way to end up in the unemployment line. Well, if Miller proved true to his word and showed up to meet her then he'd just have to like her as is and not expect some beauty queen that she wasn't.

Maybe she could stall him. Yeah, if he could give her a month's time then she'd have plenty of time to get everything done and be presentable and she'd have more time to spend with him.

Back at her keyboard, she typed.

That would be very nice for us to meet up, Miller, but unfortunately right now isn't good timing.

The pen pal project requires a lot of my time so that the Veterans Affairs Department can see how much we have been supportive of your military service. If you could give me a month that would be fantastic.

In the mean time, I'm enjoying you very much. These emails make me smile but also arouse me. I think I'll be a live wire by the time you arrive. Be warned that when I jump into your arms, I don't plan to let you go until I've had my fill. LOL. I can assure you that my nipples are hard and awaiting your touch.

Tonight I fear I will have a restless night's sleep with thoughts of our sweat-slicked bodies joined at the hips as you pump that magnificent cock deep into me. I can tell you have a superb cock just by the confidence you exude each time you write to me. You're a man who knows how to please a woman no doubt. And I'm a woman waiting to be pleased. I'll write more soon. Goodnight for now. Sweet dreams. Cambrie

****

Sex toys.

Oh, shit. She needed some if she expected Miller to fulfill her fantasies. This would be the chance of a lifetime. To have amazing sex—no limits—with a totally gorgeous man who could torment her with just words. Oh, hell, yeah. Cambrie was in this all the way. For once she would think of herself and, when Miller could visit, she'd find the time to indulge in every fantasy she could imagine.

Clicking some words into the search engine on the Internet provided Cambrie with exactly what she needed.

Sex toys for her pleasure. What a catchy advertisement.

Perusing the site only increased her arousal as she read about vibrators and dildos and anticipated what it would be like to use them with Miller. Her online cart quickly filled with the vibe, a chest harness with a dildo attached, lube, a paddle with a soft and hard side, pink fuzzy handcuffs that read “Spank Me”, and a butt plug.

Her cheeks burned once she completed the order with her credit card. Even though the total wasn’t terribly high, she still cringed knowing she’d more than blown her tiny monthly budget for novelty items, usually spent on a nice bottle of wine and girlie things like shampoo, lotion, and makeup. Now she’d be eating peanut butter and jelly sandwiches for lunch for the next three months.

Hitting the submit button, Cambrie didn’t think twice. She’d starve to allow herself the chance at sexual freedom and bliss.

During her conversations with Miller, something deep inside her had awakened. Not quite sure what it was, and not really caring because it felt too good, Cambrie logged off and stretched. After a quick check to ensure the front door was bolted, she hurried to her bedroom. If the throbbing in her pussy didn’t go away soon, she would burst into a flame on the spot.

Masturbating had never been an everyday gratification for her busy life, but tonight she needed to indulge in a quality orgasm. Stripping naked took no time at all. The cool air fanned her heated flesh. Not bothering to remove the covers, Cambrie lay across her bed and raised her knees.

Biting her bottom lip, she closed her eyes and immediately the image of Miller's naked body entered her vision. He stood there watching her massage her pussy while he stroked his huge erection.

"Rub your clit for me, baby," his rough voice whispered.

She purred, her ass wiggling on the bed, her fingers inching down her belly until they found her hard clit. The sensation of her fingertip caressing the nub almost shot her off the bed. Never had she been this aroused and so instantly on the verge of exploding. Her finger dipped lower, slipping through the wetness covering her pussy lips. With her other hand, she manipulated her clit in small, fast circles while slipping another finger into her pussy.

She envisioned it was Miller's cock slipping in and out of her pussy. The slurping sound of her arousal filled the room amidst her harsh breathing.

"Fuck that pussy, Cambrie," Miller's voice whispered in her ear. Oh, how she wished he were really here doing this to her.

The pressure built from her womb and crept up to her clit. Knowing an orgasm was strokes away, she hastened her manipulation of her clit. Her head spun when the familiar feeling of the orgasm, with its waves of pleasure flowing over her sensitive inner muscles, consumed her senses, stealing all her breath with its thrilling spasms.

"Yes!" she cried out. "Miller!"

"I'll be here soon, baby. Real soon," he whispered before leaving her.

"No! Stay!"

But his vision had evaporated, leaving her alone on her bed, her pussy lips dancing in strong aftershocks. Turning onto her side, Cambrie stared at her headboard from the middle of the bed.

What if Miller was just playing games with her? Could her heart handle it if he fucked with her mind? They hadn't even met or spoke, just emailed. She sighed, pulled the blanket over her without bothering to lay the proper way on the bed.

Closing her eyes, it didn't shock her that only blackness greeted her. Of course she read too much into Miller's emails. Maybe he only needed her to pass his lonely time while on a mission somewhere around the world. And she really only needed him to save her job.

She should be grateful to at least have enjoyed the strongest orgasm of her life thanks to thoughts of Miller's naked body. Yeah, maybe she should be.

Then why did it leave her aching for so much more?

Chapter Six

A long, month had passed with only sporadic emails from Miller, each one helping to forge a beautiful friendship and to arouse Cambrie to the point of unbearable aching. The one time he had tried to call her had been unsuccessful. Wherever he was stationed was not conducive to phone calls and the connection had been a long stretch of static before the line disconnected, neither hearing the other speak.

Now six days had passed with no word from Miller, the longest time he'd failed to get in touch with her. Cambrie kept busy with her project and had even made some progress with fundraising for the care packages.

"The Women's Choir has donated three boxes of goodies for your military man," Mrs. Ginnity announced after walking into the library. "Place them in the volunteer office, young man," she said to Greg, a member of the Teen Readers Group, drafted by the old woman to carry her packages.

Cambrie laughed at how much the other woman acted like a drill sergeant, watching intently as Greg hauled the boxes into the rear office.

"That's wonderful. Be sure to thank them for me," Cambrie replied before returning to the draft of her report for the Board of Directors outlining her progress with the grant program.

"You look down, Cambrie. Is everything all

right?" Mrs. Ginnity asked, stepping closer and gasping. "It's not dear Annabelle, is it?"

At the mention of her sick aunt, Cambrie sat up straighter. "Oh, no, ma'am. I'm sorry. I'm just a little tired I suppose." And not at all distracted by the fact that Miller hadn't been in touch with her since she'd avoided his second request to visit soon. Hopefully, he understood when she explained the need for a little more time to plan for his visit. The past month at work had been too busy for her to get anything done at home like she had wanted. And if she were to have a houseguest for a few days, then she needed—no wanted—to be there with him to enjoy his visit.

"Well, with all the crazy hours you keep between this place and taking care of Annabelle, it's a wonder you get any sleep at all." Mrs. Ginnity placed her hands on her hips and narrowed her eyes. "Why don't you go home early today and I'll close up for you? It's only another hour. And I won't be taking no for an answer." She turned to face Greg when he emerged from the back office. "Thank you, Greg. I wish all kids would be as nice as you. I'll be baking you a batch of chocolate chip cookies for your efforts here today."

The boy offered a slight smile, the most Cambrie ever saw on him. The fifteen-year-old stood tall but his slight build made him appear scrawny. He slouched when he walked away with his hands in his pockets to return to the table he shared with three of his buddies.

Mrs. Ginnity shook her head. "Who would guess that such a sweet boy could come from the loins of the meanest man in this county?"

Cambrie studied Greg from afar. She had heard the rumors of his father's temper but hadn't witnessed it herself. The younger Greg never spoke of his family when she moderated the Teen Readers Group. He was always the first to arrive for the group and last to leave. Odd because he had never really read any of the assigned books and hardly participated in discussions.

Cambrie looked back to the woman waiting for an answer. "Mrs. Ginnity, would you really mind closing for me today? I think I'd like to take you up on that offer to leave early."

"If I didn't mean it, I wouldn't have offered. Now scoot. I've got work to do. Will that be all the books today, Mr. Belfrey?" she asked, as a middle-aged man stepped to the checkout counter.

Cambrie locked her office and stopped at Greg's table before leaving. "Greg, may I speak with you for a minute?"

The kid's face paled. "I didn't do anything wrong."

She frowned. "No, of course not. I just need to ask you a huge favor."

He slowly stood and walked with her to the front doors. He stared at the ground, kicking his toe into the floor.

Cambrie held her briefcase in front of her with both hands and spoke in a low voice. "Greg, I wanted to ask if you'd be willing to email the library's adopted soldier while he serves oversees. We're competing for a special grant that could give us enough money to keep the library open."

His head rose until his gaze met hers. "Yeah, I heard you started that program. Sounds pretty cool."

She smiled. "So does that mean you'll do it?" She had hoped he'd agree. Maybe talking with a bad ass like Miller would give the kid some backbone and help him learn some self-esteem. God knew his father wouldn't do it.

"I just have to email? And say what?"

Cambrie shrugged. "Whatever you want to talk about. Sports. School. Hobbies. Anything. His name is Lt. Miller Daly and he's a pretty cool guy. See me tomorrow for his contact info, okay?"

"Sure. But I don't have a computer at home." He didn't look her in the eyes, instead staring everywhere else.

She shrugged, not seeing that as an obstacle. "There's computers here you can use after school. I'll set you up an email account."

"Cool." He walked away without another word.

Cambrie felt a stab of pain in her chest. The boy didn't look like his friends did in their happy-go-lucky teenage way. He looked lost.

Dead on her feet, Cambrie gave in to the luxury of an early end to her workday and walked to her car as fast as she could. It wasn't that she was truly tired, just couldn't stop kicking herself for appearing inhospitable with Miller. Was he mad about her last email? Did he think she was blowing him off?

God, she hoped not because that wasn't her intention. But if she were going to meet a man who blatantly expressed his interest in hot, wild sex with her, she damn well wanted to be at her best. To do that, she needed some time, time she just didn't have. She'd just email Miller when she got home and explain what she meant. Beating herself up about it wouldn't help, so the ball would be back in his court.

Driving home only took five minutes, although she was tempted to stop and grab a burger and fries. But since she'd splurged on the sex toys, every penny counted and she'd have to forego the temptation of fast food and just microwave her pizza for dinner.

After pulling into her driveway, Cambrie walked to her stairs, fumbling with her keys. She really needed to get a separate key chain for work. Finding the key she needed, she walked up the stairs only to stop mid-step, her mouth falling open.

A man sat on the wicker chair on her porch and was fast asleep. His body slumped with arms crossed couldn't hide his identity. She knew exactly who he was.

Lt. Miller Daly.

Oh. Holy. Hell.

As if he sensed her, his head shot up and his eyes opened, blinked once, and glared. There was no way for her to retreat, run, or hide until she was more presentable.

The heat from that stare was unmistakable. The dark brown eyes shimmered with amusement. A smile formed by lips made for kissing.

When he stood, the old floorboards creaked under his weight. She was totally unprepared for his physical appearance. The picture he had sent hadn't done him justice at all. Simply said, he was gorgeous beyond any man she had ever met.

"Hello, Cambrie," he said, the casual tone showcasing a deep voice, strong like she had dreamed.

What was she supposed to say? She struggled to find her voice. "Hello, Miller. This is a big surprise."

"I was hoping it would be."

She swallowed hard when he scanned her

body head to toe and focused on her face again, his smile growing. "I'm sorry. Did I miss an email or something? I didn't expect you." She stepped onto the porch and felt so much smaller. He towered over her even with her in heels.

"That's because I didn't tell you I was coming. After the last email you sent, I didn't want to take any chances of you shooting down my visit. And I really do like surprises."

That smile was intoxicating, making her feel at ease when she should be shaking. A man she barely knew had traveled halfway around the world to see her. She cleared her throat. "I'm, well, not really prepared for company. I just got off of work and, oh God. Miller, look at me. This isn't how I wanted you to see me."

With one giant step, he stood toe to toe with her. The only way to look him in the eyes was to raise her chin. When his hands landed on her upper arms, a heat so potent spiraled through her, threatening to knock her on her ass. What the hell?

"This is *exactly* how I wanted to see you, Cambrie Brasher. Just the way you are everyday. This is the Cambrie I've fallen for and not some primped up girl."

Her heart thudded hard against her breastbone. "Fallen for? How can you say that when you don't even know me?"

His breath rushed out in a long sigh. "Shit. I'm sorry. Please don't let me scare you off. Sometimes I come off as demanding. I've just been dying to meet you and, well, you're even more than I expected. Just when I thought you couldn't get any prettier, I open my eyes to find you standing here more beautiful than your pictures. I only came without notice because if you had told me not to come it would've killed me. But if you tell me to go, I will."

This guy should open a greeting card business. He said everything right, but it was also sincere. Had he blown smoke up her ass with fancy words or frilly compliments, she would've sent him packing. But his eyes said it all. They never avoided hers, each word he spoke was emphasized by his solid gaze. A man who looked her in the eye when he spoke was worthy of a chance to prove himself.

"I never sent you my address," she said, narrowing her eyes, suddenly reminded that he probably had access to all sorts of information civilians didn't. Like her private information. The sneaky bastard!

The corner of his mouth lifted into a smirk. "Thank your friend Emma for that."

Cambrie made a mental note to give Emma hell for not warning her. "You sent me the wrong picture, Miller," she said, her hand holding her keys squished between their bodies. "Looks like you've packed on some muscle since then. That wasn't fair to mislead me."

He studied her before speaking. "Okay. My bad. I sent you an older picture. But it was only a year old. That's all I had available at the time. But I'm not much bigger. Just been working out like crazy this past year after I got promoted to lieutenant."

She leveled a glare, tapping her foot. "Try again."

He glanced down at her foot then back at her face and laughed. "It's true. Besides, if I'd sent you a current pic then you might've thought I was too bulky or something."

"I'd never think that," she said, shocked at his response.

"Well, women have said that before, so I'm a bit cautious."

"Oh? Are you in the habit of sending strange women your picture?"

His laugh sounded like it came from his belly, deep and loud. "I won't lie. I've belonged to a few dating sites. But for a very short time. They weren't worth my effort."

Her heart broke. She had thought they had something special. "Ah, so you've done this before? Been a pen pal?"

He frowned. "What? No way. I've never had a pen pal. Really never even thought of having one. I've always passed the time on a mission with a good book. But once I got your email, well, I'm pretty damn grateful I have one now." His eyes twinkled with amusement. "Do you want to continue this conversation inside in privacy?"

Suddenly aware of how real this was, Cambrie was at a lost for words. Staring at the wide chest in front of her, she blinked.

His fingers lifted her chin. "I promise I won't jump your bones as soon as the door shuts or anything like that. I'm a gentleman and plan to remain one. Although, I fully admit that it'll be hard being around your loveliness. But you have my word. Besides, if I fuck things up and upset you, Finn will have my ass. I've already been threatened by the bastard," he said, the smile never leaving his face.

Cambrie's muscles loosened and her heart slowly stopped pounding like a freight train. She took his hand and tightened her fingers around it. "Come on, Lt. Daly. Let me show you where I sleep."

His low growl had her laughing as she inserted her key in the door.

"Laugh now. Scream my name soon, baby," he said roughly into her ear, his chest at her back.

When she opened the door, they practically fell through it. She had all of a second to drop her briefcase next to his duffel bag before he shut the door and faced her.

"First a kiss." His tone floated through her ears, serenading her with promises. A kiss would most definitely lead to much more. She had every intention of making sure it did.

"I think you owe me one after all those steamy emails and the promises they held," she whispered as he advanced on her.

He moved like it took no effort at all. His arms encircled her like steel, strength oozing from him. "Your emails were just as naughty, darling."

With his large hands rubbing up and down in zigzags across her back, she looped her arms around his neck and stood on her toes. Just an inch from his lips and he stopped her. What the hell?

"I just want to remember this moment, Cambrie. We only get one first kiss, no matter how many millions we share later."

She tilted her head a little to study him. "Awww. That's so sweet, Miller."

"It's true. The first kiss can make or break the rest of the evening."

"I'm not sure I understand."

The corners of his mouth lifted to show off a slight grin. "Think about it. If you don't enjoy my kiss, then how will I ever seduce you into bed so I can enjoy this hot body?" His hands trailed to her hips and rested on her ass.

Heat pooled between her legs, her wetness growing by the second. Trying not to squirm under his touch was near impossible. "Oh, I have no reason to think I won't enjoy your kiss." Her finger trailed across his parted lips before he sucked it into his mouth. The slow suckling only aroused her more. Kissing him now became a matter of life and death—she'd die if he didn't kiss her soon.

Releasing her finger, he licked his lips. One hand cradled her ass while the other skimmed up her side to slip to the nape of her neck. The heat from his touch blessed her with goose bumps so large she shivered.

His eyes stormed with desire she had never experienced before. "Glad you're as nervous as me, baby. Makes for a fucking great first kiss."

The fingers at the back of her neck pulled her into his personal space. Together they hovered with lips touching in the slightest way. His warm breath escaped his parted lips to bathe hers in it. She smelled mint and coffee. With the slowest of movements, Miller pressed his lips against hers and held. Inhaling took real effort. His fingers massaged her neck in gentle circles.

She moaned and sagged against him, her hands resting on his chest to brace for whatever he meant to share with her. She was positive that his kiss would be brutal and demanding, that he'd overwhelm her with his power. Damn, she couldn't have been more wrong.

His tongue slid across her lips, encouraging them to open, licking at them like she was the sweetest treat. Allowing him access was the easy part. Remaining upright was the hard part. Her hands grasped his shoulders to anchor herself for his possession. His hands remained on her back but ceased their movement. The steady support of his hands assured her that he meant to hold onto her.

When his tongue advanced into the depths of her mouth, lust hit her heavy in the gut. His tongue stroked against hers, each tangle more thrilling than the last. She expected to taste the coffee and mint. Instead, all she tasted was fire fueled by a desire that ran so deep within her shaking body that she lost all track of her thoughts. He devoured her with every lash of his tongue within her mouth.

Without breaking their connection, Miller angled his head in the other direction and her head moved to accommodate his. His fingers manipulated her neck again and kept her where he wanted to continue this glorious kiss.

She couldn't, and wouldn't, just stand there and not take her fill. Oh no. She loved to kiss, loved being kissed. But right now, she wanted to drive Miller so wild with need that he'd beg for more. Just the thought of making love to this handsome man made her pussy weep with a greedy need, small aches pulsing through her womb.

Needing his touch as much as he evidently needed hers, Cambrie pushed past his tongue to plunge deep into his mouth, moving rapidly like she'd never get enough of him. A firestorm grew within her, a warring of passion desperate for release.

He moaned. She moaned. It didn't matter who did. Their sounds mixed within the confinement of the kiss. Her lungs begged for oxygen, but she just couldn't bear to pull away and deprive herself of his warm mouth and hard lips.

To her disappointment, he broke the connection, but kept his lips against hers. Breathless like her, he stood holding her and sucking in air.

"My. God. Cambrie."

"Ditto." Cambrie couldn't find words to explain how she felt, how that kiss just upended the world as she knew it. Now what the hell was she suppose to do? No other man would ever kiss her like that. Shit!

"No, Cambrie. You don't understand." His words sounded desperate, or maybe it was his staggered breathing, or the wild look in his eyes when he pulled back far enough to make eye contact with her. His hands remained on her, holding her where he decided.

"Then explain," she demanded.

He rested his forehead against hers for a long moment before stepping back again and gazing into her eyes.

"I may need to take you with me." He didn't appear to be joking.

"I think I'd go willingly."

When he burst out laughing and tugged her into a bear hug, she didn't know if he had lost his mind or had suffered brain damage from lack of oxygen during that kiss. As long as he remained upright, she didn't care. Being in his embrace was the best medicine for being tired. She felt like she could run a marathon. A wicked smile crept over her lips as she rested her cheek against his shirt. In his emails, he had promised to make love to her all night. It was time to take him up on that.

She pulled away from the tight embrace but remained in his arms. "My bedroom is just through that door. Care to take this somewhere more appropriate?"

His dark brown eyes blazed like melting chocolate. "Thought I said I was gonna seduce you?"

She shrugged, running her fingers over his chest. "Maybe I'm tired of you taking your sweet ass time."

His laugh echoed throughout her small apartment. "I'm so going to enjoy spanking your very fine ass, Cambrie."

Before she could protest, he had her slung over his shoulder and strutted toward the bedroom. Only the flashing light on the answering machine could've distracted her at that moment. And it did. With her long hair hanging all around her, the blinking red light on the machine barely caught her eye.

"Wait! Miller, stop. Please."

He placed her on her feet just as quickly as he had lifted her off of them. "I'm sorry, Cambrie. I don't mean to be rough."

"Oh, hush. I don't mind rough. I'm sure I'm going to like rough with you, but I need to check my messages." She hurried to the machine and pressed the play button.

"You what!" His shock couldn't be any more obvious at the mood kill.

She wrung her hands, wishing the old machine would hurry up and spit out the phone call. "I'm sorry. Long story. Only my aunt's nursing home has this number. For emergencies. I must've missed the call on my cell phone."

Her heart pounded as the voice came across the machine. "Miss Brasher, sorry to alarm you but this is Dixieborough Nursing Home. Your aunt has taken a small fall and the doctor is with her now. Please call us when you get this message or stop by."

"Oh, no!" Cambrie yelled. "I've got to go see

her. She's all I've got, Miller. I'm so sorry." Cambrie grabbed her purse and bolted for the door with Miller on her heels. "I know you came all this way and—"

He cut her off on the porch when she locked her door. "And we can pick up where we left off once we know that Aunt Annabelle is okay. Let's walk and talk, darling. The sooner we get you to her, the sooner we can get that horrified look out of your eyes. I don't like seeing you upset." His fingers latched onto her elbow and hurried with her to the driveway. "Pity the person who ever intentionally hurts you, baby."

"Why's that?" she asked, appreciating his protectiveness.

"You don't want to know." He piled into the passenger seat. But his large frame didn't fit well in her small, practical car.

"Sorry the car's small," she said, her fingers shaking as she inserted the key into the ignition.

"Not to worry. Being six five makes most things small for me. Now drive."

Chapter Seven

Silence filled the car while Cambrie drew slow breaths to calm her nerves. Being wound up from Miller's kiss was one thing. Add her worry about Aunt Annabelle to that, and she might be a candidate for a heart attack.

"Tell me about Aunt Annabelle." Miller's soft command was welcomed as she merged through traffic.

"She's the only family I have left. She raised me since I was a little girl."

"What happened to your parents?"

She swallowed hard, harsh memories working their way back into her mind after years of being buried. She just couldn't allow them to resurface.

"I'd rather not talk about it. I'm sorry. Please don't be mad. Just some things are better left in the past."

Miller stared straight ahead. "Agreed. So why is Aunt Annabelle in a nursing home?"

Phew. He hadn't been offended that she brushed off his question. She liked how easy he was to talk with. "Um. Well, she's been there since she had a heart attack. Then they found breast cancer, but they caught it in time thanks to the heart attack."

"Lucky. If you can be at all with either illness."

"That's how I looked at it. Oh, I hope she's all right. It's just ahead."

"You're very close to her, aren't you?" Miller asked, his voice soft, soothing.

Cambrie pulled into a parking spot. "Yes."

"And what do you feel right now?"

"Scared shitless."

Offering her a smile when she glanced at him, he spoke with assurance. "Well, besides that. Your gut. Trust it."

She jumped from the car and they rushed toward the building. She looked at him. "I feel like she's fine."

Miller held the door open. "Then I bet she is."

And he was right. Aunt Annabelle was giving the home's staff hell when Cambrie bolted into her room.

"Oh, thank God, Cambrie, you came," Aunt Annabelle screeched, holding her arms up and sitting forward in her bed.

Cambrie rushed over to the bed and accepted the hug. "What happened? You scared me half to death."

"All I wanted was to go down to the lounge, and they said no. They just want to keep me locked up in here like a prisoner."

Cambrie straightened and faced the nurse who spoke with her hands on her hips. "Now, Miss Annabelle, you know that is the furthest from the truth. Really. I can't believe you, of all people, fibbing like that."

Aunt Annabelle's cheeks reddened and she pursed her lips shut, refusing to look at the nurse. Cambrie bit back a laugh. Aunt Annabelle would be just fine if she still had attitude swirling within her.

"Miss Cambrie," the nurse said, "we just

needed her to wait until after meal time. Then we would dispense meds and we could've had her go down to the lounge. It's the same routine every night. But, oh no. This woman needed to have her own way. She's awfully lucky to only have a bruise on that stubborn butt of hers. Hmmpff."

When the nurse stalked out of the room, Aunt Annabelle's mouth dropped. "Well, I say. I've never been spoken to like that. How dare she? I'll see that she's fired right away. And you, Cambrie, didn't stand up for me one bit."

Cambrie sat on the edge of the bed and straightened the sheets. "Now that's not true and you know it. And you'll not be getting Nella fired. You know she's been real good to you here. You were wrong to get out of bed by yourself. You've been warned so many times."

Aunt Annabelle shook her head, the perfectly styled short gray and white hair didn't move. "Well, I'm sorry if being cooped up in here all day makes me lose my manners. Any sane person would go nuts here." She looked past Cambrie's shoulder. "Who is that handsome young man?" Her tone had changed from bitchy to curios.

Cambrie's eyes widened and she jumped up, having totally forgotten Miller had accompanied her to the nursing home. This wasn't exactly how she wanted him to meet her aunt. "Oh, I'm sorry. Forgive my manners. Aunt Annabelle, this is Lt. Miller Daly. He's the pen pal I told you about that I'm working with to win a grant for the library." *And keep my job.*

Miller stepped into the room, instantly stealing all free space with his width and height. Taking his place beside Cambrie, he stood like a majestic statue. "Pleasure really is all mine, Aunt

Annabelle. And I must say that you have a lovely niece." He glanced at Cambrie before turning back to the older woman. "It's obvious where she gets not only her looks but her smarts as well. I don't blame you for standing up for yourself in here."

Cambrie wanted to slug him. He didn't know that he was encouraging a monster when Auntie set herself to doing something.

Aunt Annabelle sat straighter in the bed and primped her hair, an automatic gesture Cambrie had witnessed from her any time she received a compliment. "Thank you, Mr. Daly. It's nice to see Cambrie associating with such a fine gentleman."

"Thank you, ma'am. And please just call me Miller." When he took Aunt Annabelle's hand and kissed the knuckles, well, Cambrie thought she'd seen it all. With a few words and proper attention, Miller had calmed Aunt Annabelle's temper and won her over. The old woman beamed and appeared twenty years younger now that her scowl had disappeared.

Aunt Annabelle grabbed his arm and studied his tattoo on his upper arm. It peaked out just enough from under his sleeve for the edge to be viewed. "Who is this woman?"

Cambrie noticed the tattoo for the first time. It had been too hard to see on the picture he had sent. And she had been too busy being stunned at his arrival earlier to even notice. Her heart sank. Did he love the woman?

Miller looked at the tattoo and at Cambrie. "It's your niece I believe."

Cambrie gasped. "That can't be true," she said through gritted teeth. "You had that tattoo in the picture you sent. The picture was a year old. Way before I ever emailed you."

He faced her. "Yes, I know. I'll explain when we have time."

"Why don't you have time now?" Aunt Annabelle insisted.

"Because I'm just getting into town after a very long trip and I'm afraid if I try to make any sense now I won't. I'll let you ladies visit while I excuse myself to find a men's room. I hope you feel better, Aunt Annabelle. Cambrie, I'll be in the waiting room, but please take all the time you need."

When he marched from the room, Cambrie had the pleasure of viewing his ass, snugly encased in blue jeans that showcased the hard muscles of his thighs. Her cheeks blushed when her mind wandered to all the kinky things she wished to do with him.

"Well, young lady. I must say you've landed yourself a live one," Aunt Annabelle quipped, her smile still lighting up her face.

Cambrie waved her hand in the air. "Oh, stop it. He's just a pen pal who's part of a project for work." Yeah, right. More like he was the man who ruined her expectations for any other man.

Aunt Annabelle made a skeptical face. "If you say so. But I don't know of many men, or *pen pals,* that trek around the globe to meet a woman. Sounds like that would be contradictory to being a *pen pal.*"

"Would you please stop saying pen pal like that?"

The old woman rested her hand across her heart and widened her eyes. "Like what?"

"Like it's anything more than it is." Cambrie paced the room. "And if it were, it's up to me where I take it. Understood? I won't have you prying into my life and trying to force me into something I'm not ready for."

Aunt Annabelle threw her hands up in the air and let them fall back onto the bed. "There you go again, worrying I'm rushing you down the blessed aisle. All I'm saying is a proper young lady like yourself should see fit to have some romance in her life. You did say Emma and Finn know him?"

"Yes, Finn used to be his commander."

"I do adore Finn, fine young man. Well, at least you have someone that can vouch for Miller. And he seems like a fine boy. And very easy on the eyes, I might add."

"Auntie!" Cambrie stared in shock. "I've never heard you talk in such a way. What's gotten into you today? Maybe you hit your head in that fall."

"Maybe I don't want my favorite niece to pass up a good thing because she feels she owes me something. You owe me nothing except to be happy. Just remember, the best way you can repay me for taking you into my home is to make a home of your own with a man who cherishes you as much as you do him."

Cambrie studied her aunt. "You watch too many movies in that lounge, Auntie. Romance isn't what it used to be in your days."

"Which is a damn shame, pardon my language. A man knew how to properly court a woman back then. Nowadays, couples don't have a clue about how to love without boundaries. All I ask is that you open your heart to the possibility, especially when it travels around the world to meet you."

Cambrie swallowed the knot in her throat, her mouth very dry. She had to admit that Aunt

Annabelle was right about one thing. Miller had come a very long way just to meet her and had gone through a lot of effort to avoid her telling him not to visit. And they hadn't even talked on the phone, just emailed. But the tattoo on his arm had to be discussed before they could become any more intimate. Looking at another woman on his muscles while Cambrie made love to him would really be a killjoy. It was supposed to be her…did he think she was born yesterday? She didn't take him as a man to play head games but, then again, she still had to get to know him.

"Well, it's good to see that you're not arguing with me, Cambrie. Shows you're thinking about what I just said. Good for you. Now your young man is waiting. Go to him. I'll still be here in this prison when you can visit again." Aunt Annabelle held her gaze on Cambrie.

"Fine. I'll get going but you, Auntie, had better follow the rules. Mr. Hackler has commented on how you are one of the last true Southern Belles. You wouldn't want to damage that reputation by causing trouble. Would you?"

Aunt Annabelle's mouth dropped open. "Now that's not playing fair."

Cambrie smiled. At least she could get through to her aunt when it involved people's perception of her. "Sure it is. Behave and you have nothing to worry about." Cambrie kissed her cheek. "I'll call tomorrow and come by soon."

"I can't wait to hear stories about Miller."

Cambrie waltzed from the room before her blazing cheeks could stir up more questions. No one would ever guess the wicked sexual fantasies Cambrie kept hidden deep inside her. They'd think she was some kind of freak.

Walking into the waiting room, she caught a glimpse of Miller standing at the window peering out. When he turned and smiled, Cambrie no longer cared what anyone thought. She wanted Miller and planned to fulfill all of her fantasies if he'd allow it.

"All set?" he asked, striding toward her.

She smiled. "I am now. Let's head home and see if we can find where we left off."

Chapter Eight

"What's in the box, Cambrie?" Miller asked, hovering over Cambrie's shoulder while she attempted to push the box to the far side of her kitchen counter.

Of all the things she hadn't had time to put away, it had to be the sex toys delivered last week. Before she could stop him, he picked up the box and studied it. Now that shouldn't have been a problem since the company used a discreet business name on the return address label. But Cambrie jumping at him like he had stolen her diary had stirred his curiosity. He hadn't stop badgering her since they walked through the front door five minutes ago.

"None of your business," she said, hoping her carefree reply threw him off of his nosy quest. "Are you hungry? I'm afraid all I have is frozen pizza or pasta."

"Oh, I'm very hungry. But not for food, darling." The glimmer in his dark brown eyes sent a delicious tingle down her spine as memories of where they had left things re-surfaced.

"Mmmm. I do like the sound of that, Miller. Kiss me."

The devilish smile creeping across his face held warning. "Sure. Open the box first."

Christ, did he never let up? "Why are you so fascinated with that box when you could be dragging me into the bedroom to drive me wild like you promised?" She hoped the purr in her voice would be enough to force him to concentrate on her instead. She'd much rather open her package in private to discreetly have the toys in a drawer in the bedroom for their use. She shouldn't have put off doing that. Damn!

His finger swooped over her ear to push her hair behind it. The innocent touch sent a blistering shock wave through her body. Shivering was a reaction she couldn't stop as his gaze remained on hers. "I'm betting there are some things in that box that will help me drive you wild, baby."

She gasped. How the heck could he have guessed that?

His knuckles skimmed her cheek, the warmth of her skin heating more by his touch. "And by this pretty blush on your cheeks, I'd say I figured out your dirty little secret, Cambrie. I might add here that I like dirty."

A battle between embarrassment and annoyance grew within her. "Okay. Fine. I ordered sex toys." There was no escaping his embrace. She was forced to stand her ground in front of him under those watchful eyes. "But how did you figure that out? There's nothing on that package to indicate what the contents are or where it came from."

He lifted the box to point at the business name. "ABC Company. Who the hell names their business that? A generic name like that always indicates something from the sex industry."

"Oh." Now didn't she feel foolish thinking she'd be so smart trying to cover up her naughty side?

Oh, God then the mailman probably knew where it came from too. How would she ever face him again? Worse, what if someone in town started gossiping and it got back to Aunt Annabelle. Cambrie sighed inwardly—the challenges of living in a small town—too many nosy people with boring lives always looking for gossip on another poor soul.

Miller's voice filled with humor and acceptance. "And I've ordered enough porn in my lifetime to recognize those labels anywhere."

His admission provided her comfort. "You have?"

He smirked. "Well, of course. I'm a guy. Now stop driving me wild wondering what you ordered and open the damn thing."

She laughed, her belly swarming with butterflies. This was even more exciting than perusing the naughty website. She could open her presents with Miller here to watch. Miller's silent respect made her feel like there was nothing she couldn't do. For the first time in her life, she didn't have to worry about impressing someone or following rules.

Cambrie quickly opened the brown package and dug through the bubble wrap to the contents. The vibrator, butt plug, metal handcuffs encased in pink fuzzy fur, paddle, and lube were all in plastic packages. The chest harness came in a black box with a picture of a woman straddling a man's chest while he fucked her with the dildo. Cambrie swallowed hard.

"Holy shit," Miller exclaimed, his wide eyes glancing between her and the toys. "You have to run away with me, Cambrie," he vibrated with excitement while he grabbed the harness. "We think so much alike, it's scary. Have you used any of this before?"

Shaking her head with a little too much force,

she answered without looking at him, her gaze never straying from the toys. "No. Never. Well, except for a vibrator. A girl goes without sex as long as I do, she needs a little something to help keep her sane."

When she dared to look up, she caught him studying her. "Are men around here fucking blind?" He held up his palm. "Don't even answer that because I know they are if they've allowed a beautiful, sexy woman like you to walk around unclaimed. But their idiocy is certainly my fortune."

He kissed her forehead, the simple touch swelling her heart like nothing ever before. Feeling desired and cherished, she fought to keep from shaking and focused on the muscular arms inches from her. "I like you, Miller."

He smiled. "Yeah? Well, that's pretty darn good because I'm liking the hell out of you too, Cambrie Brasher. Now pick a toy and let's have some fun."

Feeling brave, she chose the paddle. Always wondering what an erotic spanking felt like, she set her mind to find out with Miller.

"Good choice. That should warm your pretty little ass nice. Then I'll use the softer side to caress the marks I leave on your flesh."

Her pussy convulsed, causing her to squeeze her legs together, but then she'd forgotten to breathe. Her breath sucked in loudly and elicited a devastatingly powerful smile from Miller.

"Damn. I love your reaction to me, baby." He scooped up the remaining toys. "These are what I choose." His grin held promise and warning, adding to her desire. "Now lead the way to your bedroom and let's have that fun we promised each other."

Walking on shaky legs proved more difficult than she expected, and the short trek to her room seemed longer than she remembered.

"Good thing none of these require batteries…well except your vibrator, but I think we can postpone using that for now," Miller teased.

She pressed her palm to her forehead. "I never thought of batteries. I was just in such a hurry to order them…never mind."

He strutted to her side. "Why were you in a rush?"

Open mouth, insert foot. She sighed. "I…I wanted. Christ, if you must know, I just wanted to have some stuff on hand to use with you." She stared at her hands and wrung them, not knowing where to look or what to think. "I've never used sex toys before except my vibrator and, well, I'm a bit curious is all." She forced her head up until she caught his gaze. There was no judgment in his eyes, just desire. "I wanted to try them with you because you seem very open and adventurous."

"Hold that thought, baby." He left the room and returned with his duffle bag. With a quick motion, he unzipped it, dug inside, and pulled out a plastic shopping bag. "I stopped at a sex toy shop on the way here. Was hoping I read you right and you were the adventurous type, too. See what I mean, we think alike."

He dropped the goodies back into his bag. When his hand rubbed her upper arm, she felt comfortable, a little giddy. What was it about this larger-than-life man that kept her at ease when she should be worried in the face of his obvious sexual experience? Would he be disappointed by her lack of skills? Remembering his promise to make love all day or night made her wonder if she could actually keep up with him. It thrilled her to hear a sexy man tell her that he wanted her in his bed for hours. But how did someone like herself, so inexperienced and lacking a sex life, really match his powers in bed?

He stopped touching her. "Tell me I'm not scaring you off, Cambrie." His voice rang of concern and care, interrupting her thoughts.

She blinked a few times, staring at his face, mesmerized by the hardened features with small scars. "What? Why would you think that, Miller?"

He offered a simple shrug, but never removed his gaze from hers. "I don't know. You looked worried, distracted. I would never make you do anything that you didn't want to, okay? You have to understand that hurting you is the last thing I'd ever do. That, darling, is a promise from my heart and soul. Plus, Finn would beat me senseless if I harmed a hair on your head—which I wouldn't."

A sigh escaped her lips. "I believe that, Miller. Really. I do. I just wonder if I can live up to your expectations is all. I'm not, well, really experienced. Haven't had a whole lotta sex." She forced a smile to hide her embarrassment. Better to warn him now than to let him down without a heads up.

This was it. This was the moment. She held her breath. He'd run now. Probably would realize he had chosen the wrong woman to get involved with. And once he ran, there went her job, the library's chances of the grant to remain open, and Aunt Annabelle's future. Not to mention Cambrie's one chance to fulfill all those fantasies, those deep, dark desires that she had conjured up since first emailing Miller.

Standing with his hands on his hips, his height was magnificent. "You expecting me to turn tail and run as fast as I can, or something?" Miller said softly but with an edge to his tone, like he was aggravated.

"How did you know what I was thinking?" She couldn't keep the shock from her question.

"Baby, I make a living reading people. In my line of work, it keeps me alive." His hands grasped her arms and he leaned down to her ear. "I don't plan on leaving unless you tell me to go or my orders come in. The only place I ran was here…to meet you."

With a whoosh of air from her lungs, she relaxed as he leaned back and studied her. The friskiness welling up inside her became overwhelming. "Can you tell what I'm thinking right now, Miller?"

His eyes darkened. "It better be about getting naked with me."

She laughed and began unbuttoning her blouse. His eyes fixated on the movement of her fingers. "It's exactly what I'm thinking. But I need to make a request."

"Christ, anything."

"The first time we make love, no toys. Just you. Okay?"

His gaze rose to meet hers. "Agreed. Just us this first time." Long fingers grazed her shoulders after she shrugged off her blouse. "Feeling all your softness and beauty. Then I want to feel the wild woman hiding inside here." His thumb brushed across the swell of her breast to her heart.

When his lips landed on hers, something deep inside her awakened, a feeling of finding what was missing. His kiss was sharper this time, like he claimed her. Delving deep into his mouth, she relished the feeling of heat and strength. Strong hands gripped her sides, pulling her against his hard chest, never breaking the connection of their mouths.

She moaned, the sound swallowed up by his mouth. The way his tongue roamed inside her mouth, like he was sipping at sweetness, unnerved her with its patience. Leaving her mouth to trail along the side of her neck, Miller's lips left a fiery wet path wherever they touched. Leaning her head back, she offered him the access he demanded, wanting his kisses to pamper her skin with their attention.

Her hands busied themselves, wandering over the hard muscles of his arms and shoulders. Crossing over the tattoo on his upper arm brought her crashing back to reality.

"What's wrong?" he asked when she stiffened and pushed back.

"The tattoo. I need to know who she is before we continue. I need to know if there's another woman in your life. I…I just don't operate that way. I won't be anyone's plaything."

The frown covered his face, reflecting slow burning anger. "Don't ever insult yourself like that. I'd never use you, Cambrie. Let's get that straight right now. I sure as hell wouldn't hightail it from my mission the second it was over if I wasn't totally into you."

She crossed her arms, vulnerability rearing its ugly head. "Then why'd you say that tat is of me when you know damn well we only just met. The picture you shared with me was a year old and you had that tat then. Explain."

He crossed his arms to match her stance. Not

backing down a bit, he spoke slowly. “I love temper in a woman. Good to see you have one. Now I don’t have a clue how to explain this tattoo. You’ll only think I’m crazy.”

“Try me.”

The corner of his mouth raised a bit to soften his hard stare. “You’ve come to me in my dreams for over a year now. It’s driven me crazy and preoccupied my waking hours. I can’t explain why I know it was you.” He sighed and continued. “This tat, well, I had it done after one particular mission. I was cornered in a building owned by a drug lord. After my team extracted me, I had your face permanently etched into my arm. Wanted to carry your image with me. If something were to happen to me, then you’d come with me into the next life. May sound fucked up…I don’t know how to explain it. But you have my word, there is you and no other woman, Cambrie.”

She moved his arm and studied the artwork. “I’m hardly a mermaid, Miller.”

He laughed, the deep sound filling the small bedroom, easing the awkward tension. “I made the tat a mermaid because she was unique like I knew you’d be. She’s a mystical creature, one that can’t be explained, wasn’t predictable. That’s how I felt about every dream. I couldn’t explain you, and really didn’t want to. I was just glad you kept coming back. The nights you didn’t appear in my dreams, well, I’d wake up in the worst of moods. God help the poor fuck that got in my way.”

Wow. She did all that to him? “Can I tell you something and promise you won’t laugh?”

He smirked. “Darling, did you not hear what I just said? I’m the last person to laugh. Now spill.”

She rubbed the tattoo with a gentle rhythm,

admiring the detail. She had to admit, as odd as it was, that the woman did resemble her. The long, dark brown hair flowing around her like a halo, small face with a defined jaw line, lips parted and waiting for a lover's tongue, eyes half closed with lust. "You said earlier that the men around here are blind because none of them have claimed me. That's partly my fault. Besides having absolutely no time to date, none of them compared to the man I occasionally dreamt of on many restless nights. A man larger than life. Someone I could imagine being myself with, no pretenses, no fakeness. Someone I could share what's inside here." She placed his hand over her heart. "The part of me that even I don't really understand. The part of me that goes against how I was raised. So while you dreamt of me, I like to think you haunted me at night as well. My dream man."

"Am I now?" His voice vibrated with lust.

She swallowed hard. "I'm glad you're here, Miller. I'm sorry if I made you feel unwelcome in my previous emails. I just didn't know how to deal with my busy schedule, and I wanted everything to be perfect when you arrived."

"Then thank you, Cambrie, honey."

"For what?"

"For making everything perfect. You continue to surpass my expectations in every way." He stepped closer until they stood toe to toe, the twinkle in his eyes lit up his face. "I'm about to seduce you. Last chance to back out."

Clearing her throat, she asked the question she really didn't want to hear an affirmative answer to. "There's no other woman in your life?" Just because the tattoo was of the woman he dreamt of, didn't mean there wasn't another woman in his life.

His gaze remained on hers. Never flinching, he spoke clearly. "No. Hasn't been for a long time. And you? Any guy I need to pound on?"

She laughed. "Nope. So let the seduction begin," she said, flipping her hair over her shoulder while angling her head, not feeling shy standing in her bra.

"God, we think alike. Love it," he said, pulling his shirt over his head, baring a chest rippled with muscles and a fine mat of brown hair that disappeared in a V into his pants.

His hands roamed up and down her back before inching over her ass. Long fingers kneaded her cheeks through her skirt. Her hips pushed forward grinding her clit against the hardness of his thigh. Her pussy awakened with jealousy, needing attention desperately. Oh, how she wanted his hands everywhere on her body all at once. Didn't matter that it wasn't physically possible. She just *needed* it.

When Miller's lips covered hers, she melted against him, loving the way he held her up with no effort at all. He tasted of heat so potent, she swore he burned her lips. But there was nothing she'd change about his approach. She came alive under his ministrations, like an electrical wire sparking in all directions. The manipulation of his fingers on her ass cheeks warned of his strength and his seduction. The patient massaging, crawling inch by inch, over her ass drove her insane with the need to feel his hands on her bare skin.

"The skirt. Take it off. If I do it, babe, I'll only rip it," he choked, his voice strangled as he laid wet kisses across her jawbone.

With shaking fingers, she found the clasp on

the back of the skirt and undid it. Stepping back from him, she immediately missed his body heat. Feeling sexier than ever before, she slowed down her movements and allowed the material to shimmy over her hips and down her thighs until it pooled at her feet and she could step out of it. Standing before Miller in beige thigh highs, tiny panties and demi bra, Cambrie should've felt the urge to cover up, her strict upbringing never too far from her thoughts. But instead, the look in his eyes, pure animal lust, gave her all the prompting she needed to continue her teasing moves.

"Don't stop. I want you naked. I've endured too many tormenting dreams. Strip now, baby. Or I can help you." His tone thrilled her with its manly demands and the lust hidden behind each word. No doubt he meant what he said.

Oh, what a feeling to be the center of Miller's attention right now, knowing that he had seen so much more than she had in this life. And yet, here she was, standing half naked in her bedroom, captivating him beyond his control.

Hell, yeah! Now this was addictive. More powerful than anything she had ever experienced.

"I'll tell you what, Miller." She ran her fingers under her bra straps. "Get naked with me."

A low growl emanated from his throat, but his gaze remained on her while he sat on the edge of her bed and untied his boots, leaving them neatly on the floor once he shoved his socks inside.

Standing before her, he wasted no time undoing his pants. When he pulled each leg free of the jeans, he tossed the pants to the side, stood and crossed his arms facing her. She studied his long frame dressed only in dark green boxer shorts and felt a little cheated since the material hid the bulge that lay behind it.

Without a word, he waited for her to continue, his breathing increasing and the swell of his chest showcasing magnificent muscles with each rise and fall.

Reaching behind her back, she unsnapped the clasp, loosening the lacy material. Keeping her attention on his face, she watched his gaze roam down to her breasts as his jaw tightened.

"You're killing me, Cambrie."

The warning fell on deaf ears. She was enjoying his torment too much to fear pushing it too far. Driving him wild was part of her plan to give him the ultimate pleasure tonight. She didn't feel as inexperienced as her history proved.

"What a shame," she said, inching the bra down over her breasts until the rosy tips were exposed. Tossing the lacy material onto the floor, she whipped her hair back over her shoulders with a quick flick of her neck before taking each nipple between her thumbs and fingers and pinching them.

Without a sound, Miller leapt forward, lifted Cambrie by the waist earning a loud squeal of pleasure. He lowered her onto the bed with his massive body as a blanket. The weight of him pressed her deeply into the soft mattress. She reveled in the moment, in the closeness of this sexy man whose hard body was so gentle.

Without warning, his lips latched onto her nipple and sucked hard, his tongue lapping at it like she were a special treat. Arching her head back, she cried out. "Oh, yes!"

With her hands unable to fist in his hair because it was too short, she resorted to holding him by the back of the head to keep his delicious attention on her breast. Her short fingernails dug into his scalp, but the low growl escaping from his busy mouth only proved he was as aroused by her actions as she was by his.

Within seconds, he had her so aroused and needy. She yearned for rougher, harder, faster. He'd made her vibrator an obsolete toy. Now what the hell would she do to achieve an orgasm once he left and she couldn't replicate what he was doing now?

She'd be doomed to crave him like a potent obsession. And she'd yet to even feel an orgasm brought on by Miller's attentions but, from the way it built deep inside her womb, like a smoldering flame bursting to life, she expected to be addicted to him as soon as the climatic sensation captured her.

Losing herself in the moment, she was swept away by the desires swirling around them. The heat from their bodies fed her pulse until her heartbeat roared in her ears. With every inch of her body craving Miller's touch, Cambrie squirmed under his massive body. Pinned in place with not much room to move, she was desperate to keep his hungry mouth on her heated flesh until he brought her the explosion her pussy begged for.

Above her, Miller's body trembled. Was it from holding his weight off of her? Doubtful. The guy looked like he bench-pressed refrigerators.

"Cambrie, honey. I want to go slow. Really. But I can't promise anything once I'm inside you. I'm afraid I'll lose any control I have." His mouth struggled to form the words as he kissed the swells of her breasts.

Keeping her hands busy massaging his firm muscles, she didn't want to stop touching him. "I don't want slow. Just want you, Miller. All of you. Inside me. Now."

Her breathing hitched against the side of his neck when he climbed up her body, his heat encompassing her in a blanket of warmth. Her hands had a mind of their own, running along his upper body. They glided over his smooth skin, memorizing every outline of the muscles on his back, shoulders, arms.

Each time her fingers ran over his mermaid tattoo, she felt a sense of pride, believing that she resembled his dream woman. She believed in the romance of it all, the fairy tale likeness. For once in her life, it felt right to do something for herself, temporarily forgetting every responsibility or other aspect of her orderly life.

Miller's strong voice interrupted her giddiness. "Need a sec, baby. Touch yourself for me," he commanded, lifting off of her.

With the loss of his body heat, she shivered, not wanting to let him up and not understanding why he needed to leave her bed. Had she done something wrong?

It had been a very long time since she'd had a man in her bed, but things between her and Miller were heating up very fast and progressing as nature intended. So why would he need to jump up just when they were reaching the point of breathlessness? Oh, how she loved that oxygen-starved feeling.

Leaning up on her elbows, she watched as he removed a condom from his bag and sheathed his cock with the latex. His tall, muscular frame appeared massive in the light of her small bedside lamp.

With a sigh of relief, she dropped back onto

the bed and did as he had requested. She strummed her hands over her breasts, stroking the hard nipples. Electric sensations swirled deep inside her belly. Feeling the bed sink, she turned her head to watch Miller creep over her again but this time he began his kisses at her navel.

Damn right the man should feast on her! Cambrie succumbed to the wanton woman hiding inside her. She had everything to offer Miller, everything that any other woman had. Just so happened that she had Miller, too.

Cambrie sucked in her breath. The cool wetness left behind on her simmering flesh by Miller's kisses only made her whimper for more of the delightful contact.

"Miller, what are you waiting for? This is pure torture."

His laugh should've irritated her, but it didn't. She enjoyed his easy-going approach and patience. God, if only she could borrow some patience from him then she wouldn't be squirming all over the bed, thrusting her hips into his to coax his cock into her throbbing pussy.

"Maybe I'm waiting for you to beg me to fuck you, Cambrie. Or maybe I want to take my sweet time with you, enjoying every inch of your hot body. My God, I never expected this kind of sizzle." His last words were rushed, like he couldn't catch his breath.

"Sizzle? What the hell is sizzle?" she demanded, looking over her belly. If she didn't feel his cock inside her soon, she may very well find the strength to flip him onto his back and straddle him. Well, she could at least give it a good try.

His smile lit up his face. The sharp angles had softened now with his focus on her. Nothing else mattered but her. The warm feeling left her oozing with giddiness, like a schoolgirl preparing for her first kiss, that awkward thrill of the unknown.

"Sizzle," he repeated. "A serious spark. Don't you feel it?" He stared, waiting on her reply.

"Feel it? Are you insane? I'm about to burst into flames and all you can talk about is sizzle?" She wrapped her legs around his hips. "Fuck me, now, Miller. You want begging? How about demanding?" His raised eyebrows earned a smirk from her. "That's right, Miller. You put me into this state, now you can damn well finish the job."

"Is that so?" he asked, dry humping her, his engorged cock rubbing against her clit.

She moaned some inaudible words before shrieking. "Miller! For God's sake. Fuck me. Now! Oh, please," she whimpered, her head thrashing side to side as a wall of pleasure built inside her, so deep she thought she'd melt into the bed before he finished with her.

"Soon. Very soon. But first I want to taste you on my lips," he said against her heated flesh as his mouth returned to her breast, sucked hard on the nipple for a few teasing seconds, before descending down her body with a trail of slippery kisses.

His intention was obvious and Cambrie willed herself not to squirm out of his reach. But she feared she hadn't hidden her nervousness when Miller looked up, his head hovering above her pelvis.

"I'm guessing no one has ever gone down on you before." His directness stunned her.

"No. Never."

"Mmmm. Good. I like that I'm the first to taste this sweet pussy."

Before she could bask in the glory of his words, his mouth landed on her mound. He made no effort to hide his pleasure. Hot kisses smothered her pussy lips like she was a lollipop, his tongue stroking up and down her swollen lips, swiping the clit with the tenderest of touches.

"Oh Christ, Miller!" Cambrie yelled, her nails digging into anything to keep her from launching off of the bed. Grasping the sheets, she made an effort to keep her hips settled for his mouth to continue its delicious feast.

He interrupted his work to look up, his dark eyes dancing with lust. "I love that you shave your pussy, Cambrie. So smooth for me. So sweet. I think I'm already addicted to you, baby girl."

With a wink, he slowly lowered his head and focused on driving her to a place she never knew existed. A place where her mind hovered somewhere in the clouds and her body twisted in the greedy hands of lust, unwilling to fight free from the waves of pleasure enveloping her, yet unable to attain gratification.

Keeping her head still did nothing to calm the dizziness rioting through her system. With her breathing out of control, her temperature continued to rise as her body ignited in too many places to count.

Sounds of Miller indulging himself between her legs only drove her closer to the edge. He made no effort to hide his satisfied groans. Her pussy begged for the pleasure but she hesitated, not wanting to lose this feeling of floating between body and soul.

"Oh, Miller. Oh, wow. I can't. I mean…" She couldn't even form a sentence and he didn't stop to let her. His continued sucking and licking where no other man had tasted her, kept her in a dreamlike state, but far from the orgasm she so desperately needed.

When his tongue darted from her aching pussy lips to torment her clit, she shot off the bed like a firecracker. The orgasm so powerful there was no preparing for it. Everything around her blurred as she rode the pulses within her core, bucking and twisting like a mad woman.

Cambrie feared there'd never be another orgasm like this. Although, with her body reeling from the spasms deep within her pussy and on her clit, she wasn't quite sure she could survive another orgasm. Coming this hard had never been possible with either man or machine. What would she do once Miller left?

"Miller," she managed the soft plea through ragged breaths.

With her eyes half open, she watched as he rose above her, his sleek body moving over hers, his focus concentrating on her face. Her shaky hands reached for his arms, grasping onto the muscles in his forearms as the weight of him pressed her firmly into the mattress.

She sighed with contentment, never wanting this moment to end. Never wanting to forget the lust filled gleam in the dark chocolate brown eyes that seemed mesmerized by her features.

When his gaze met hers, it held. His cock nudged against her wet pussy. With the slowest movements, he inched inside her, his hips barely pressing into her. The tightness was immediate. Christ, how long had it been since she fucked someone? Too long to remember, and now Miller would think she was even more inexperienced than she had admitted.

"Oh, my, God, Cambrie," he said, his voice shaking, the first sign of emotion defeating his usual control. His arms trembled as he looked toward the ceiling. She almost expected him to howl or something.

She didn't know how to react to him. What was going through his mind? The nip of pain as his cock pushed deeper into her anxious pussy had her biting down on her lip in an effort not to cry out in pleasure for fear he would mistake it for pain and stop. Much larger than she expected, his cock stretched her pussy and the pleasure grew by the second.

His warm gaze melted her heart with the intense focus he showered over her. "You feel so amazing, my sweet Cambrie. How can a guy be any luckier than me right now?"

Miller had stopped thrusting and her pussy adjusted to the thick head of his cock. "Don't stop. I want to feel you so deep inside of me, Miller. Don't stop," she whispered. Her lips found the side of his neck to nip and suck while her hips edged upward, encouraging his cock to bury itself deeper into her wetness.

"Aw hell, Cambrie. I'm losing control here. I don't want to come before I'm buried inside you. Christ."

She felt his pain, his anguish, having lived it moments before. The bite in his words revealed his frustration. Well, too bad. He had teased her enough tonight. It's about time he got a taste of his own medicine, um, in this case, torment.

"Payback sucks, doesn't it?" she said against the side of his neck. Her words rushed out as she gasped for air, the weight of him making breathing a challenge, but she couldn't bear for him move off and steal the warmth that encompassed her.

He angled his head to stare at her. "Payback? And what's that suppose to mean, darling?" There was a hint of machismo shining through his words. It didn't mean shit, not after he'd put her through exquisite torture to give her the best orgasm of her life.

"It means, how's it feel to be driven wild? Just like you did to me."

Brown eyes danced as he spoke. "If I remember right, you were squealing with delight."

"And you will too, babe, if you move that cock. Fuck me, Miller. Like you promised."

The corners of his mouth rose to form a giant smirk. "I have never squealed in my life."

With that declaration, he thrust his cock deep into her pussy until he was fully seated in her. Her cries echoed throughout the room. The tightness caught her off guard. But the glorious feeling of him filling her was worth it.

Miller stilled instantly and glared. "Christ, you're so fucking tight, honey. You sure you're not a virgin?" Then he crooked his neck to the side to offer a few curses before turning back to her. "I swear to God, if you are and you let me fuck you this hard, I will paddle your ass until you can't sit for a week."

God, didn't he look like he meant that particular threat? She could only stare into his serious face. She probably should've been scared at his declaration. Maybe even fearful to continue. But something deep inside her, somewhere she'd only begun to discover, broke free and released a wildness that had been caged for too long. Yeah, there was no more room for any maybes.

Cambrie simply opened her mouth and spoke

slowly so she couldn't be mistaken. "I'm not a virgin, just have a sad love life and, as a result, my pussy has lacked from any serious attention. Could I still get paddled?"

Now Cambrie could've wagered on a multitude of reactions from Miller except the one she received. It appeared she was playing with fire and had better learn the game fast. And she was positive she would love to play the game!

Miller growled, slammed his lips onto hers and devoured her mouth in the most demanding kiss she had ever experienced. Gone was the slow, calculated loving he had shown her so far. Replaced with an animalistic longing, a determination so powerful it stole her breath.

But she matched his power and met his conquest with her own. Her tongue wrapped around his as his hips thrust into hers, pummeling her pussy walls with stroke after stroke of that magnificent cock. She screamed out with the building tension, but he only swallowed her cries.

Her hands were most likely scratching him as she clawed at his back, but it was beyond her power to stop. If she didn't cling to him, she feared she'd fall into the abyss hovering around her.

The smell of hot male flesh tinged with a spicy aroma sent her senses into overdrive and spiraling out of control. With her lips locked with Miller's, it prevented Cambrie from inhaling as deep as she wished to memorize the scent of this sexy, wild male in her arms.

His hips, powerful and unstoppable, thrust into hers over and over, his cock swelling as each stroke became more sensitive than the last. She had to breathe. Breaking the kiss, she gasped, her lungs filling with much needed oxygen.

"Miller! Oh, Miller."

"Ride me, Cambrie. Ride me hard." Without effort, he rolled under her, dragging her on top of him, keeping his cock deeply seated in her throbbing pussy. Could she ever get used to his strength?

She reveled in having control of the loving. Rocking her hips back and forth, she rode him as he had demanded, but she did it her way. Swiveling her hips in circles earned her a deep groan and flex of muscles as his upper body twitched off of the bed.

"Christ, woman. You're gonna kill me."

But he didn't tell her to stop. Instead, he settled back down, sucking deep breaths through his lips, reminding her of a bull with a red flag in front of him.

"I promise not to kill you, Lt. Daly. Maybe just brand you a little."

He laughed, between gasps. "God. Help. Me."

Feeling like a new woman, Cambrie rode his cock like she was riding the toughest bull around. She bucked and lifted, bucked and lifted, setting a pace that would surely destroy both of them if they didn't come soon. Her gaze settled on Miller's distorted face, his cool composure replaced with flushed skin and gritted teeth. Hell, yeah. She'd make damn sure he never forgot her.

Pivoting her hips again allowed his cock to stroke a fascinating place just inside her vagina. God, had that spot always been there? How come she'd never felt it until now? Not wanting to lose the sensation, she fucked him harder and faster as his hips thrust upward.

Her pussy tightened, sending shockwaves

throughout her womb. Little spasms grew into massive ones until she screamed out, "Miller! Yes. Oh, yes."

His body tightened into one long stretch of muscles from toes to head, signaling his release. But she couldn't hold on any longer and collapsed onto Miller's chest, the fine mat of hair lightly dampened with perspiration. The coolness against her cheek was welcomed.

"Cambrie. My God. Cambrie." Miller chanted her name about a dozen times, each time thrusting and holding his cock deep inside her as his hands gripped her sides to keep her anchored to his hips.

She regretted the need to use a condom, wondering what it would feel like to have him shoot his hot load into her aching pussy. To feel his wetness after he removed his cock from its place in her pussy.

When his hips stopped flexing, his arms circled her back and just held her. Not tight. Not possessive.

Just…intimately. That was the only way to describe it. The sheer romance of his embrace causing her to sigh when he urged her aside to clean up.

Rolling onto her back, she felt no shame in lying on her messed bed completely naked because she didn't have a lick of energy to make herself decent. Miller removed the condom and turned to her. "Bathroom?"

"Second door on the right. Don't worry. If you make a mistake, you'll just end up in the linen closet." He grinned when she laughed. "You can't get lost in this small apartment."

"Baby, not to worry," he said, taking two

giant steps back to the bed before leaning down and kissing her lips with a loud smacking sound. "I can't get lost with my training. I'll always find a way back to you."

With that, he left her on the bed, feeling more alive than she ever had. And wondering what to do now about Lt. Miller Daly.

Oh, Emma wasn't going to believe how this was turning out.

Chapter Nine

Peering inside Cambrie's small freezer, Miller made a mental note to hit the grocery store and prepare a real meal for the amazing woman sitting only inches away on a kitchen stool.

"Told you," Cambrie's voice interrupted his perusal. "Choice of frozen pizza or mac and cheese. I never claimed to be a chef. Guess I should've warned you that there'd be no five-star accommodations if you came here. I'm sorry, Miller."

He shut the fridge door and faced her. Now didn't she wear the cutest little pout? Although he really wanted to spank her for worrying like that. "Cambrie, I came to see you. Not your apartment, not your freezer. You, baby."

For emphasis, or maybe because he just couldn't keep himself from touching her, he pulled her from the chair and into his arms, staring at her lovely face. Her long, dark brown hair was mussed from their lovemaking. He could imagine grabbing a fistful, tugging her head back to bare her slender neck and sinking his teeth into her delicate skin.

Those light brown eyes staring up at him had been dancing all night with amusement and sparkling like stars. He loved that the most, mesmerized by just looking into the wide brown circles, knowing the lust was all for him.

God, he would never think about librarians in the same way again! He liked the wild woman under that polished exterior. Thoughts of silently fucking her in the bookracks at her library roared his imagination to life.

The sex toys' empty box sat on the counter, and he could see it in his peripheral vision and remembered each toy awaited them in the bedroom. He looked forward to using each one of them with Cambrie.

But first, they needed to fuel their bodies for the lovemaking he planned for the rest of the night. "I vote for pizza. Quick and easy," he said.

"I second that vote," Cambrie replied, slipping past him to remove a box of French bread pizza from the freezer. "They're microwavable so we'll save some time."

"Oh?" He maneuvered his arms around her waist and kissed the indent between her shoulder and neck. "Save time for what?"

The apartment was a bit chilly but the heat between their bodies was unmistakable.

She giggled at his kisses, pressing her fingers on the keypad to start the microwave buzzing. When she turned into his embrace, a slap of lust hit him like a sucker punch to the gut. His cock had remained in a semi hard state since they'd left the bedroom and now came back to life, the hard length of him pushing against his boxers and into her belly.

Her soft eyes studied him, a hint of confusion hidden in the frisky brown depths. "For making love again. Don't you want to? I mean if you're tired then, of course, we could just wait and—"

He couldn't listen to another word and swallowed the rest in a kiss. Was she insane? Why the fuck would he ever want to sleep when this gorgeous woman kept him in a state of constant arousal just by standing next to her? How the hell he was expected to sleep in her bed with her naked body—and she damn well would be naked—all cuddled against him was beyond him.

She purred under his hold, the simple soft sighs reverberated through her sleek body and tickled his hands where they massaged her back. Her innocence shone through each touch like a bright beacon on the sea. But wasn't that what drew him to her? How she could walk the fine line of classy and wild?

Breaking the kiss, he stared at her. "Does that answer your question?"

She licked her lips, the simple act stirring jealousy in his cock that those lips weren't around his throbbing hard-on. "Um, no. I don't think I quite have the answer. Maybe you'd better kiss me again just to be sure."

He laughed, not remembering when he had ever enjoyed a woman's company more than now, standing in Cambrie's simple kitchen with her sexy body begging to be dominated. The microwave chose that moment to ding. "We eat fast. Then I have many plans for you in the bedroom."

He prayed she enjoyed the sex toys. Christ, since they opened the box, his imagination had run wild with vivid images of how they'd use each one. He knew he'd start with the paddle. That was Cambrie's choice, so who was he not to oblige the lady?

"Do you now? Does that mean you don't want to catch some sleep?" Her teasing tone was just as arousing as the way her hard nipples dented the thin cotton T-shirt she had professed as her favorite nightshirt.

"Oh, I promise we'll get sleep, darling," he

said, biting into the hot pizza. "But first I plan to exhaust you."

"I like how you think," she offered before taking her own bite of pizza.

They sat at her small, round kitchen table sipping iced tea and devouring the pizza. She had obviously worked up an appetite like he had by the way she dug in heartily.

Wiping her mouth with a napkin, Cambrie sipped her drink and spoke. "So, Miller, are you on vacation or something? You had mentioned getting leave after your assignment was done. Does that happen after each assignment?"

Miller didn't want to think about having to leave her now that he had finally found her. Dreaming of her nightly was one thing. But now that he had held her, well, that changed everything. His job was his job, but now he had to figure out where or how Cambrie would fit into his life.

"Technically, I'm on a mini vacation. I begged for a few days leave once we completed this last mission. But I'm still on call."

Her hand wavered between the table and her mouth, holding the pizza. This time her pout broke his heart. "You mean you could be called away at any time?"

And there it was. The nature of the military life. Something civilians had a hard time grasping-the need to move at a moment's notice, leave loved ones behind for God knew how long, to endure what most could not. It sure did make having a relationship hard.

"Yes, Cambrie. When my team needs me, I'm there. No questions. No complaints. That's my job. What I was trained for. I know that when I'm activated, it's because my special skills are needed somewhere and fast."

"What's your specialty?" Her genuine interest pleased him more than he wanted to admit.

"Scoping out enemy territory to locate known perpetrators."

She watched him for all of two seconds until that little temper she kept well in check reared its beautiful head. "Do you take me as some lame female, Miller? What kind of friggin' answer was that?" She jumped up, mimicked his words while getting two slices of pizza from the counter. Coming back to the table, she placed a slice on his plate before sitting again. When she caught him staring, she asked, "What?"

"You're beautiful even when you're chewing my ass out. But I don't know if you have the right to do that yet, since we've only been with each other for like eight hours or so." Teasing her probably wasn't in his best interest since he hadn't really gauged that adorable temper, but he'd never been accused of being overly smart.

"Seriously, Miller. Your answer translates into 'I hunt down the bastards that no one else can catch and make them regret ever meeting me.' Am I close?" She took a bite of the pizza and watched him with a very cocky look.

He stared in shock. No one had ever pegged him down so well, describing him to the letter. How did she do that? "You're dead on, honey. For the record, I wasn't trying to talk down to you. I've just learned that civilians usually don't care to hear the details of what I do. Guess it just brings the war and terror threats too close to home for them or something."

"Well, for the record, Miller. When I ask a question, I'd like an answer that doesn't scream of bullshit."

He laughed so hard it hurt his sides. Damn, he couldn't wait to spank her pretty little ass. He loved the fiery side of her and hadn't expected her to have one. But then again, there's a lot that goes unnoticed when your only form of communication is emails.

"Yes, ma'am. You have my word it won't happen again."

She nodded and continued eating, a satisfied smile pasted on her sexy lips.

Ah, but he could be cocky, too. "And, Cambrie, you have my word that I plan on spanking that pretty little ass of yours. You have my cock so fucking hard and it's all I've thought about doing since you pulled out that paddle."

Now to say the look on her face was priceless would have been an understatement. She lost all interest in her pizza as a slight shade of pink covered her cheeks and her mouth slowly opened into an 'O'. Funny how her cockiness disappeared only to be replaced with wide-eyed curiosity. She took a long sip of her iced tea, peering at him over the rim of the glass.

She wiped her mouth on her napkin and spoke with a huskiness he hadn't heard before. He loved it. "I hope you don't get called away tonight. If we don't get to use all those toys, then you'll leave me a very horny girl until you can come back and finish the job."

Miller sat astounded and kept his face emotionless for fear of sharing too much of himself. She couldn't have said anything that would've have touched him more. Her simple statement offered an understanding for his work and the commitment that came with it.

She didn't complain that he would have to leave even after only a brief time with her. She didn't try to lecture him about staying longer or demanding that he did. Her quiet acceptance rang loud and clear. Having her respect for that part of his life intensified his feelings for this woman who continued to surprise him with every minute they spent together.

"As long as you tell me I'm welcome, then I promise, I'll be back, baby girl."

"I hope so. Can't let this sizzle go to waste."

Her forced giggle told him she hid her feelings well. She had almost fooled him into believing she'd be okay with him leaving on missions. When in fact, she meant to shoulder the burden of his absences alone and silently.

Did she even realize the remarkable woman that she was? She would hide her own pain if it meant he wouldn't worry about her. And she was definitely the type of woman to become attached. He didn't think she entered into any relationship lightly or without serious thought of the consequences.

Why his thoughts were jumping ahead and thinking of more than a few nights in Cambrie's bed, he couldn't say. Nor did he wish to dwell on that right now. His life was very complicated, as was hers.

"We've only just begun to sizzle, baby." He kept his tone reassuring, hoping to just enjoy the moment.

He chalked the excessive analysis of the situation up to his lack of sleep and the excitement of meeting Cambrie. Maybe he'd just been working too damn hard lately. Being away from his team after spending the entire past year with them on one mission after another took some getting used to.

He couldn't help glancing around the apartment as if he were still doing surveillance in the Afghan deserts and villages. That kind of training was hard to shake even when he returned to civilian life, which wasn't too often now that his team had been assigned a special sector of the Afghan nation.

Rubbing his tattoo, he smiled, knowing Cambrie would be with him everywhere.

"You never said where you lived when you're not fighting bad guys or meeting pen pals, Miller."

Too far away from you. "When I'm not on a mission, I live near my duty station in Little Creek, Virginia."

"That's where you're stationed?"

"Yes, ma'am."

"And you can't move anywhere else, right?"

He hated the truth to be so definite. "Right. Otherwise, it'd be too difficult to assemble the team with the time limits usually involved. I mean, we need to be ready to run at a moment's notice and, seriously, every second counts."

Cambrie leaned forward and rubbed her knuckles across his cheek. "I want to hear so much more about your job, but I'm afraid right now I'd rather be using our limited time together to try out some of those sex toys."

If ever there had been a need for a change of subject it had been just then. Miller was very grateful to Cambrie for doing it. His job was an obvious obstacle with them being together in any real relationship since he couldn't expect her to leave her life behind to come live with him when he'd be disappearing each time his team was called to duty.

"You read my mind, baby. I say I drag you into the bedroom and we begin round two."

She stood and laughed. "Dragging me would imply I didn't want to go willingly. I say, catch me if you can."

The challenge in her soft, brown eyes was all the coaxing he needed to bolt from his chair. With a screech, she laughed and ran toward the bedroom. He caught her around the waist and lifted her wiggling body into the air with one arm.

"Show off," she scolded as her fingers latched onto his forearm.

He took the opportunity to nip at her ear lobe. Her soft flowery scent tickled his nose and reminded him of a cool summer's night on a lake with crisp fresh air. God, he'd love to peel her sexy body out of a bikini.

"Not showing off at all, Cambrie. How else am I to put you across my knee to be spanked?"

Her loud gasp stirred his cock to a hardness that made walking painful. The little witch. She was just too damn sexy for both their good.

"You mean I'm getting spanked now?" Her words, while filled with a bit of shock, carried an excitement that thrilled him.

He placed her on her feet to face him, using his finger to edge her chin up. Once he caught her gaze, he spoke. "I need your safe word."

She cocked her head to the side. "Safe word?"

"A word that you will use so that I know to stop what I'm doing immediately. No questions asked. It'll signal you've had enough of whatever play we're doing." He rubbed her upper arms with gentle caresses to ease her anxiety. "I said I'd never do anything to hurt you. Everything has to be for your pleasure or we don't do it. Okay?"

"So when you spank me it won't hurt?" She looked disappointed.

He loved her naivety. "Oh, your ass will be on fire, baby. But I promise you'll enjoy every second of it." His hands roamed over her ass, massaging the round curves.

"Hanky panky. That's my word."

He cocked an eyebrow, confused at her choice. "Any particular reason for that one?"

She shrugged, the material of her T-shirt almost see-through and the outline of her nipples obvious. "Not really, except my Aunt Annabelle used to warn 'no hanky panky' when I'd go out on a date. So since this is far beyond any hanky panky I've ever had, I thought it fitting to use that word. I could choose another."

He smiled. "Nope. Hanky panky will work fine. But I'm hoping I never hear the word again, darling. I want you to trust that I'll give you the ultimate pleasures this sexy body deserves."

She wrapped her arms around his neck, a slight humming emanated from her body. "So what about you?"

"Me?"

"What's your safe word, Lt. Daly?"

He bit down on a laugh. The woman didn't have a clue about this situation. "Why the hell would I need a safe word?"

"Because when I drive you insane with my mouth, it's only fair that you, too, have a way to stop the torment."

He could only stare at her. This woman was made for him. There was absolutely no doubt in his mind. Just when he expected her to turn tail and run because the game got too hot, she surprised him. Not only did she walk the walk, but she brought her own agenda, too. "Ah, so you think you will get me to beg for mercy?"

She shrugged in that non-flustered way he enjoyed more and more. "Don't really know especially since you're so muscular," she said in an overly husky voice. For emphasis, she ran her hands along his shoulders and arms while wiggling that hot fucking body against him. "And you're so strong. But I enjoy a good challenge, so you'd better have a safe word because I won't be responsible for any whimpering because you were too smug to choose a word to save your ass."

Christ! How did she manage to arouse him with a few frisky words? He was doomed if only words and wiggles could torture his cock into a raging hard-on.

"Oh, you are so spanked, Cambrie Brasher." He kissed her forehead before gazing back into her seductive eyes filled with clouds and a carefree easiness. "*Mercy*. That's my word. Because if you can make me rely on a word to stop the attention of your pretty mouth, then I will need all the mercy I can get. And then you are so spanked again, baby girl. That…I promise."

Chapter Ten

Spankings and paddles. Butt plugs and dildos. Cambrie had never been more curious about anything until Miller had stepped into her life. Now just the thought of using the sex toys was enough to heat her body and scramble her brains.

"Nice choice of paddle, Cambrie. Hard side for punishing. Soft side for comforting," Miller commented.

"Thanks. Not bad for a first time buyer," Cambrie said as she watched with amazement as he removed the paddle from its casing and slapped it into his palm. The sound, a quick thud, had her swallowing hard. Her pussy spasmed with an awareness of what was to come and all she could do was squirm while standing in front of him. Squeezing her knees together did nothing to relieve the ache growing deep inside her pussy.

The determination on his face was neither menacing nor mean. All she saw was a man so focused on her that all else around them stood still. She didn't know how he would get summoned back to work, whether it would be via cell phone or pager, but right now she didn't care. All she wanted was to have these few stolen hours with Miller, to experience things that, up until now, she had only read about or watched on TV.

When Miller took small steps toward her, she used all of her willpower not to back up. She could do this. She could role-play and enjoy experimenting sexually. It had puzzled her how much she had wanted to try new sex acts, to be spanked and dominated, to give herself to this man she hardly knew but felt a special connection, a special bond with him.

To trust him with her body asked a lot of her, but she had agreed because she trusted him. He had earned that trust by being up front with her since their first emails. Her eagerness to get started had shocked her even more so than her vivid visions of sucking his cock and being tied up while he fucked her hard.

Miller grasped her hand in his, the firm hold tugged her to the bed where he sat down and hauled her over his lap. Staring at her bedroom floor with her hair hanging down, she squashed the sense of panic rising within her, reminding herself that her safe word would stop the spanking if she didn't like it. And this was a fantasy of hers that he was about to fulfill. What better gift could he give her?

Cool air wafted across her bottom when Miller lifted her shirt up, baring her ass. She could picture the sight she made, stretched out across his lap, naked butt high in the air.

"You have the most beautiful ass, Cambrie," he said, the casual tone quiet as his hand glided across her bottom with smooth caresses. "I can't wait to add some color to it. Think I want to start with my hand first."

The slap landed on her ass cheek without further warning. It wasn't hard, but it was real.

"Oh," she yelped just as another slap landed again. Okay, this was different.

"Trust me with your pleasure, Cambrie, and I promise you will enjoy this more than you know."

"I do trust you, Miller, or this wouldn't be

happening." And that was the truth since she had never been this experimental with anyone else.

Two more slaps rained down on her naked ass. "I enjoy seeing my hand print on your white skin. Can't wait to see what the paddle does on your delicate flesh."

"You promised me a spanking, not a play-by-play." With the snippiness in her words, she had hoped to egg him on, encourage him not to hold back. "Make me come, Miller. The heat on my ass…it feels so good."

Spank, spank, spank.

"Should warn you now to be careful for what you ask for. Because I aim to please, baby girl."

Spank, spank, spank on one cheek. *Spank, spank, spank* on the other cheek.

Wow, was her ass getting hot. His hand spared her bottom a moment's break, and she thought that was the end of the punishment. Until the paddle cracked her ass and she couldn't hold her reaction in. "Oohh!"

Miller used the paddle, alternating cheek after cheek, each blow a little stronger than the last. The room filled with a whacking sound. Her ass heated to an unbelievable temperature, the fire spreading quickly to her pussy. Little spasms ran along her swollen and drenched pussy lips as she squirmed over his legs.

"Oh, Miller. Please. I need to come." She was so close. The power building within her womb had her rocking her hips attempting to rub her clit against his leg, but it was futile. His strength easily held her in place and movement wasn't allowed.

When his fingers traced the cleft between her ass cheeks, she stilled. No one had touched her like that. Ever. After all her and Miller had done so far, it was silly to be concerned with the area his finger edged closer to.

"I can't wait to fuck your ass, Cambrie, but not tonight. I want to get my fill of that sweet pussy first." His finger skimmed her anus on the way down to her pussy. "Mmmm. Someone's pussy is plenty wet for me. Good girl. But I'm still not done spanking you."

The instant he removed his fingers from her wetness, she wanted to protest. She swallowed hard, her breath caught in her throat. He what? "You're not?"

"Nope. I'll decide when the spanking ends, unless you use your safe word."

Oh, God. It was such a turn-on when he talked like that. She needed to come. "Miller." That was all she could say, his name and nothing more, as groans escaped her throat.

When his hand landed firmly on her ass again, she cried out, the pleasure too much to withstand. "I wish you could see this beautiful ass of yours, baby. Pink from my hand and the paddle. Hot to the touch. So adorable wiggling with each slap."

Spank, spank, spank on one cheek. *Spank, spank, spank* on the other cheek.

She knew he tested her, wanted to see how much she could endure. And to her complete surprise, she realized that she didn't want the spanking to end. "Don't stop. Please. Oh, yes!"

She didn't even recognize her own voice, it was filled with a husky desperation. Never had she expected a spanking to be so arousing, sending waves of pleasure throughout her vaginal walls and swelling her clit until it throbbed.

"Oh, God, what did I ever do to deserve you,

baby?" he whispered, like he hadn't meant to say the words out loud.

To her disappointment, the spanking had ceased. When did he stop? With her breaths ragged and her lungs desperate for oxygen, she gulped air. She hadn't even realized she had been so breathless. Every cell in her body was alive, filled with an energy that had her believing she could match Miller's strength, or collapse trying. Every inch of her pussy wanted Miller's attention, but he was preoccupied with caressing her warm ass cheeks.

Her moans echoed throughout her small bedroom. Miller dragged her off of his knees and cradled her back on his chest. Blinking her eyes, the room spun. With one strong arm wrapped around her waist, the other dipped between her legs. His fingers stroked her clit, creating a firecracker in his arms, shaking, vibrating, twitching.

Her back arched and she screamed, "Miller! Yes! Oh, please. Harder."

Miller increased the pressure on her clit, rubbing circles over the hard nub until she thought she'd pass out from the orgasm riveting through her womb. How could it be stronger than the one earlier? All Cambrie knew was she could get used to this wild lovemaking. A roller coaster of pleasure circled deep inside her vagina, each wave creating another spasm of bliss to steal her breath and blank her mind.

"That's it, baby. Come hard for me. I love the feel of your juices on my fingertips."

When her energy should've been depleted, a burst of passion renewed her stamina. Miller loosened his grip around her and she spun to straddle him. All he wore was boxers. Her fingers grabbed at the elastic band, tugging without success to free the material from his body. She needed him naked. She needed to feel that hot male flesh against her skin.

"Take them off," she demanded through harsh breaths.

He stood holding her with no effort at all, pushed his boxers down his legs and kicked free of them.

"Now you," he insisted, his dark brown eyes heated with a fiery desire not hiding his intentions.

Pulling the T-shirt over her head, she stood before Miller with only the small lamp to illuminate their bodies. This man had been professionally trained in patience and control, a part of his world that she would never quite understand having no patience skills herself. But the low growl emanating from his throat as his eyes skimmed her body was only the first warning that she had managed to breech that schooling.

Now she witnessed the total breakdown of that impeccable restraint. One glance into his eyes showed a wild hunger that had Cambrie's blood pressure rising along with her libido. She had already come more times today than she had in a whole month and still she wanted, needed, more. Would she always crave his touch to the point of madness?

Leaping into his arms, she clung to his neck with arms that felt more like spaghetti noodles than limbs. Her mouth landed on his, the need to taste him unbearable. Fusing her mouth to his, her tongue dove between his lips into deep, hot passion.

Not able to get enough of him, she clawed

and scratched at his shoulders, willing to apologize later for any unintentional damage. But the greedy lust rising within her was too powerful to fight, so she flowed with it, enjoying every second in Miller's strong arms. Her pussy, already slick with her juices and swollen from her orgasms, begged for his cock.

Breaking the kiss for a necessary breath, she whispered against his lips. "God, how can I need you so badly, Miller? Tie me up while you fuck me."

The words shocked her once they fell upon her ears. Where had that come from? She hardly knew her own body anymore with all its kinky cravings.

But in true Miller fashion, he moved calmly to the pile of sex toys and in no time at all had the pink fuzzy handcuffs free of their package.

He may be trained to hide his emotions, but there was no mistaking that gleam in his eyes, the one that warned she had stirred him beyond what she could handle. But with her body humming all over, she was willing to give anything a try to reach that awesome climax again. And she had her safe word.

Panic consumed her. Her safe word? Oh, God. What the fuck was her safe word?

Miller advanced on her too quickly for her to organize a sane thought. His arms dragged her back into his embrace while his head lowered to capture her mouth and sear her lips with a kiss made of fire and confidence. He controlled the kiss, the way his tongue traced the line of her lips, plunged inside, darted around like a flame licking at her with its heat.

She could remain in this position forever

without a complaint, surrounded by Miller's strength and adoring attention. The smell of hot male flesh only enticed her more to dabble in their domination games.

Curiosity may kill her someday but not tonight. Tonight, she had freed her spirit with Miller's help and awakened a side of herself long kept hidden. It was about damn time she considered what she really wanted, what she deserved.

And she deserved Miller Daly…every blessed muscle of him.

Turning her away from him, Miller brought her arms behind her back, gentleness evident in his every move. Cambrie reminded herself to breathe to ward off the anxiety sneaking up on her and to face the rising excitement inside her. The first cuff attached to her wrist so fast and expertly, she didn't have time to resist, not that she would've. The metal link seemed cool against her heated flesh even with the pink fuzzy fur around it.

When the second cuff bound both her wrists behind her back, Cambrie was surprised there was no rush of panic within her. Instead, her pussy throbbed harder and she arched her neck back, hoping the offer would entice Miller to nibble her sensitive spot along the shoulder blade.

To her disappointment, he had other plans. With careful movements, he lifted Cambrie onto her knees on the bed, settling her face gently against the blanket. Her ass high in the air should've had her squirming, but all she could do was control the thoughts racing through her mind, guessing his next moves. She heard the telltale ripping sound and pictured him pushing his cock into the condom.

The bed dipped behind her and the heat from Miller's body pampered her thighs. The thick head of his cock teased the entrance of her pussy, probing it.

"Oh, Miller, let me feel your cock deep inside me."

"Is that what you want, Cambrie? My cock?" he asked, kissing her spine driving her wild with need.

"Y-yes," she whimpered.

With one long thrust, he pushed inside her, his groans mixing with her cries while he held his body still. Her pussy stretched, accommodating the width and length of his cock, while each thrust along her vaginal walls created a fiery flash of spasms.

"Christ, I can't get used to your tightness. You feel so good, baby. So damn good."

"Show me then. Show me how good I make you feel," she spoke in rushed words, needing him to pick up the pace or she'd resort to begging. The cuffs served as a reminder of her willingness to expand her sexual experiences and the thrill that came with that openness.

Miller's hand roamed over her tied ones. "You be sure to tell me if the handcuffs hurt, okay?" he demanded, concern etched into the statement and touching her heart.

"Mmmm. I'm not complaining."

Latching his hand onto her cuffed ones, Miller began a steady thrusting, pulling almost completely out of her pussy before driving back in. Each new stroke found new places in her pussy to awaken and increase her arousal. The slapping of flesh against flesh filled the room, matched only by their rushed breaths as Miller fucked them closer to orgasm.

"Come for me, Cambrie. I want to feel your pussy grip my cock and milk me dry. Come for me." His tone held an urgency that suggested he couldn't hold off exploding for long. His stamina was impressive but no match for the heat between their bodies, a heat fueled by lust and desires so powerful it rocked their control.

Listening to his dirty talk heightened her awareness of their intimacy. While new positions and sex toys were new to her, so was the explicit talk Miller shared with her. She felt adored, cherished, and appealing.

"Oh, God. I'm so close, Miller," Cambrie yelled, the cuffs kept her from touching him, anchoring him while he thrust and driving her insane with the need to feel his muscles, his heat, his power.

"Then come for me."

He increased his pumping until the entire bed shook with the force. The heat on her ass from the spanking reminded her of the erotic episode over his knees. The angle of his cock from this position allowed him to hit what she believed was her G-spot for the powerful electric shock it created each time he slammed into it.

His hips pummeled into hers, over and over, until she screamed as the explosion ripped through her pussy.

"Miller! I can't. Do. This. It's. Too. Much."

"It's a little late…now…babe," he yelled, achieving his release and holding his cock deep inside her core while he grunted inaudible words and his hand at her back gripped her with his usual strength.

She rode the orgasm and each wave that came

with it. Her clit had a heartbeat of its own, throbbing, pulsing, throbbing, pulsing, until it faded to leave her spent as his cock slid free. When the mattress bounced, she imagined he stood to discard the condom. She never even felt Miller remove the handcuffs, but when he dragged her into his arms and cradled her against his chest, she sighed. Wrapping the blankets around them, Miller's arms swallowed her up.

"Damn." Miller's voice whispered into her ear.

"What?"

"Forgot the light," he said, then offered a huge yawn before crawling from bed, snapping off the light, and returning to her side.

She turned to face him. "Miller? What's the charge for holding a military man hostage?"

He cocked an eyebrow, seen in the moonlight sneaking in from the half-open curtain. "Why? Plan on kidnapping me?"

"Gave it some thought now that you've stirred this wild woman in me."

"Give me time. I'll stir some more."

She laughed. He looked so exhausted. "I can't leave Maddyville." She hadn't meant to just blurt it out, but it had been on her mind since their conversation earlier.

His expression turned grim. "I know."

"It's just that, well, my job pays for the nursing home for Aunt Annabelle. She raised me. I have to take care of her. I'm all she has left. I could never move away and leave her." Tears tickled her eyes.

"I understand, honey," he said, his words comforting. Kissing the top of her head, he continued to hold her.

She was so bummed that nothing could come of this wonderful connection with Miller. This special thing they shared had been doomed from the beginning. Aunt Annabelle had made sacrifices to raise Cambrie, the least she could do was make the same so her final years were as comfortable as possible. "I have to work in the morning. Taking time off now would just get me fired, and the library needs me to do all I can to win the grant that will keep us open."

"I might tie you to the bed, baby girl."

She gasped. "Don't you dare, Miller."

He laughed and yawned again. "I'm sure I can keep myself occupied until you bring this sexy body back home to me. I'll work out, maybe go for a run. I've got some calls to make to family and friends now that I'm back in the States for a bit."

For a bit. Those three words stung, but Cambrie brushed off the feeling not wanting to add to Miller's stress.

"And I have a laptop to do some work. Since you ordered the sex toys online, you must have wifi, right?"

"Yes, of course. But you said you're on vacation. Why would you have to do work on your days off?"

"Ahh but, honey, the military is never really on vacation. I just have special permission to be away from my duty station. Allows me a little extra time to respond to orders."

And she knew he'd be called away. That was his job. Maddyville could offer him nothing when there was a world of bad guys needing an ass-kicker like Miller to teach them a lesson.

"Do you mind me staying here while you're at work?"

The question was absurd. "Uh. Duh. We just had wild and kinky sex. Why would I mind?"

"Just didn't want to assume, that's all," he said with a half grin.

"So, any idea how long I have with you?" she dared ask.

"I've got a week before I have to report back. That doesn't mean I can't get called back sooner. Chances are good I'll get to stay the week." He kissed her forehead. "I'm beat. If I continue talking, I'm afraid I won't make much sense."

"Me too," she said with a slight giggle. "Miller?"

"Yes, baby." His sluggish voice sounded so different from the confident, strong tone he'd used earlier but was just as sexy.

"I'm so glad you came. I'm happy you're here with me."

His arm tightened around her. "Mmmm. Me too. At least now you're in my arms, not just my dreams. Sweet dreams, Cambrie, baby."

"Sweet dreams, Miller."

Cambrie snuggled into Miller's warmth, amazed at the contentment settling over her. A week. They had at least that much time. Then what? How could she ever rebound from a man like Miller Daly—so passionate, so intense, so…captivating?

Chapter Eleven

Cambrie slipped out of bed and into the bathroom quietly so Miller could get the sleep he needed. After all, he was on vacation. He should rest.

The cool morning air raised goose bumps on her skin while she waited for the shower to warm up. What an odd twenty-four hours. She had met the most interesting man of her life, had the most amazing sex she'd probably ever have, and had that same sexy man fast asleep in her bed snoring lightly, his hard muscled body hogging most of the mattress and sheets.

Stepping under the water, she thought about how just twenty-four hours ago she had been a totally different person. This morning, she awoke remembering all that she had discovered about herself while making love with Miller last night. The naughty side that she craved, now yearned for, and feared she'd never have after Miller left. How could such a wonderful night become bittersweet?

"If you were going to sleep standing up you should've stayed in bed." Miller's voice scared the shit out of her. She spun around with her hand on her heart and the other wiping the water and her hair out of her eyes. She wasn't used to having someone else in the house with her.

"Shit, Miller. Don't sneak up on me."

With palms out, he offered an apology. "Sorry. I didn't mean to startle you." He stepped into the shower, his massive body taking all available free space. She was forced under the stream of water and had to angle her head to avoid the water and open her eyes.

"What are you doing?" she demanded.

"Um, I think it's obvious. Joining you for a shower." The cocky smile he offered didn't amuse her.

"No you're not. Get out. You'll make me late for work." And she didn't need to be distracted by his sexy body.

An evil smirk creased his lips. "I hope so. You need me to wash your back."

She placed her hand on his chest to keep him at arm's length or she'd lose all track of time. "I've managed fine all these years, Miller. Now out." She swung the shower curtain over to compel him to step out of the tub, but he only shut it again and remained with her.

"Then I'll help you wash that sweet pussy and your hot ass." There was that damn patience of his again.

Before she could protest again, his hand rubbed between her legs, the touch instantly igniting a fire within the walls of her pussy. Oh, God, his fingers felt so good caressing her pussy lips, reminding her clearly of their hot loving last night. She sank against his chest, capturing his mouth in a kiss meant to taste and explore. The warmth of his mouth was no match for the heat from his body as every inch of her skin came alive under his touch.

"Ever make love in a shower?" he asked against her lips.

She looked at him like he had three heads. "What do you think?"

"Awesome. Another first all for me." His

bragging finished with another kiss, only this time he lingered on her lips long enough to pull her leg up around his waist so he could trail his finger to the puckered entrance of her ass and push inside. She gasped and tore away from the kiss. "Relax for me, Cambrie. It's just my finger. I want to get your ass ready so I can fuck it with my cock one of these nights."

Liking the intrusion of his finger, her body seemed to purr, wanting to feel more. The intimacy made her look forward to that time, helped her understand what it would feel like. "Mmmm. Feels good, Miller."

"Me too. So tight, like your pussy." With his words tickling her ear, his finger maneuvered in and out of her ass. The slight pinch aroused her with thoughts of more anal play, maybe with toys.

With a series of flutters, her pussy hummed. "You destroy me with your dirty talk, Miller. This isn't fair." Pushing her ass back onto his finger to encourage him to move faster, deeper, she sighed. "I need to get to the library and you've got me all worked up."

With a devastating smile, he had placed her under his charm. "Now, do you really believe I would send you off to work without finishing what I've started here?"

Before she knew what to expect, his finger withdrew from her ass as he lifted her to straddle his hips, easing his cock inside her pussy. The stretching was minimal this time as he eased fully into her. How good it felt to have him stroking inside her.

"Wait! Condom," she yelled, her voice echoing over the spray of the water.

The strength of his arms easily held her up.

"Already taken care of. I put it on before coming in here. Waking up in your bed, surrounded by your lovely scent, gave me a massive hard-on. Thought you'd like to help me out with that."

She laughed. He had a way with words for sure. "Glad to be of assistance."

His slow, deep thrusts were different from the heated passion of last night, but they still served to make her a horny mess in his arms. With the warmth of the steam around them, Miller fucked her with deep, long strokes, kissing her neck and shoulder.

Leaning her back against the tile, she forgave the coldness on her warm flesh when his fingers skimmed around to her breast and gripped the slippery mound, squeezing and kneading. Taking her nipple between his finger and thumb, he pinched until heat shot to her pussy.

"Yes, Miller. Don't. Stop."

With her hands clinging to his back and shoulders, she bucked her hips with each thrust he offered, wanting to heighten his arousal and drive him as wild as he did her.

"Cambrie. Oh, baby. You are my dream."

Mist circled them in wisps of rose and vanilla scents from the oval soap in the soap dish. Until Miller, she would've had a hard time believing this kind of loving existed outside of romance novels, but she had found it. Or rather, it had found her. Oh, God, Miller was corrupting her normal good habits.

Miller sped up his hips until they pumped into her with a steady force, increasing the spasms deep within her core. All the sensations swarmed into one. With her hips grinding into his, the movement allowed her to crush her clit into his pelvis, each connection sending throbbing spasms humming deep inside her core.

The orgasm built quickly, the dull aches deep within her pussy grew at an uncontrolled pace. Soon she clawed at his head to hold on, fearful of collapsing from the powerful waves of pleasure consuming her.

She screamed, unable to contain her emotions. “Miller! Yes. I’m there. I’m coming! Fuck me harder. Oh, yes!”

The swiftness of his thrusts increased, amplifying her pleasure. With his cock buried deep inside her pussy and her ass tingling from his finger’s earlier attention, Cambrie allowed the orgasm to sweep over her, to take her under its control. Soon her pussy rippled with wave after wave of pleasure, each spasm stronger than the one before it.

“Cambrie!” Miller yelled, before burying his face into the curve of her neck.

Water sluiced over their joined bodies, until Miller regained his composure, slipped his softening cock from her wetness, and stood her on her feet. With her pussy still humming, Cambrie stood quietly under the water. Miller stepped out to dispose of the condom before re-joining Cambrie under the showerhead.

“I’ve got to hurry. Work,” she said, rinsing shampoo from her hair.

Of course he’d understand being accountable and on time. He soaped her body using her fluffy sponge with an impressive efficiency. She admitted she could get used to this kind of treatment. But her head warned her to be cautious. They came from two different worlds and lived totally different lives.

Still, with bubbles slicking her skin and a sexy man standing in front of her, Cambrie gave in to the moment and enjoyed the shower until the water cooled and forced an end to their playing.

He helped her from the tub and wrapped a large towel around her before flinging one around his hips.

“For the record, I’ve never done that,” Miller said matter-of-factly.

Wiping her skin dry, she stared up. “Done what?”

“Made love in the shower. Never had someone that interested me enough to bother.” He tweaked her nose. “Until now.”

****

Once at work, Cambrie discovered it was impossible to concentrate. Her usual dedication warred with daydreaming of Miller. But she had managed to get some things done while the morning dragged by. Her most important project had been to set up an email account for Greg on the library’s computer network. Now he’d be able to email Miller when he left again.

She sighed, not wanting to think about having to say goodbye to Miller. Memories surfaced throughout the morning to keep her smiling and floating on air. Every time she thought of Miller’s hands or his kisses on her body, her cheeks warmed and her heart fluttered, not to mention she had creamed her panties after one enchanting remembrance.

Sorting the papers on her desk, she bundled a group of envelopes with a thick rubberband and tucked them into her briefcase to bring home to

Miller. The Teen Readers Group had done a wonderful job writing the correspondence as part of their support for the grant. But since Miller had surprised her with his visit, then she no longer needed to mail them. She made a mental note to hand them to him when she got home.

Mrs. Ginnity walked in the front door with two other women, all dressed in skirts and heels and each carrying two shopping bags. "My goodness, Cambrie. Just look at all these donations for your military man."

"Wow," Cambrie said, pleased at the overflowing bags. "Where did those come from?"

Mrs. Ginnity stopped in front of the checkout desk where Cambrie stood dutifully awaiting customers. "From our bridge group last night. The ladies thought it'd be a great idea to collect them at our weekly game night. I'll put them in the back. Follow me, ladies." The other women followed Mrs. Ginnity and they disappeared into the volunteer's office.

When they returned, Mrs. Ginnity waved goodbye to her friends.

"Thank you very much," Cambrie called out after them.

"Now I'm sure you're up to your eyeballs with work, Cambrie," Mrs. Ginnity began. "Would you like a break to go hide in your office for a bit and work without the constant interruptions?"

The woman was an angel. "That would be super, Mrs. Ginnity. Just holler if it gets too busy or if Mr. Hackler needs me."

The older woman just waved her hand in the air. "Not to worry. I have it all under control. And Mr. Hackler needs to get through me to interrupt you. Now scoot and let me get to work here."

Cambrie swore she saw a twinkle in Mrs. Ginnity's eyes at the mention of Mr. Hackler. Really? Could the woman be attracted to the stuffy old man? Would explain all the hours she was willing to volunteer at the library lately and why she liked to watch the front desk that Hackler walked by to get to any other part of the library. Cambrie smirked. What a pair they'd make!

Once in her office, she shut the door and logged onto her computer. Remembering all of Miller's sexy emails warmed her heart. She missed that communication and the excitement of logging on and finding an email from him. But she was happier with him here in Maddyville at her apartment.

Okay, time to get back to work and stop daydreaming. Mr. Hackler had given her specific orders to prepare a detailed summary of her efforts to secure the grant to share with the library's Board of Directors. She blushed—if he only knew what she had done with her pen pal.

Time passed as she became so engrossed in writing her report that she didn't pay attention. A knock on her office door broke her concentration.

"Come in," she said, looking up from the computer screen.

When Miller's tall, muscular frame slipped through the door, Cambrie's heart did somersaults. "Hey, there," he offered, his casual tone hinted of enthusiasm.

"Wow. This is a pleasant surprise," she said, remaining seated for fear of running and jumping into his arms.

He shut the door behind him, sauntered to her seat, leaned down, placed a gentle kiss on her lips, hovering long enough to make her crave more, and then sat on the corner of her desk, resting his jacket to the side. "Let me steal you away for lunch."

Now wasn't that the best offer she'd ever had? Smiling couldn't be helped as she looked up. "That's sounds wonderful. Wait a minute. How did you get here? Oh, my God. How rude of me? I didn't leave you with a way to get around."

"Well, ma'am. The last time I looked, I had two good feet, but that's not how I got here. I rode my motorcycle. Can't wait to take you for a spin and have your sexy little body cling to me while the wind whips around us."

Of course a man like him would own a motorcycle. Probably had an army tank, too. "Miller, I'm wearing a skirt. I can't possibly ride on a motorcycle."

"Not now, silly. There must be somewhere around here to grab a bite to eat."

"Oh, of course. Let me just tell Mrs. Ginnity that I'll be stepping out," she said and stood.

"My so formal. So professional," he said, not hiding his teasing tone. His hand moved quickly to wrap around her waist and haul her against him as he continued to sit on her desk. "There's no rush. I wanted to see where you worked first. See if you'd give me a tour of the library. You know, for the grant."

The mischief in his eyes warned her that he might have other objectives. "I think you have naughty intentions, Miller. What are you really up to?"

A squeeze from his hand resting on her side drove goose bumps over her skin. "Busted. Okay, I was doing some work on my laptop when the image of fucking you in the bookracks drove me so wild that I jumped on my hog and came to find you."

She gasped. "Are you insane? We'd never get away with that." Although, she wished they could because she grew hornier by the minute. "Mrs. Ginnity is all eyes and ears. Nothing would get by her."

He laughed. "Let's see about that." His hand trailed down her side and disappeared under the hem of her skirt. The quick ascension up her leg to her panties sent warning bells blaring in her head.

"Miller!" she whispered through gritted teeth. "At least lock the door." Had she lost her mind to want sex in her office of all places for Christ's sake?

"Did when I shut it, Cambrie. I just want to touch you. Feel the slickness of your bare pussy lips on the tips of my fingers, wishing it was my tongue running along them."

That did it. She melted into his embrace and allowed his fingers to dip beneath her panties. His finger slid through the wetness gathered there, her head arching back while biting on her lip to keep as quiet as possible.

With her hands anchored on his shoulders, she stood with his knee lodged between her legs and his finger caressing her clit. The slow circles he pressed onto the hard nub sent electric shocks throughout her core. A humming built from deep within her womb, the familiar urgency building.

"Oh, damn, Cambrie. You're so fucking hot right now," he said in a soft voice. Grateful for his quietness, Cambrie rocked against his hand. "That's my girl, rub that beautiful pussy over my fingers."

My girl? What the hell did that mean? Too aroused to think straight, she buried the question for now.

"Makes me so fucking hot, baby, knowing people are just on the other side of the door, and I have you in here all to myself." His words sped up her heartbeat. Someone could interrupt them. The thrill of being discovered shocked her with its power to stir her libido and increase the fire already in her belly.

When he inserted one long finger into her pussy, she swallowed a scream. The orgasm took control from there and exploded throughout her pussy, each muscle convulsing with greedy nerves and transferring heated sensations deep into her womb.

Miller never stopped, just stroked and rubbed, caressed and fingerfucked her pussy with two fingers now, the tightness of her pussy growing over the delightful intrusion. When the vibrations slowly trickled away, she was left mesmerized by what had just happened. Since when did she participate in such wanton behavior and so easily too?

"I love knowing there's a hidden firecracker under that librarian persona, baby girl," Miller said, removing his fingers from her panties and bringing them up to his lips.

With a determined slowness, he licked them clean, his tongue wiping her juices from his skin. Wasn't that the most erotic sight she had ever seen? She almost forgot to breathe while she took it in.

"Taste how sweet you are, Cambrie," he whispered before pulling her into his arms and devouring her mouth in a kiss so deep and possessive she swore he branded his name on her lips.

Every swipe of his tongue against hers made her want to beg for more—more kisses, more loving, more Miller. Tasting her juices on his tongue, the creamy sweetness, only served to make her want to take his cock into her mouth to savor him. Her hands ran through his short hair, wishing it was long enough to grab hold of it.

Ending the kiss tore a cry from her throat before she remembered where they were, in her office, in the library and surrounded by nosy people. "Miller, you are so spanked," she spit out, echoing the words he had used on her so many times.

Her statement served to stun him as he faced her with a cocked eyebrow. "Now I've never had that said to me before."

"Well, you deserve to get your ass kicked coming in here and making me a blubbering, horny mess." Her complaint came with no heat. Truth be told, she didn't want him to stop touching her. If she thought they could have privacy long enough, she'd drag him to the floor to show him how horny he had made her. "I just wish we were at the apartment to finish."

"Mmmm. We'll finish later. Now give me that tour and you can tell me how you plan to finish later."

"Or maybe I won't finish and I'll leave you aching like you do to me."

"Try that, honey, and I will paddle your ass until it glows," he responded, his eyes simmering with desire each time he spoke of spanking her.

"Let's begin that tour. If we stay in here too long, the gossip mongers will have a field day." She stepped into the hallway, her heels tapping on the tile floor.

As expected, Mrs. Ginnity stood at the front desk with a curious glare etched on her painted face. "Cambrie, who's this handsome, young man?"

Oh, God. Cambrie now regretted letting the old woman hang around to help her out. "Um, Mrs. Ginnity, meet Lt. Miller Daly. My pen pal for the library grant."

"Pleasure to meet you, ma'am."

The elegant woman shook his hand and studied him too intently for Cambrie's liking. "Oh, I've heard so much about you from Annabelle. I must say, she didn't exaggerate."

She what? Cambrie's jaw dropped. "From Auntie?"

"Why of course. We just spoke this morning. Said you rescued her, Cambrie, from that mean nurse who insists on keeping her locked in her room. Honestly, that was so awful."

"Aunt Annabelle misstated the facts. She took a fall because she refused to listen to the nurses' orders and give them time to accommodate her request to go to the lounge." And why the hell was Cambrie explaining herself?

"Well, that's neither here nor there. So tell me, Lt. Daly, how long are you in town?"

"Please, it's Miller. For about a week, less if duty calls."

Cambrie's heart squeezed like a vice had clamped around it. She refused to think of him leaving. "Excuse us, Mrs. Ginnity, but I've promised Miller a tour of the library so he can personally see how wonderful it is and why we deserve the grant."

"Nice to meet you, ma'am," he said as Cambrie led him away.

"You too, young man," Mrs. Ginnity said with a little too much sugar.

"She picked up the phone and is dialing, right?" Cambrie asked, walking up the stairs with Miller.

He glanced over his shoulder in a casual manner. "Sure is."

"Oh, Aunt Annabelle's going to have lots of questions now," Cambrie complained.

"I'll do my best to answer them as truthfully as I can," he suggested.

Cambrie faced him and noticed the smirk on his face. "Careful, Miller. I don't care what kind of training you have. You're no match for a southern woman like my aunt when she sets her mind to something."

"Hhmmm. Now I know where her niece gets it from." He laughed when she shot him a warning glare over her shoulder. "This is a huge library, Cam."

His use of the nickname that only close friends and family called her caught her off guard for a moment, made their acquaintance even more intimate. "This library has served generations in this county. It's the only one for about fifty miles so you can understand the importance in keeping it running."

"Of course," he agreed, strumming his finger along the books neatly stacked in rows. "I love reading. Biographies, history, mystery. In my line of work, when I'm not fighting the bad guys or training, then I have lots of down time, so I spend it working out and reading mostly. If I didn't stimulate my brain and body then I'd go stir crazy."

"And now you can add writing erotic emails

to that list."

He laughed but kept his voice low. "True."

Walking through the three floors of the library gave them time to talk since making out wasn't an option no matter how much Cambrie craved his kisses. "I want to hear all about your job. It sounds so interesting."

"Oh, without a doubt it is. I've seen parts of the world I wouldn't have without the military. But it's not like in the movies where there's always action. Gets pretty boring sometimes."

"Do you mean not a lot of women available to spend your time with?" Somehow she couldn't picture him as the type to be alone.

"Women are a rare thing on missions, darling."

Well, that was a relief. "Answer me something, Miller."

"Sure."

"Why would you need to join an online dating site?" So what if the question had been burning in the back of her mind since his admission after arriving.

He shrugged, his wide shoulders stretching the material of his T-shirt. "Just hard to meet women in my line of work. I'm never usually in one place for very long. Thought it'd help when I got lonely. I can only look at the guys' ugly faces for so long before I need to see a pretty lady."

"Is that so?" Yes, jealousy had reared its ugly head.

"Uh oh. Did I say something wrong? Fuck!" he said, still in a quiet tone. "I knew there'd be no good answer to that damn question."

"Stop it," she whispered and swatted his arm. "You don't owe me any explanations, Miller, especially about something you did before we met. I just wondered, I guess, how many women you talk to online."

"Just one," he said without hesitation.

Her heart sank. She should've known that he'd have other women to chat with. A gorgeous, confident man in uniform who exuded sexual charisma wouldn't need to be lonely. "I'm sure you have your choice of any woman."

"That's true."

Okay, now she wanted to choke him. Did he have to carry the honesty thing so far?

"But the *only* woman I choose to speak with is currently standing in front of me ready to take my head off for no reason. I don't lie, Cambrie. There are no other women in my life. Yes, some friends are female, but they're strictly friends. The online thing wasn't for me. That's one of the reasons I blew you off after that first email you sent. I hated the online dating meet-and-greet thing and thought you'd be more of the same."

Didn't she feel silly? "Oh, well, that makes sense. I'm sorry to act like an insecure teenager. I guess I just expect you to get bored of me. I mean, our lives are so different that mine must seem so dull to you."

He leaned forward and whispered into her ear. "Remind me to spank you later for putting yourself down. You're the most interesting, fun lady I've ever met. I happen to envy your lifestyle, how you're settled in one place with friends and family surrounding you, and have a heart as big and bright as the sun. You're spanked. I promise."

She cleared her throat not knowing how to respond and not wanting to get hot and bothered in the middle of the library under the watchful gazes of the customers. A change of subject was a must. "Here's where we're storing the collections for the care packages I wanted to send to you, but then you surprised me with a visit."

He studied the bags of goodies. "The only care package I want is you wrapped in a bow so I can slowly unravel it to find my treat." He grinned with a wickedness not to be mistaken for anything else. "Sorry, there's nowhere to send anything to me since I move around too much."

She giggled, his company so refreshing. "Somehow I don't think I'd be allowed to enter Afghanistan or wherever you go. What should I do with all of these donations?"

"I'll give you the address of a homeless veteran's shelter back in Virginia. They can use the care packages more than me and I'd be honored if you'd focus on them instead."

"Oh, of course. That's a wonderful idea. Consider it done."

"Did you enjoy the tour, Miller?" Mrs. Ginnity asked once they came back out to the lobby. "Mr. Hackler, this is Lt. Miller Daly, Cambrie's pen pal for the grant program. This is Mr. Hackler, director of the library."

Mr. Hackler offered a hand to Miller. "Very nice to meet you and, on behalf of Highland Library, we really appreciate the opportunity for a chance to keep our doors open but also to support your service to our country. From what I've heard from Mrs. Ginnity, we're very lucky to have you on board with this project."

Miller offered Mrs. Ginnity a smile and turned back to the director. "Thank you, sir. I must add what a fantastic employee Cambrie is. So knowledgeable and caring about the library. She just gave me a lovely tour and renewed my interest in books. You're very lucky to have her on your staff. I hope you realize that."

Cambrie enjoyed the way Hackler's pudgy face reddened with Miller's stern compliments and the veiled statement she was positive Miller chose to ensure her job security. In the presence of a massive man like Miller, it was no wonder Hackler nearly choked on his own tie in the face of Miller's open adoration. Good, served him right for threatening her job and Aunt Annabelle's future.

"Mr. Hackler," Mrs. Ginnity began. "Why… I think it's important that Cambrie spend some time with Miller to show him around our town. How else would he realize what a special community we have? Don't you think so? I mean, I'm already watching the desk and I could stay until closing if you agree."

Mr. Hackler glanced at Cambrie then Miller and spoke after clearing his throat. "Yes, of course," he said, having no room to disagree.

Mrs. Ginnity lightly applauded. "Then it's a plan. You folks go and enjoy the afternoon. Miller, I think you'll find that Cambrie is an excellent tour guide."

"I don't doubt it, ma'am," Miller offered.

Being shooed away from her job was one thing, being set up on a date was another.

"Were we just set up?" Miller asked, reading her mind as they walked away.

"I believe so and it has Aunt Annabelle written all over it. I just know it."

After getting her briefcase and pocketbook and Miller's coat from her office, they walked to Cambrie's car. "I owe Aunt Annabelle a thank you. I now get to spend the afternoon with you and not with my laptop," Miller said.

"And I like that idea, too, but I want to keep the level of our relationship a secret," Cambrie said at her car, opening the back door to place her briefcase and pocketbook inside.

A scowl covered his face. "Oh? Embarrassed by me?"

She stopped to stare at him before getting into the driver's seat. "What? No, of course not. Never. I just don't want them thinking we're dating when we're not. You don't know how the people are in this town. Gossip spreads like wild fire here."

"Sure, whatever you say," he said from the passenger seat, looking very uncomfortable with his long frame squished into her little car again.

Sighing, she rested her head on the headrest and angled her neck to look at him. "I'm sorry. That didn't come out the right way. It's just that I'm a very private person and, well, people can get the wrong idea about us."

"Then we need to talk about where we go from here. You know, once I leave and get back to work. I hope you'd at least want me to return. I would as soon as I could."

"Yes. I'd like that. But I don't have an answer for you. I guess we just take our time and see where life leads us." She couldn't face the fact that they could have no more than whatever visits Miller's job allowed. And just how long could that go on for? Too much to think about.

His smile lit up his eyes. "Okay. I can live with that. For now." He drew her knuckles up to his mouth and kissed them, not releasing her hand. "I'm starved. No matter what else we do, I want to eat first."

She started the car. "I know just the place."

Chapter Twelve

At the River's Shack Grille & Bar, a very courteous elderly man greeted Cambrie and Miller with enthusiasm before seating them in a window booth.

"What's in your hands, Cambrie?" Miller asked, eyeballing her before sitting.

"Running pants, shirt, and sneakers. I keep them in my car for when I get the urge to exercise after work. Who knows how long I've had them in the trunk." She laughed, the sound mixing with the din of the restaurant. "Since I don't have to return to the library, I thought I'd ditch the skirt and heels. Be more comfy."

"A shame. I like you in heels," he admitted, fire flashing in the depths of his eyes.

"Sshh, naughty boy. Be right back. Gonna hit the ladies room and change."

For a woman, Cambrie was remarkably fast with her fashion change, returning to the booth in under five minutes.

They placed their orders and were served their drinks immediately even though the place was packed with a lunch crowd. Voices and laughter filled the air, a welcomed treat for Miller who was used to the solitude of missions.

"This is a charming town, Cambrie. Is everyone so polite and happy all the time?" Miller asked before sipping his soda.

Glancing around the room, he thought the charm appropriate for such an authentic neighborhood restaurant in a small town. The wood walls sparkled, probably from a weekly polish. The entire place was uniquely decorated with deer head, bobcats, and some kind of massive fish all stuffed and adorning the walls.

It was fascinating to sit so close to predators that, when alive, would have been just as vicious as the human ones Miller fought on his deployments. Photos of famous actors and people were scattered around the room, some with scribbled messages in black marker. Strings of small white lights stretched from every wall and hung from corner to corner to soften the otherwise bustling ambience.

With her chin resting on her hand, Miller caught Cambrie watching him with those beautiful brown eyes so full of life. He never wanted her to lose the innocence he saw in their depths, never wanted to see shadows of pain where joy should be.

"Most in Maddyville are friendly. It's in our nature to be pleasant to others. I guess we've got it pretty good here, more than most. I mean, if someone falls on a bit of bad luck then there's plenty of people to pitch in and help each other out. And we take an interest in our neighbors, so stopping for a quick 'hello, how are you?' and listening to the reply is never seen as a bother. I couldn't imagine living anywhere else or having to give this up." She looked around the room with a wide grin plastered to her pretty face.

A sharp stab of pain hit Miller right in the middle of his chest. He knew she'd never leave Maddyville or Aunt Annabelle-that was painfully obvious!-but hearing her admission did something to his heart, like it could shatter into a million pieces. *Suck it up, Miller, you have nothing to offer her.*

"Anyone with all this would be a fool to give it up, Cambrie. Trust me, I've been all around the world, and, well, Maddyville, is truly one of a kind, a very special place." *Because of you.*

"Don't get me wrong. We also have our fair share of problems and, being a small town, most people grow up and leave chasing dreams elsewhere."

"But you stayed." Miller didn't intend for his words to sound so morbid, like she had made some unbelievable sacrifice.

"Yeah, kinda," Cambrie whispered and stared at her hands a moment before looking back up. "I came back."

Her tone had turned from spirited to sad. Christ, it killed him to hear her be anything but happy. "You lost me, babe. Came back? Meaning you left?"

Her glassy eyes stared back. "I had a dream job in Nashville a few years ago. I was the editor for a national fashion magazine. Had impressed the publisher so much during my first month that he quickly promoted me to editor. I was in charge of the New York fashion spotlight, so my hours were grueling, but I never noticed because I loved the work I was doing."

He enjoyed the sparkle in those brown circles when she spoke of Nashville. He tried to understand how she went from being an editor to being a librarian. "And?"

She sighed. "And then Aunt Annabelle suffered a heart attack." When she choked on the words, he reached for her hand and held it without a word. "I'm sorry. I hate talking about it. She almost died, but the doctors were saints and saved her. I…I knew that she needed me…like I had needed her once. I only went back to Nashville to empty my apartment and give my notice. I was fortunate that the Highland Library needed a librarian and I qualified."

"Sounds like you're *overqualified*."

She attempted a smile, but it was lame. "True. But the job paid the bills. Then the doctors discovered that Aunt Annabelle had breast cancer. They said the heart attack actually saved her life because, if not for the heart attack and follow-up care, then the cancer would've gone undetected and killed her."

His heart constricted once again not knowing how to ease the pain of her memories. "Believe me, Cam, if I had known you then, I swear you wouldn't have spent one minute alone to worry by yourself." And that was the God's honest truth. Never would he leave her to fight demons like that alone, no matter what fucking terrorist was on his agenda.

Her eyes fluttered. "That is so sweet, Miller. But, believe me, I wasn't alone, even when sometimes I just wanted to be. There was always a neighbor or friend there to wait with me for test results or a prognosis." She sat up straight and pushed away from the table and offered another smile that didn't quite glow. "But I admit, I would've preferred your company, Miller."

Their food came and the waitress disappeared, leaving them to their privacy. Miller dug into his sandwich to ease his hunger pains.

"Now that you know something about me, how about sharing something of yourself, handsome," Cambrie said with a heightened curiosity. He admired how quickly she could reign in her emotions and continue on like nothing had happened. If he didn't know any better, he'd swear she had some kind of military training.

Miller wasn't interested in divulging family secrets and spoiling the mood. Skirting the question was best. "Oh, I plan to share a lot of me with you, baby girl. Just as soon as we can be alone."

The pink flush that covered her cheeks in a slow ascent was alluring. Knowing he had such an instant affect on her was the sweetest aphrodisiac. "Now that veiled promise may pique my interest," she began. "But I'm not letting you avoid the question. So far, you know much more about my life and me. Now it's only fair that you share a part of you. I won't ask for specific info. Just share what you're comfortable with, Miller."

He knew she wouldn't allow him to weasel out of a decent answer. She was too smart to be distracted with sexual innuendos. "Not much to really talk about. My mom and dad still live in Florida where they raised me and my sisters. I'm the middle child, spoiled rotten since I'm the only boy." The smirk couldn't be helped when he remembered his sisters' constant complaints of how he always got his way. "My older sister is studying to be a doctor. The younger one is trying to be a model. Me? I'm just trying to keep the world safe from bastards that think bombs are the only answer to their problems."

"It sounds like you had great parents who raised y'all well."

Miller shrugged. "My dad was a work-a-holic who showed his love by buying me everything I wanted when I would've preferred him spending some time with me, you know, like throwing a ball around or shooting some hoops. But I guess he did what he could. My mother was always more interested in her status within the community than taking time to spend with her kids. So me and my sisters just found our own way in life. Marie, the doctor, follows after Dad's work-a-holic tendencies. Catherine, the model, takes after mom's need for attention. And me, well, I just look for things that hold my interest. That's why the military was perfect. Always something to do."

"I'm sure your parents did the best they could. And, it doesn't surprise me that one of your sisters is a model. Great looks must run in the family."

Watching her sip her drink through the straw created visions of those pretty lips sucking his cock with the same enthusiasm. He squirmed in his seat, adjusting the semi-hard cock pressing into his jeans. Fuck! Now she had him squirming. Oh, she was so spanked.

"Well, you see, there's no impressive story about my past to spill. I graduated fourth in my high school class, went to college on a partial football scholarship."

"Shocking," she teased. "Like you don't look like a wide receiver or defensive back."

That piqued his interest. "You know a little bit about football, do you?"

She blew out a breath and waved her hand in the air. "When you grow up in a small town like Maddyville, well, you either know about sports or you'd die of boredom. I'm a mean quarterback. I can find my target every time as long as my offensive line keeps me from getting blitzed."

God, she was the woman for him. "Keep

talking like that. It's fucking arousing."

"Ah, ah, ah, I still want to hear more about you."

He cleared his throat. "Okay. After college I tried a few jobs, but nothing interested me. I hated sitting behind a desk doing lame reports or financial comparisons. A military recruitment ad on television caught my eye one day and the rest is history. I signed up and haven't regretted it once." *Except when I have to say good-bye to you.*

"And what if you could no longer be in the military, then what would you do?" she asked, pushing her plate to the end of the table and sipping on her drink.

He had to dismiss thoughts of her mouth wrapping around his cock or it'd be impossible to form words. "I have enough experience to fall back on any number of jobs. But I haven't really thought about it since I plan to be a lifer, well, or until they throw my sorry ass out." He laughed, hoping the casual response would ease the seriousness of the question.

She leaned over the table and whispered. "I admire your choice of career, Miller. No matter what happens between us, I'd never ask you to give that up. Just thought you needed to know that up front."

His heart melted, the odd feeling leaving him woozy. He didn't like woozy. Then he was vulnerable. "Thank you, Cambrie. And no matter what happens, I'd never string you along. I promise to always be up front."

Her slender shoulders offered a shrug. "We all have to make hard decisions sometimes in life, like when I chose to give up my career to take care of the only family member I had left just like she had done for me. Was it heartbreaking to do so? Yes. Do I regret doing it? No. But I had to be the one to make that choice. If someone else forced me to make it, then I'd be bitter and resentful of that person and my situation. I'd never want to force someone to do something they couldn't, just like I wouldn't want them to force me to do something that I just couldn't."

"Like move away from Maddyville?" The question hung in the air between them like a sledgehammer, no matter the answer it was bound to shatter one of their hopes.

"Exactly." Her tone filled with a cloaked sadness, still trying hard to hide the emotions swirling in the brown depths staring back at him. "So as long as we both know where we stand, then neither of us will have unrealistic expectations."

He was ready to answer her, hell he wanted to argue with her. There was no reason to worry about a future that they both hadn't a clue about yet. The obvious connection between them, both physically and mentally, was worth at least trying to figure out how to make a relationship between them work. And he would've argued had the shrilling tone of his cell phone not interrupted them.

One glance at Cambrie and Miller noticed her expression freeze, her face go pale, and her eyes widen before she slowly lowered her gaze to the phone he removed from his front pocket.

Fuck! Not now. Not when they had just gotten some time together.

"Daly," he answered, not caring if his tone was harsh.

"It's Wallace."

"Yes, sir." Miller kept his gaze on Cambrie

but she wouldn't look at him, just stared out the window.

"Listen, I'm afraid I'm going to have to cut short your R&R, Millcr. Need you back in three days. We're going after some new intelligence. Wanted to deploy tonight, but ran into a few snags. You're just going to have to stop playing house and tell the pretty lady you'll send her a postcard."

"Understood, and believe me, asshole, I'm going to kick your fucking ass for that last remark." Chance may be his team leader, but that didn't mean Miller had to take shit from his best friend.

"Bring it on, buddy," Chance said, his laughing tone contagious as Miller cracked a grin. "See you when you get your ass back to work."

The call disconnected and Miller replaced the phone in the front pocket of his pants. Cambrie faced him.

"Do you have to leave now?" Her nerves reverberated across the table.

"No. Just had my vacation shortened by a few days. I've got three left before I need to report back."

Her shoulders loosened and her expression relaxed. "Would you like to take a short ride, Miller? It's such a lovely day and I would love to spend it walking in the woods with you. There's some great fall foliage coming out."

The waitress cleared their dishes and left the check.

"Don't even think about it, Cambrie, or I'll spank you and won't give a shit who's around to watch," Miller stated when she reached for the check.

She gasped. "You wouldn't dare."

He cocked an eyebrow and stared. "Care to find out?"

The wicked smile that creased her unpainted lips challenged him. "I know the perfect place I want to take you. We'll have all the privacy I'll need."

Throwing a few bills on the table, Miller stood and Cambrie followed. "And what will you need privacy for, darling?"

When she stood on her toes to whisper in his ear, he never expected to hear, "I can't wait to take your magnificent cock deep into my throat and taste your cum on my tongue."

Mercy!

He growled, unable to control the sound escaping his throat. When the little witch turned and walked from the restaurant, sashaying that tight little ass in front of him, Miller's thoughts were consumed with visions of her sucking his cock and then him fucking her ass. God, she was slowly killing him.

Walking with a hard-on proved torturous. Once inside the car, he adjusted his cock the best he could before taking her hand and placing it over the bulge in his pants. "See what you started?" he complained. "How fucking long until we get to the forest?"

She roared the engine to life, laughing. "About half an hour. You'll survive."

"Barely." He rested his head back on the headrest, wishing there was room to stroke his cock.

"Don't lie back, Miller, or you'll miss the foliage."

He stared at her, incredulous. "Honey, if you think I'm interested in the color of a few friggin' leaves after the image you just planted in my mind, then I think you're stoned."

Her giggle only made him want to feel the warmth of her mouth on his dick more.

"Christ, just drive, Cambrie. Get us there."

****

Miller followed Cambrie into the woods after she put on a sweatshirt, each step torment for his hard cock.

"I used to hike up here for the exercise and the peacefulness of the forest. But I don't have time lately to do much of anything, so this is a special treat for me today," Cambrie said, striding along a path abutted by thick brush and tall trees.

A special treat for her? Hell, once those lips circled his cock, he'd be the lucky one. She had at least been correct about privacy. Much to his relief, there were no other cars in the parking lot when they had pulled in. If he didn't get that blowjob she promised, he expected to collapse from the torture of waiting.

"This is one of many fantasies, Cam, that you're about to help come true," he said, enjoying her energy as they trekked forward and deeper into the solitude of the woods.

"What is?" she asked, flinging a quick glance back over her shoulder.

"Public sex. Always wondered how intense it'd be."

She stopped in front of a massive boulder. "You're about to find out. We've reached our destination, Lt. Daly. Welcome to Boulder Ridge, a local hangout."

He glanced around. They stood in a small

clearing where fallen tree stumps formed a circle near a makeshift fire pit. The fall air was crisp and clean. Inhaling, he wanted to steady his pounding heart to prevent coming the second her mouth touched his dick.

When her slim hand moved over the front of his jeans and her smile flashed with mischief, he thought again. Now he'd have to worry about coming with just her touch.

Arching his head back, he drew on his intense military training to control his emotions, but the task seemed impossible as Cambrie maneuvered her hand inside his pants once she unzipped them.

Looking down, he saw heaven. Cambrie knelt before him, gripping the length of his cock, licking her lips.

"I've wanted to taste you on my tongue forever, Miller," she purred, stroking his cock with a grip that had him grinding his teeth against the pure pleasure shooting through his body.

"Nothing stopping you now, baby. Oh, God, if you make me beg, I'm going to light your ass on fire for it," he blurted out, making fists to control his edginess.

After a quick peek around, Cambrie slipped her lips over the thick head of his cock. The pleasure of that intimate touch shook Miller to the core. When he tightened his body against the unbelievable urges filling him, his head banged off the boulder. But even the slight pain on his scalp didn't distract him from how great her mouth felt around his dick.

She sucked with little tugs, her tongue darting out to lick the sides and the head of his cock, paying particular attention to the slit. When she removed her mouth, he wanted to beg for mercy.

"Am I doing it right? I've never done this before, Miller."

Oh. Holy. Fucking. Hell. Did he just hear her right? "Baby, you have no idea what it means to me that my cock is the only one to enjoy the pleasures of your mouth. Don't change a thing you're doing." His words rushed out with his breathlessness. "Suck my cock, Cambrie. Show me how that pretty mouth can drive me wild."

Her smile lit up her face. Taking his rod back into her mouth, she kept a steady pace, sucking the length of him in and out of the warmth of her mouth. Each time the head of his cock brushed against the back of her throat, he cringed, not wanting to come yet and end this thrill.

"Damn, Cambrie." It hurt to speak the words through gritted teeth.

She stopped the sucking for a bit and licked her tongue up and down his erection. "What if someone comes, Miller? You'll have to keep an eye out."

Yeah, right, as if he could! "Fuck them! Just don't stop. Feels too damn good."

"Mmmm. I know." She swallowed his cock again.

That was it. She was a threat to national security if she could single-handedly take a killing machine to his knees with just her hands and mouth. The jagged rock at his back couldn't deter him from the explosion rising.

He wanted to rip his jacket off as his temperature rose, but there was no way to do it without breaking connection with Cambrie. And no way in hell did he want that to happen.

Every inch of his body quivered, mesmerized by Cambrie's sensual exploration. If she hadn't admitted never giving a blowjob before, he wouldn't have believed it the way her mouth worked magic over his cock—sucking, licking, slurping, sucking, licking, slurping. Christ, it was too intense. His knees threatened to buckle under the weight of his need.

His head rolled side to side, his eyes stared up at treetops against a partly cloudy sky. A noise to the right caught his attention, the sound of a breaking branch. He'd kill whoever interrupted them. Looking toward the source of the noise, relief consumed him when he noticed two squirrels jumping through the brush.

Glancing down at Cambrie while she had his cock buried deep in her pretty mouth was the most erotic sight he had ever seen. His hand fisted in her long hair, directing her motions. The move only served to make her suck his dick harder, pushing at the orgasm that lingered just over the horizon.

"Oh, Cambrie, baby." His few words exhausted him, his thoughts only for the woman on her knees in front of him.

"Mmmm." Her enthusiastic response sealed the deal.

"Cam, pull back. I'm…going…to come. Pull back…or swallow."

With a grunt, his body tightened, his hand let her hair go for fear of pulling it too hard. Grasping at the boulder, he bucked, spilling his cum into her mouth. She hadn't pulled back, but surprised him as she swallowed his load, greedily sucking until the last drop was cleaned from his cock.

Gasping for breath and willing his legs to continue to hold him up, Miller found the strength to lift his head from the rock and stare down at Cambrie. She sat licking her lips, a satisfied look on her flushed face. Her eyes glanced quickly around the woods before looking up at him.

He offered his hand to help her stand. While she brushed leaves from her legs, Miller shoved his cock back into his pants, amazed at how sensitive it was, how it still hummed with the vibrations still swirling within him. Usually after a blowjob, he went limp and forgot the pleasure within minutes. Cambrie's had stunned him with its intensity.

But even after coming so hard, his dick still remained semi-hard. It would take only one touch from Cambrie to be rock hard again. He adjusted his jeans for ultimate comfort before pulling Cambrie into his arms. Wrapping her in an embrace against his chest, he kissed the top of her head, staring into the peaceful land surrounding them.

"There's a waterfall I want to show you," Cambrie said, her words muffled against his jacket. She pulled away and smiled up at him. "It's a small one but still beautiful. It's a five minute walk and then we should head back before it gets dark."

"This place is beautiful, Cambrie," he said, holding her hand as she led the way back through the forest. Birds flew from tree to tree, bushes rustled with the small animals hiding within, and the soft breeze carried the scents of the forest-dirt, pine, flowers. "But its beauty can't compete with yours. I'm having an amazing time, Cam. Just wanted you to know that."

Her smile did things to his insides that he had never felt before. The way his heart constricted like it was in a vice grip, the way his chest felt like someone stood on it, the way his flesh came alive with tiny goose bumps. Christ. What was this woman doing to him?

"And I just want you to know, Lt. Daly, that I've never had so much fun in my life. You bring out a side of me, well, that I never knew existed."

"That's only because you never gave yourself a chance to follow your heart and know the happiness you try so hard to give to your aunt, the library, your friends."

Her slender shoulders gave a shrug. "Maybe. But before I met you, I could never imagine giving a blowjob in broad daylight in the middle of the woods where anyone could have seen us."

"It was thrilling, wasn't it?"

She laughed, the sound a soft music to his ears. "Oh, hell yes. I really got into it."

His cock twitched in his pants. "Oh, I know you did."

"I felt…free. I felt…sexy. The feeling was simply amazing. I feel like a new woman around you, Miller. Thank you."

"Thank me? For what?"

She shrugged again. "For agreeing to be my pen pal."

He returned her smile with a wide one of his own. "Best damn decision I've ever made. That is the God's honest truth."

They stepped onto a small ledge overlooking the falls. Water sprayed from a rock ledge across from where they stood. Green foliage covered every inch of land. Nature sang as birds chirped, insects buzzed, and butterflies hummed.

Wrapping his arms around her, he held her back to his chest and kissed her neck. "It's gorgeous," he spoke against her skin. "If it weren't so chilly, I'd suggest making love right here. What I wouldn't give to hear your screams of pleasure echo off of that waterfall."

She turned into his embrace, burying her hands inside his jacket to rest on his sides. “Mmmm. That sounds divine, but since we can’t then I’ll settle for a kiss before we head home to make love. We’ll drive by the library to get your motorcycle.”

Lowering his head, he captured her lips, surprised when she matched his power. He held her tightly for fear of losing his balance. He thought he tasted a little of himself on her tongue, tanginess mixed with her usual sweetness.

Their tongues danced together in a slow battle of wills, each wanting to conquer the other, to devour the heat flowing from their connection. When her fingernails dug into his shoulders, his dick stirred to life at the twitch of pain. His lust grew with each swipe of her tongue against his. Damn, this woman was like the sweetest addiction. He feared never getting his fill.

What was it about Cambrie that he lost his thoughts at her touch? His mind blanked of all other matters in his life and filled only with visions of her naked body lying beneath his while his cock slipped into her bare pussy lips. His hand slid under the sweatshirt and scanned over her belly to her breast, capturing the soft mound in his hand. Squeezing, he wished he had the nipple between his lips sucking it hard until she cried out in pleasure and begged for more.

She chose to break the connection, stepping back gasping for air. The flushed skin on her cheeks highlighted her delicate features. There was no doubt in his mind he could wake up staring into those dancing eyes for the rest of his life. With an inward sigh, he wanted to kick himself. Thinking like that would only make his departure that much harder when the time came.

"I'm cooking you dinner, Cambrie. Come on, we should head back," he said, needing to walk and leave the romantic waterfall behind them.

A peel of laughter from Cambrie caught his attention. Just what the hell was so funny?

As if she read his mind, she spoke up. "We can feast on frozen pizza or mac and cheese. Take your choice, but neither really can constitute a real dinner. They just barely pass as sustenance. Consequences of being single and not knowing how to cook. If I have any more fires at my apartment, the Maddyville Fire Department has threatened to issue a 'No Cooking Allowed' order. The chief, who knows Auntie, has even promised to have the Town Council make it a law."

Miller joined in her laughter and walked with his arm around her shoulder. "Well, rest assured, my dear, that I know how to cook without setting the place on fire. And since I went to the market before I came to see you at work, I picked up dinner. And it's real food, not frozen or canned or boxed." He kissed the top of her head before they stepped over a fallen log. "We'll enjoy a romantic dinner before I ravage you all night."

There had never been a romantic bone in his body until Cambrie. The woman stirred him to do things that he had never imagined. And he had enjoyed every second with her so far.

"Okay, then I'll take care of dessert," she said, back at the car.

He glanced at her. "And what will that be?"

"Me with whipped cream." Her mischief was an instant turn-on.

"Damn, woman. I think you could make me go AWOL."

The car filled with laughter as Cambrie sped home, the sun offering its last rays of the day as the temps fell with the loss of the sun's heat.

And Miller's heart swelled with an emotion so strong he just couldn't figure it out. For the first time, his training couldn't help him.

Chapter Thirteen

Cambrie inhaled the mouth-watering scents coming from the kitchen where Miller dutifully cooked dinner. She peeked in, adoring the sight of him at the stove stirring a chicken stir-fry.

"Okay, I've changed my clothes," she said, standing in jeans and a clean T-shirt. "What can I do to help?" she asked, stepping to his side and peering into the steaming pan.

He kissed her forehead before whisking the contents of the pan. "Just set the table, hun. This is done."

She was pleased to at least have decent dishware even if frozen pizza typically adorned it. When she'd sold Aunt Annabelle's house, there were a few things she managed to keep, like the antique China plates she cherished and used now for her romantic dinner with Miller.

When he plated the stir-fry and took his seat, Cambrie joined him. Digging into the food, she tasted heaven. What a treat to actually have a homemade meal.

"God, Miller. You don't have to worry about going AWOL. I'm not planning on letting you leave." She sipped her iced tea. "I haven't had a home cooked meal like this since Aunt Annabelle dished one up."

Miller offered a slight smile before forking more food into his mouth. Every time she looked up, she caught him watching her.

She waved her fork. "You're going to make

me self-conscious if you keep watching me so intently while I eat, Miller."

"Not to turn the mood somber, but how old were you when you lost your parents?"

She never saw that question coming. Holding her fork, she used it to toy with her veggies. His hand covered hers and stopped her motion. Forcing her eyes up, she saw the quiet determination in the depths of his soft gaze.

"I know it must be hard as hell to talk about, but you'll have to tell me eventually how you came to be with Aunt Annabelle." With a tender tone, he spoke in a manner that comforted. "I won't force you to talk about it. Hell, I know there are some things that can be just too damn difficult to talk about. But someday I hope you trust me enough to share that part of you because it's made you who you are, Cambrie Brasher. A wonderful, brilliant, adorable woman who takes my breath away." He gulped his iced tea. "Aunt Annabelle is a major part of your life. I'd love to hear more about her. When you're ready."

Miller didn't pressure her, didn't demand answers, didn't complain that she hesitated to speak of a past she wished not to relive. But he was right. She owed him at least an explanation about why Aunt Annabelle was important to her.

Taking a long sip of her drink, she was thankful for the coolness on her dry throat. "My parents were expecting my baby brother. Mom went into labor so they rushed me to a neighbor's house and sped off to the hospital because Mom was in a lot of pain. It was a beautiful summer's night. You could see every star in the sky. I went to bed that night hardly able to sleep because I really looked forward to being a big sister."

She took a long, steadying breath. "But sometime during the night I started having bad nightmares, like scary monsters all around me. I heard adult voices but didn't want to spy. I wanted my mom but remembered she was with Daddy at the hospital. Sleep finally overcame me and I woke up in the morning. Aunt Annabelle was already there speaking with the neighbor lady."

Cambrie sipped her drink again, fought back the tears that threatened each time she allowed that horrible day to resurface. "Aunt Annabelle told me I was going to go live with her, that my parents had been…killed in a car accident…hit by a drunk driver enroute to the hospital. None of them survived, not my parents or my baby brother. Just the drunk driver lived." She looked at Miller. "Some fucking justice that is, huh? The guy slaughters three people and he gets to live. The useless bastard." Anger vibrated throughout her body. She hated re-living the nightmare. "I was seven-years-old."

"Sometimes justice isn't always served immediately, honey," Miller said, his voice soothing and understanding. "But I firmly believe that somehow that bastard will pay for the pain he caused you and your family."

Cambrie sighed, her shoulders heavy. "Aunt Annabelle had just retired the year before. She had to go back to work to support me. Imagine a retiree being forced to raise a child? She should've been enjoying herself, traveling, relaxing, doing all the things she had looked forward to."

"Unfortunately, it happens all too often for various reasons. And I'm sure Aunt Annabelle didn't do anything she didn't want to." He scooped a forkful into his mouth.

She finished chewing her last bite before speaking again. "My parents had life insurance but it was just enough for the funerals. So Auntie gave up her retirement for me when I had no one else. I could never abandon her now. I'm all she's got. Just like she was all I had. All that's left are distant relatives that I've never met and live out of state. Auntie did good by me all these years and I intend to do just as good by her until the Lord takes her." She scooped one last bite into her mouth.

A smile creased Miller's lips. "Have I ever told you what a remarkable woman you are, Cambrie?"

Returning the smile, the tension slipped from her body now that she had pretty much bared her soul. "Remarkable is Aunt Annabelle. I'm just a product of good upbringing."

"With a great heart to go along with the gorgeous package. There's more stir-fry if you want some. Looks like you were as famished as me," Miller said eyeballing her plate, standing to carry his to the sink.

She looked at her empty plate, not remembering eating it all. But with her belly full and her heart aching with bad memories, Cambrie set out to save the rest of the night and make the most of the time she had left with Miller.

"Care for a nightcap?" she asked, hoping to discuss more entertaining topics than her past. "I've got a nice bottle of red wine."

"That, my dear, sounds fantastic." He winked. "I want to seduce you, drive you wild until you beg for my cock to drive into that sweet pussy."

She purred, leaned her hip against the counter, and angled her head. "How do you manage to do that?"

He looked puzzled. "Do what?"

Opening her cabinet, she chose two crystal glasses. "Make me feel like the sexiest woman in the world while getting me hornier than I've ever been?" she demanded, poured two glasses of wine and handed one to him. Taking his hand, she led him to the couch and pulled him down until they were both seated, their legs touching, the heat from his body warming hers.

Sipping his wine, he watched her over the rim, before lowering the glass and speaking. "You *are* the sexiest woman I've ever met and I'm just speaking the truth. I wish you understood how aroused you get me. First, with your hot emails. Then with that first kiss. Baby, the fire in my belly isn't lying."

"Maybe it's heartburn," she teased, almost choking on a laugh as she sipped the wine.

His cocked eyebrow warned of his playful mood. "Smart ass." His knuckles trailed down her cheek to her jawbone earning a shiver. God, she loved his touch. "I love how I feel when we're together, Cambrie. Love that hidden naughty girl side that only I've been allowed to see. And as my pen pal, your mission is to please me." The smirk he offered was more mischievous than teasing.

As his words melted her heart, her frisky side heated up. "And as my pen pal, you had better fulfill those fantasies you conjured up in my imagination."

His hands lifted her onto his lap and snuggled her into his arms. This was heaven. Sitting on her couch with a sexy man who couldn't take his eyes off of her. This was one dream she never wanted to wake up from.

"Pick a sex toy to use tonight, Cambrie," Miller whispered into her ear after placing his glass onto the coffee table. "Which fantasy shall I fulfill for you tonight, baby girl?"

A tingle ran up her spine to where his breath tickled the side of her neck. "Just one toy?"

His laugh was heartwarming and too damn sexy. "Hell, pick them all."

She might just have to. "Well, I am a bit curious about the butt plug, but I'm also hesitant. Do you think it'll hurt?"

He twirled a strand of her hair, speaking in a quiet, strong voice. "I promise I'll prep you so well with plenty of lube that any pain you feel will be the pleasurable kind. The first time I insert the plug, it'll be tight and maybe uncomfortable, but I swear I'll do everything in my power to keep it from being painful. Once your muscles stretch, they'll accommodate the plug easier and the uncomfortable feeling will dissipate very quickly. If not, and you don't like it, we stop. Plain and simple."

"The safe word, right?"

"Well, yes, that and, as your lover, it's my responsibility to gauge how much your body can take to prevent any harm or pain. You trust me to give you pleasure, baby, that's a task I don't take lightly. And I've learned a lot about your body since I've had the delight of making love to you. I've been trained to read a person within minutes of meeting them and I'll admit that you're a tough one to read, Cam. You present me with one of the greatest challenges I've ever had, which is very enjoyable. But most importantly, I've got a good idea of your physical reactions at least."

Tipping her glass back, she drank slowly

before responding. “Wow, you make me sound like a boring book.”

His brows crossed, highlighting the faint lines at his eyes. “Hardly. It’s just like when I think I’ve figured you out—bam!—you do something that goes against everything I expected. You keep me on my toes for sure.”

“I also want to use the chest harness. That looks wild. Although that dildo may be too big for my pussy.” What was her curiosity getting her into?

His arm encased her in steel strength, and he continued. “Can you feel my hard-on against your leg? I swear I’ve never been more turned on than I get with you. Sitting here, discussing sex toys like an everyday subject, having you be so comfortable with me is like a natural high. My cock throbs wanting to be buried in that hot pussy all the time.”

Did her heart just skip a beat? “Hhmmm. Does it throb when I say I can’t wait for you to fuck my ass the way you fuck my pussy? Hard and fast. Mmmm. Deep.”

A growl escaped his throat. “I think we’d better move this to the bedroom. Hate for the sex toys to be lonely.”

“I like that idea. But first give me a minute to change into something…sexier.”

The harsh gasp from him sounded painful. She scooted off the couch and dashed across the room. “What the hell for? I’m only going to rip it off of you,” Miller yelled.

She disappeared into her bedroom and stripped as fast as she could, dressing in the lingerie she had laid out earlier when she changed her clothes after they got home. The baby blue teddy and matching thigh highs had to be put on with care since they'd rip if she rushed too much.

Hurrying, because Miller wouldn't wait much longer to enter the room, Cambrie slipped into the black stiletto heels she had only worn once before at work. The four-inch heels just didn't cut it at the library.

A quick spritz of perfume and she had barely finished getting dolled up before Miller stormed into the room.

"What's taking…so…long…" His words trailed off as he came to a halt, his mouth hanging open as his stare moved from toes to head, while his eyes were wide and menacing.

Cambrie stood with one foot strategically placed in front of the other to offer the most alluring pose. One hand on her hip, the other holding a finger over her pouty lips, she batted her eyes and smiled, wishing she had remembered lipstick.

"Hot. Friggin'. Damn. Cambrie, I swear, as God is my witness, no other man had better ever see you dressed like that. I'm not opposed to murder to protect what's mine."

His? "And just how am I yours, Miller? Are we dating?"

"We can work out the details later. I don't care. There's just no friggin' way I could allow a guy to live if he saw you dressed like that. Christ, Cambrie, just when I thought you couldn't get any hotter." He stood, hands on hips, practically licking his lips. "Now do you understand why I can't read you like I can everyone else?"

Two giant steps and he had her lifted into his arms.

"I don't know what you mean, Miller. I'm as ordinary as they get," she said, clinging to his neck.

"Like hell," he said, laying her on the bed. "There's not an ordinary bone in this hot body. You just like people to think that you're plain. It helps you keep people at arm's length, doesn't it?"

His words touched a sore spot and she didn't know why. "That's not true." Did she keep people at a distance?

"That's a debate for another time and not when you're lying in front of me covered in sexy lace and satin with come-fuck-me heels. Just let me take my fill of you, baby. I want to remember this moment."

While his hands roamed every inch of the body his eyes studied, her skin heated to sizzling. She wanted to feel those long fingers on and in her pussy and ass. Arching her back off of the bed only allowed him to concentrate on her breasts, circling the material around her nipples like he traced a picture.

"Miller, my fantasy. Make it come true. You're the only one I've ever wanted to try things with. The only person I've ever trusted."

His eyes smoldered with heavy lust. Lifting her nylon clad leg in the air, his hands ran up and down it at a slow pace, his mouth kissing her thigh and knee. Damn, did he realize how potent a lover he was? She was about to combust with raw need.

"First, I want these legs wrapped around my shoulders while I taste your sweet pussy."

She gasped, not expecting this. But when he settled between her legs and lifted her calves to rest on his shoulders, she was a goner. His hand pulled at the snaps holding the material together between her legs. Once freed, it was brushed aside with obvious impatience, a striking contrast to his usual patience.

His mouth clamped onto her aching pussy with one hard wet kiss. She would have shot off the bed except his forearm over her hips kept her in place.

His tongue wasted no time in licking the tender folds of her pussy lips. Heat spread throughout her womb as the pressure within her rose to a spiraling level so out of her control. With his free hand, he fingerfucked her pussy, inserting one finger into her wet heat, then two. Reaching deep into her core, he touched on something that was absolutely glorious.

A bolt of intense spasms flowed from her womb. Her body heated with fever, twitching and quivering deep inside until she thought she'd incinerate with sheer lust. Every inch of her pussy responded to the exploration of Miller's fingers with a greedy need to experience the same touch.

"Oh, Miller. Yes. Right there. Please don't stop."

He listened and kept a steady pace, slamming his fingers over and over across that secret spot. Pressure built inside her from every direction. Breathing became hard as she gasped for air to compete with her racing heartbeat. When her orgasm ripped through her pussy, stars exploded behind her eyelids. Maybe she had squeezed them shut too hard or maybe the lack of oxygen finally affected her brain. Either way, she didn't care for anything except the pleasure riveting throughout her womb to her pulsing pussy. Spasm after spasm gripped her swollen lips, the sensations earning a loud cry.

"Miller! Miller! It's too much. Oh, holy hell. Too much."

His mouth remained on her clit even as she floated back to the bed. When he removed his mouth, cool air swept across the wet kisses he had left behind on her throbbing lips. Opening her eyes awarded her the view of Miller stripping. Funny how she hadn't felt him move from the bed. Was he always so quiet?

"Onto your belly, Cambrie," he ordered, coming back to the side of the bed holding the butt plug.

What? He really expected her to have the energy to move after that orgasm. "May need a minute to recuperate."

No chance in that. Miller took her heels off and helped her roll over then scooted her ass into the air. His massive hand covered her ass cheeks with two spanks on each side.

"Oh!" she cried out more in surprise than pain.

"Just can't help myself. Love spanking this ass." For emphasis, he landed two more slaps to each cheek. The sound aroused her as much as the tingle left behind.

Her pussy came alive again with tiny pulses hovering around her clit. She moaned, enjoying the heat increasing on her ass cheeks while the slippery touch of his finger prodded her dark rosette.

"Relax for me," he commanded from behind her. "My finger's going to play with your ass, make sure it's nice and lubed. Damn, I wish you could see how fucking sexy you look with this very fine ass for me to view and play with."

"Oh, that's…different feeling," she said, gasping as his finger slid deeper and moved faster.

"You're so tight here, Cambrie. God, my

cock is as hard as steel wanting to replace my finger. But I promised to make this enjoyable for you. There's no way in hell I'm going to rush it. You just concentrate on relaxing your body to allow me easier entry."

He removed his fingers and re-inserted them after a few seconds. The cool liquid on them helped him slide two fingers in this time.

"Oh, um. Oh." What exactly did she say to a guy who had his fingers in her ass, elevating her to a new height of arousal? "Don't stop." The words rushed out without any embarrassment or need to censure her needs. For the first time in her life, she didn't have to think if what she wanted was acceptable. With Miller, everything was acceptable and that left her feeling so sure of her wants and desires that nothing could hold her back.

"I like it when you demand more of our loving, baby." He slid his fingers from her ass. The emptiness noticeable, earning a whimper from her. "Just lubing the butt plug. Now don't tense up." With the tip of the cool plastic pressing against her ass, he shifted his weight on the bed. "I'll go slow. You just breathe normal. Think of how good my cock is going to feel buried deep inside this pretty ass while my fingers rub your clit."

Oh, she wanted it all now. Waiting proved more painful than the prepping of her ass. The invasion of the butt plug into her ass provided a moment of awareness, this was really about to happen. She and Miller would have anal sex and fulfill another one of her fantasies.

Life as she knew it was forever changed and the future would be dim without Miller in it, but she couldn't dwell on that with the plastic toy pushing further into her anus. She concentrated on breathing and staying relaxed.

"Doing great, Cambrie." Miller's reassuring tone soothed her. "How's it feeling?"

"Tight. Very tight. But I'm fine." Was that husky tone hers?

His free hand massaged her hips and ass, the attention welcomed and calming. "Ready? One more push and it'll be in."

"Oh! Wow," she yelped, once the plug was all the way in her ass. She couldn't resist wiggling her bottom to adjust to the fullness within her ass. "Touch me, Miller. I need to feel you close to me."

The mattress shifted again as he stood and lifted her onto her toes. Using a small towel on the nightstand, he wiped his hands. His arms wrapped around her in an embrace so loving, she melted against his chest. The tightness and slight pinch in her ass subsided, leaving behind a sensation of heat that ignited her pussy with sharp pulses. Oh, God, she never imagined her body could feel this alive, this on fire with a desire so powerful it could rob her of breath.

Miller eased away to lift her chin until his lips could claim hers. Opening her mouth, his tongue swept in to possess her. She could taste the remnants of his wine and her juices. How erotic to taste herself and know what he had experienced between her legs. Being open to this new type of sex offered her the most unbelievable freedom to fulfill her every deep, dark secret desire. There were no barriers to what she craved or to the new experiences she would have with Miller.

When he ended the kiss, he stared into her eyes. "Take me into your mouth, baby. But I don't want to come. I'll wait to be in your hot ass."

With an offer of a hand for support, Miller

helped her kneel before him. The snug fit of the butt plug in her ass was a constant reminder of what was to come. Her body hummed hotter with each passing minute as muscles she hadn't previously felt relaxed.

Taking his thick cock into her hand, Cambrie squeezed while sliding her hand up and down the huge shaft. This close she could study him, feeling a naughty side awakening and wanting to learn every inch of Miller's body. His cock was heavy in her palm, the purple bulges of veins throbbed with her touch. The head mushroomed and the slit already glistened with pre-cum. She licked her lips, wanting that pearly white drop on her tongue, greedy for the taste of him.

"You're teasing the shit out of me, baby girl," Miller exclaimed from above.

When she glanced up, she caught him studying her, fascination written all over his face. "Just admiring how thick and heavy your cock is, Miller."

His head slumped back with a growl.

Okay, maybe she had tortured him enough. Leaning forward, she swiped her tongue across the swollen head and licked at the pre-cum. The salty liquid bathed her tongue in small droplets while she worked more of his cock into her mouth. She felt his body stiffen and held her hand on his hard thigh to keep her balance.

Stroking his cock up and down the steel length with her hand and mouth, she stole her hand away to caress his balls.

"Christ, Cambrie! You're killing me. Christ."

His body was strung so tight and the thick muscles of his leg flexed where her free hand roamed. His breathing, filled with sharp gasps, whispered through the air, proof of how much she was driving him wild.

She didn't allow the exasperated tone to deter her. Determined to drive him even wilder, she swallowed his cock to the back of her throat, taking the engorged muscle fully into the warmth of her mouth. His hips flexed, pushing the head against the back of her throat. Moans and groans filled the room along with the heady scent of arousal, hers and his mixing together.

His hand ran over the top of her head, fisting in the hair, allowing his dominance to control the way she performed the blow job, holding her close or pulling her back when intensity overwhelmed his cock. Sucking on the length of him filled her with a power so intense that she shook. She held this man's pleasure in her hands and could hold him in the cusp of that bliss for as long as she desired. She held his attention and no other woman. It was her name that he yelled, her name heard after every moan from his throat. And it was her pleasure that he always kept in mind.

Her mouth released his cock to allow her tongue to swipe over the slit. His salty flavor teased her taste buds and shot heat straight to her pussy, vibrating the butt plug that remained nestled in her tight ass. With her mouth, she urged him to explode on her tongue. She wanted to swallow his cum, suck the pleasure from him until he was sated and happy.

"Cambrie. Stop!" With his hand under her chin, he eased his cock from her mouth. "God. Please. Baby, I want to come in your ass. Any more of this delicious mouth and I'm a goner."

Leaning over her, he helped her onto her feet, placed a soft kiss to her forehead, and laid her onto the bed on her belly. "Can I go bare-back in your ass or do you want me to use a condom? I'm clean. We get tested every time we leave the States."

"No condom. I want to feel you."

With a scoop of his arm under her hips, she was on her knees. "Just removing the plug."

When his hands tugged at the toy in her ass, she gripped the bed sheet. The sensations rioting throughout her body were too much to handle. Every inch of her body begged for Miller's touch, his kiss, his heat. Once the plug left her ass, the emptiness seemed overwhelming. She had enjoyed the intrusion and the naughtiness it offered.

She turned her head to catch Miller lathering his cock with the lube. The sight made her body hum like a burning ember. "Miller, hurry." If she didn't feel his hands on her soon, she'd be reduced to begging.

When he climbed onto the bed behind her, she reminded herself to stay relaxed. He had prepped her body well and had taken good care of her up to now. There was no reason he wouldn't continue to keep her comfort and pleasure in mind.

The thick head of his cock pressed through her tight rosette and stopped. The sensation of taking his cock into her ass was so much different than the butt plug had been. The heat from his erection warmed her anus, easing the tender muscles. His pulsing thickness slid into her dark channel with a tender slowness that drove her wild with desire.

"Oh, hell, Cambrie. You're tighter than I even imagined. Am I hurting you?" His fingers gripped her sides, whether for possession or comfort, she didn't care. It added to her arousal knowing that he held her so firmly.

The genuine concern in his voice touched her and swelled her heart with a feeling that made her lightheaded and giddy. "No, Miller. I'm getting used to it. I…I like it."

With his hands still gripping her hips, he eased his cock deeper until he was fully seated in her ass. He ceased movement and allowed her body to adjust to his invasion.

"Oh," she gasped as the tightness gave way to a firestorm of intense yearnings. Feeling the fullness of his cock in her ass, her body tingled with the need to feel him moving in the tight channel. "Miller, fuck me. Now." She craved his possession, releasing the wanton woman hidden within her.

His growl indicated that he had heard her loud and clear. But it was his hips that spoke volumes as they pummeled into hers. The slow speed turned into a determined one. Each thrust of his cock into her anus brushed across tender nerves and sent shockwaves to her pussy, which throbbed in response. The slapping of his hips against hers filled the air, competing with the noise from their heavy breathing.

"So. Fucking. Tight. Hell." Miller said, sounding like his teeth were clenched.

"Please. Miller. I need to come. Fuck me. Harder."

He obliged and slammed his cock into her ass over and over, crying out—curses, her name, and many other inaudible words. She could barely pay attention to his words as she clung to the bed to keep on her knees, the sheer power of his movements almost flattened her to the mattress.

"Come with me, Cambrie. Come with me now," he yelled, his words caught on intense gasps.

When his hand reached under their bodies to run a finger over her hard clit, a bolt of fire shot through her pussy to her womb and then to her ass. “Miller! Yes! Yes!”

Her body bucked like a bronco. Her head whipped around, her hair flew everywhere. Behind her, Miller held his body against hers as his cock pulsed deep inside her ass, filling her channel with his hot cum.

“Cambrie!” His lone word echoed his lust.

With her body on fire, Cambrie’s orgasm crashed over her like a runaway train. The sheer force of the orgasm stole her breath and sent her in a spiraling free-fall, floating through bright lights and flashes. Her pussy lips spasmed until she thought she’d pass out.

Each sensation reached her ass where Miller’s cock was buried deep, its thickness rippling against the tightness of the forbidden canal. His fingers gripped her side while the other hand worked its magic over her clit. Slow, steady circles pressed into the aching nub, keeping merciless pressure that fueled the orgasms. Another wave of pleasure tore through her body, stronger than the first and more intense.

“Miller! Oh, God. More.”

It shocked Cambrie how much her body could endure and still want more. Miller’s hands moved from her hips and clit to grasp her breasts, tweaking each nipple between rough fingers. The slight pain fanned her desires more and kept her body humming in a constant state of arousal even as her orgasms slowly died out.

Exhausted, Cambrie sank forward onto the mattress as Miller withdrew his spent cock and stepped off of the bed. Wishing she could catch her breath, she just lay there with closed eyes and focused on easing her heart from its relentless pounding. When a warm, wet cloth rubbed between her ass cheeks, she gasped.

Looking back, she noticed Miller washing her ass and wasn't ashamed to admit that it felt so good. "What are you doing now, Miller?"

He glanced at her then back at her ass. "Just taking care of my baby. You have the nicest ass, Cambrie. God, you drive me wild."

He disappeared again before returning a few minutes later. Lifting her up, he pulled the covers down and stripped her lingerie from her body.

"Love the outfit, baby. But would much rather feel your soft skin against me while we sleep," he whispered before placing her on the bed, shutting off the light, and scooting in beside her.

She really craved sleep. Having her energy level sapped with world-altering sex was the best sleep medicine she could think of. "Good night, Miller," she said through a sleepy yawn.

"Night," he replied, kissing the top of her head and pulling her into his tight embrace. Sleeping with that strong arm wrapped around her, felt like a dream.

She didn't want it to end if it were.

Chapter Fourteen

Cambrie feared the house was on fire the way Miller bolted from the bed and grabbed the cell phone out of his pants pocket.

"Miller," he yelled into the phone, ending the shrilling ring.

Cambrie sat up, blinking the sleep from her eyes. Squinting in the light beaming from the nightstand, she read the alarm clock. Two in the morning. Who could be calling Miller at two in the morning?

Oh no!

"Yes, sir," Miller said, disconnecting. "Sorry, Cambrie. My orders changed. I've got to leave now."

He threw his clothes on while she sat in the middle of the bed, trying to comprehend what she'd just heard. He was leaving right now?

"But, I thought, well, you didn't need to leave for a few more days?" she wondered, slipping from the bed without a thought for her nakedness.

"That's the nature of my job. Things can change second to second."

"Well, where are they sending you?"

His gaze caught hers. "I can't tell you that." He rushed from the room.

Cambrie threw on a nightshirt and ran after him. He had his gym bag packed and shoved his arms into his jacket. She didn't know what to say. Shock settled deep into her bones.

So this is what it was like to have him stolen

away in the middle of the night? This abruptness was daunting.

She bit her lip and stayed out of his way as he tightened the laces on his boots and glanced around like he had forgotten something.

"Oh, wait. I almost forgot to give you something," Cambrie exclaimed and tore through her briefcase.

"Hurry, babe. I need every second to get back to base." His cool tone didn't hide the anxiousness in his eyes. When she handed him a bundle of envelopes, he asked, "What are these?"

"Letters from our Teen Readers Group. Read them while you're away. It's just part of the pen pal program for the library."

"Okay," he shoved them into his bag, gripped her waist, and kissed her with a big smacking sound on her lips. "I've got to run. I don't know when I can call or email. But I promise I will." He brushed his knuckles over her cheek. "Talk soon, Cam."

With those few short words, he shut the door behind him, leaving Cambrie stunned at the speed of his departure. Boy, he sure didn't lie when he said he would have to leave at a moment's notice.

She placed her hands on her hips and stared at the front door. How dare he leave her with just a quick kiss? Would it have killed him to take an extra second for a decent good-bye?

She hated to think of him being vulnerable on the highways at this late hour, just like her parents twenty years ago. If she focused on being mad at him for leaving so quickly, then she wouldn't have to worry about his safety.

As she turned back toward her bedroom, a pounding on the door stopped her. She hurried to open it, stepping back to allow Miller's massive body back in.

"I should be shot leaving like that. I'm so sorry, baby. I've just never had to worry about rushing off until now. Come here." Miller's chest rose and fell in rapid succession. Outside, his motorcycle roared with life in front of the house.

Cambrie jumped into his arms, wrapping her legs around his waist, anchoring her body to his. His strong hands gripped her ass and squeezed. God, his touch was addictive. If only she could lock him away in her bedroom. But a man like Miller wouldn't be happy doing any other job. He said so himself.

Without further hesitation, his lips found hers and his tongue dove deep inside her mouth. She went wild with need, holding his shoulders and battling his tongue for control. She needed to taste him one more time before he left to the unknown. The heat from his body warmed her against the cool breeze coming in from the open door. His heart pounded under her palm when she ran her hand over the tight muscles of his chest.

Moaning into the kiss, pain tore through her knowing this was the last touch of Miller until God knew when. When he broke the kiss, she wanted to cry, but understood he had to get going. At least he had come back for a proper good-bye. She wouldn't hold him up any further.

She climbed off of him and held the door. "I'll miss you, Miller, and will look forward to when we can talk again. Be safe."

"Cambrie." He appeared to be ready to say more but didn't.

Her forced smile required every bit of acting skill she had. He walked through the door into the darkness of the night. She couldn't watch him drive off, so she shut the door and lights and walked to her bedroom, her arms crossed over her breaking heart.

With the roar of the motorcycle fading as he drove away, Cambrie crawled under the covers and refused to cry. Miller would return. He promised.

Holding his pillow to her face, she breathed deeply, lay on it, closed her eyes, and wondered just why her dream had to end so damn soon.

****

With the wind whipping in his face and the hint of the morning sun over the horizon, Miller kept his motorcycle racing back toward Virginia. The trip back would take four hours if he didn't hit any morning traffic. But if he kept his speed ten miles above the limit then he could possibly shave an hour off that time.

He didn't want to break the law, but he needed to get back to base. The last thing he needed was to keep his team waiting and then never be granted a leave to visit Cambrie again because he couldn't get back in a decent amount of time.

Cambrie.

God, he didn't want to think of that startled look in her wide, brown eyes when he had to haul ass out of there. She looked confused and bewildered and who could blame her after being rudely awakened in the middle of the night to say a hasty good-bye to her lover. How he wished he had the remaining days with her and his mission hadn't changed. But the job was the job and nothing was ever set in stone.

Damn! He had never been pissed about being called back to base early or having a leave interrupted because he was needed for a mission. Until Cambrie. Now he was angry at having to leave her and her sexy body. This was the first time he ever wanted to be somewhere more than on a mission. What the fuck!

Maybe it was good that he had to leave earlier than planned. It would give him time to think about how Cambrie had such an impact on him. He couldn't let his emotions for the lovely woman get out of control. She'd made it clear there was no way for her to leave her aunt or Maddyville. And it sure wasn't possible for him to make the trip back and forth between missions when his team could be activated at any time.

Miller roared down the interstate into Virginia. He was almost home.

A few days of working and chasing bad guys would help him expend some physical energy and get back to his daily regimen. Then he'd figure out what to do now that he had found the woman of his dreams but couldn't have her because they were stuck in two different worlds. She might as well be from anther planet given the distance between them. Fuck!

He revved the engine and concentrated on the road as more vehicles joined him for morning rush hour as he neared Little Creek. His heart felt like someone had reached into his chest and ripped it out. The only reason he knew his heart was still there was the ache every time he thought of Cambrie.

It was going to be hard sleeping without her in his arms or hearing her sexy voice or contagious laugh. Even harder to accept that he didn't know when he'd see her next.

Visions of her naked body danced in his memories, how pretty her curves were, how supple her skin was, the way she blushed or gasped. She had been a willing lover, trusting him with her body as well as her pleasure and then demanding more.

His cock stirred just thinking of her inquisitive sexual nature and how she had ordered those sex toys for them to use. What a stroke of luck that he'd found this amazing woman—well, for her to have found him.

He made a mental note to shake Finn's hand for this one. Even if he'd thought his friend and former commander was busting his balls at first by sending him a pen pal, Miller couldn't be more pleased with the outcome.

Back in Little Creek, Miller faced a full day with little sleep. Wherever his team was headed, he hoped he could get sleep on the plane without worrying about how Cambrie was holding up. She wasn't used to the military life and it hadn't been fair for her to have to experience it first hand so quickly.

Parking the bike in front of his house, Miller stepped off and fought the memory of arriving at Cambrie's the other day. Now, he just wanted to get back to her.

****

Cambrie rose earlier than usual the next morning, unable to sleep after Miller left. Sipping a cup of coffee, she sat before her laptop wondering what to say in the email she had started for him. He needed to know that she supported him and would be here when he could get back.

Hi Miller, just writing a quick note as I head out to work. Hope your ride home went well and you get some rest soon. Had a wonderful time with you and hope you can visit again soon. We'll have more fun. Wink! Write when you can, but if I don't hear from you, I understand you're working hard to protect us and you'll get in touch when you can. I won't lie. I found it very hard to sleep without you in my bed. I'll keep your side of the bed warm for you. Mwah! Hugz, Cambrie

She wiped the tears from her eyes, refusing to get upset. He had a job to do just like she did. She'd had a life before Miller Daly and she'd continue to have one no matter how much she missed him. She had learned a long time ago that life managed to go on and stopped for nothing. It wasn't like she'd never see him again. They'd find a way to get together, even if only for a few stolen days here and there.

At work, the morning dragged on. Cambrie was bummed when no response came from Miller, but she hadn't really expected one.

"Do you have your report ready for the Board of Directors, Miss Brasher?" Mr. Hackler asked, stepping into her office.

"Yes, sir," she replied with no real enthusiasm. He expected her to give a briefing on Miller when it tortured her just to think of him, not knowing when she'd see him again?

"Then let's head in there. I think they've all arrived."

In the large meeting room, the six Board Members had assembled, drinking coffee and talking. When they saw Hackler and Cambrie enter the room, they took their seats and the chairman spoke. "I call to order this meeting of the Highland Library's Board of Directors. First on the agenda, a report by Miss Brasher on her progress with the Veterans Affairs grant. Miss Brasher, if you will."

Cambrie stood at the end of the table. She had only spoken before this group once before and had been terrified. But those feelings didn't surface this time because she heard Miller's voice in her ear offering her the encouragement she needed to believe in herself. He may not be beside her, but his presence would always be with her.

"Ladies and Gentlemen, I'll be brief as I've only just begun work on the grant program. Support has been immense from our community for which I am grateful. Donations have come in steadily as have the volunteers to collect more. I had an opportunity to meet our pen pal, and Lt. Miller Daly is an exceptional man of strength, values, and character. We should be honored to support him while he serves our great country."

"Where is Lt. Daly now, Miss Brasher? We'd love to meet him," the chairman said, the others nodding their heads in agreement.

A sudden jolt of pain struck her heart. Clearing her throat, she spoke calmly. "Lt. Daly was called out of town earlier than expected. He had to return for a mission, sir. But he assured me we had his complete support in our quest to receive the grant."

"It sounds like you've gotten to know the young man quite well in such a short period of time, Miss Brasher," another board member said.

Cambrie's cheeks warmed and she prayed they couldn't see her blushing. Remembering just how well she'd gotten to know Miller had her squeezing her legs together as her pussy awakened with the memories. "Well, with the wonders of modern technology, I've been able to communicate with him via email a lot. Since the grant is vital to our survival, I've also made plans to dedicate part of the library's website to this program."

"Will there be an additional expense to do that?" an elderly female member asked.

"No, ma'am. It's just a matter of me setting up a page. Will that be all?"

She needed to stop talking about Miller and the grant. Getting involved with Miller while he was a project for work was not her smartest decision, but she couldn't have regrets now.

"Thank you, Miss Brasher."

She quickly left the room and walked as fast as she could to her office where she shut the door for privacy. "Oh, Miller. I hope you're safe."

Her belly felt queasy so she sipped from the water bottle she kept on her desk. Her computer stared back. But she wouldn't keep checking for a reply from Miller. Instead, she'd reach out to her friend for comfort and much needed advice.

She began to type then erased the words. Picking up the phone, she dialed Emma's number. She needed to *talk* not just email. Christ, when did technology replace the common phone call?

"Hello." Emma's voice sounded upbeat as usual on the other end.

"Hi, Emma. It's Cambrie. I hope I'm not catching you at the wrong time."

"Oh, wow. Cambrie! What a surprise. Oh, it's so great to hear your voice. What's going on? Everything okay?"

"Yes, I'm fine. Well, just wanted to say thank

you for introducing me to Miller. He's been a fantastic pen pal."

"Oh, you're so welcome. I really hope it gets you that grant."

Cambrie toyed with the telephone wire. "He came to visit me the other day."

"What? He's there now?"

"No. He could only stay two days and got called back. That's why I called you. Hoping you could give me some advice on how to handle the nature of his job. I mean, we were just getting to know each other and, wham, he's called away."

"Aw, honey. I know it's hard. I don't think you can ever get used to sending your man into battle." Emma's soothing voice was genuine. But she was oh so sneaky.

"He's hardly my man, Emma. We're not even dating. We, um, we just hung out during his visit."

"Oh, my God. Was he good in bed?"

"Emma!"

"Oh, hush. There's no way Miller didn't seduce you. He's a lot like Finn and, honey, we ain't got a chance against testosterone like that." Emma laughed.

Cambrie smiled. "Miller was magnificent, but then I had something to do with how amazing sex was, too."

"I'm sure you drove him insane with lust."

"Yeah. He did threaten to go AWOL once or twice." Peels of laughter came through the earpiece. "I miss him already, Em. I know it sounds stupid, but I got used to him being here with me."

"I don't think that's stupid at all. He made an impression and probably was a great match for you and not just in bed. The man has a great head on his shoulders. Finn would never steer a dumb ass your way." Now it was Cambrie's turn to laugh. "Listen, Cam. It's nerve wracking to wait to hear from them, but you need to keep busy."

Cambrie asked the question she didn't even want to think about. "What if something happens to him, Emma? I'd never know."

"Of course, you would. Finn would tell you any news he got, good or bad. Miller's family. So are you, Cam."

"Thank you, Emma. I'm at work so I've got to run. Just wanted to ask your advice."

"Any time, love. I'm here. Don't forget that. Lots of love."

"Same to you and give Finn a hug for me."

Hanging up the phone, Cambrie decided to take Emma's advice and keep busy. She developed a page on the library's website dedicated to the grant quest. She used the picture Miller had sent her, but wished she had thought to take a newer one while he was here. She didn't even have one of them together. Well, they did have better things to do. She smiled, allowing the memories of their loving to warm her and keep her company while she worked on the pen pal page.

****

Miller rushed into the crumbling brick building, the earpiece his only connection to the other team members. The hunt for the missing U.S. Marine over enemy lines had been the mission that had called Miller's team back into action.

Extracting the POW depended on if the team had received the correct coordinates for where his captors held him. The Marine had been fresh out of boot camp and deployed to Afghanistan only weeks ago. The Marine's convoy fell under enemy fire and all were killed but the young man reported MIA.

A local terror group released a photo confirming that they held him. Sons-of-a-bitches didn't know who they were fucking with when they held an American hostage. Miller kept his cool, relying on his training to make his every move.

Short phrases rang in his ear. The team said only what they needed and nothing more. The stench of piss and dust filled the hundred-degree air. Under his armored vest, Miller's shirt was soaked with his perspiration, but this was all in a day's work. The military had never promised a cozy work environment.

Miller sensed movement as he approached a room that showed signs of a previous bomb attack, the walls crumbling and piles of debris covering the floors. He blinked for focus and came upon the hostage. He whispered into his mouthpiece and waited for his team to rendezvous at his location.

Waiting for backup was one of the hardest things Miller had had to do. He was helpless to aid the young man being tortured. He had to await the team because, on his own, he'd be useless.

The bloodied Marine sat in a chair with his hands tied behind his back, while his captors fired questions at him, punching him, spitting on him, kicking him. The man's head hung low, his voice barely audible with each answer he offered.

"What you say? Speak, you American asshole," one captor shouted an inch from his face.

With guts Miller wouldn't have expected to see under such tactics and from someone so young, the Marine raised his head and spoke clearly, his eyes fixated on his captor. "Go. Fuck. Yourself. Mothafucka."

Bravo kid.

Miller's team arrived. Taking thirty seconds to discuss their tactical measures, they rushed the room. A spray of bullets filled the room and bodies fell to the floor. Miller grabbed a knife, sliced through the Marine's bindings, helping him to a more protected position.

"Give me a weapon," the Marine yelled.

Miller handed him a spare handgun. "Let's get you outta this shit hole, Marine."

"Yes, sir."

The team left as they had arrived, quickly and organized. On the street, they boarded their vehicle and raced to the safety of the American camp four miles away.

"Hell of a job back there, men," Chance yelled over the hum of the engine as the army truck sped across the desert kicking up dust. Hoots and hollers echoed from the men.

"You're a tough fucking Marine," Miller said. "Never seen steel balls like you displayed back there."

Miller shook his hand while the kid's fat lip attempted a smile. Entering the relative safety of their camp, Miller jumped from the truck and prepared to debrief.

He wished he could email Cambrie or even give her a call. Maybe once he got done with his work and with a great deal of luck, the Internet connection would be stable enough for him to send a quick note. Cambrie had to be fast asleep half way around the world far from the dangers that surrounded him. That's what made his job worthwhile, keeping people like Cambrie safe in their beds at night.

The camp didn't offer any comforts of home, just the basics for survival. Miller sacked out on a wooden carton and cleaned his gun. Thanks to the fucking sand flying around, if he didn't clean it then the damn thing would jam.

He found himself thinking of Cambrie during the tedious chore. Looking forward to her emails and seeing her again, Miller knew he wouldn't be able to stay away for long. He'd figure out some way for them to be together. For now, he'd just enjoy getting to know the wonderfully refreshing woman.

Maybe, if he ever had privacy again, he could entice her to play with him a bit at some cyber sex and use that web cam on her laptop. Shit, seeing her naked body flash across his computer screen would just about give him reason to beg for Section 8.

Chapter Fifteen

Cambrie couldn't decide what made her more proud, the military boardroom filled with local citizens highlighting their military service or the wad of money she held in her hand that had been raised by the Teen Readers Group for care packages to the homeless veteran's shelter. Never had a project given her such a sense of pride for her country.

When Cambrie put out a call to local vets to submit their photos for a Military Board of Honor for Maddyville to be displayed at Highland Library, she never expected the response to be so great. But it had been and now even more citizens took advantage of the library's services.

A group of vets gathered to make new friends, see old friends, and share stories. Cambrie couldn't listen because it brought Miller's job too close to home. She was better when she thought of him being bored in a desert somewhere rather than him facing enemy combatants and running out of ammunition like some of the vets had talked about. It was also hard to see their war wounds up close. Limbs maimed or lost. Eyesight or hearing lost. Scars etched into skin now wrinkled with age. Cambrie admired each and every veteran she had met.

It had been almost a week since Miller left and still no word from him. But Cambrie reminded herself that he'd get in touch when he could.

Meanwhile, she had responsibilities to see the

pen pal project through and emailed Miller each day, keeping him updated on the happenings around Maddyville, the heartwarming letter she'd received from the shelter's manager so grateful for the first donations sent, and Aunt Annabelle's constant efforts to get out of the nursing home.

Aunt Annabelle even had gone as far as writing Miller a letter under the false pretense of supporting the pen pal program. Cambrie at least had the good sense to intercept that letter, read it, and confiscate it.

"How could you write Miller that you're being held prisoner and needed to be rescued?" Cambrie had admonished her stubborn aunt. "Honestly, don't you think the man has more important things to worry about than a stubborn old woman who is too set in her ways for her own good?"

"Well, someone needs to help me. I'm wasting my days in here."

Cambrie had made some phone calls to see about bringing Aunt Annabelle home, but her physicians thought it was too soon. Until her medications could be regulated, then Aunt Annabelle would receive the best care in the nursing home.

Supervising the Teen Readers Group was always the highlight of Cambrie's week. But today, a bruise on Greg's cheek distracted her. The boy had been his usual quiet self and didn't make eye contact. Just kept his head hung low while the other kids discussed the book of the week. The story had been about a boy who ran from each foster home he was placed in because he was being abused.

"Greg, what do you think the boy's friends or

family could've done to protect him from the abuse?" Cambrie asked, hoping to give the kid a forum to discuss his troubles with his peers.

Greg shrugged his shoulders. "Maybe they couldn't do anything because they weren't strong enough."

The answer stunned Cambrie for its insight and honesty. "Very true."

"Or maybe the boy tried, maybe he tried to tell someone he thought would be a match for the abuser, but that person did nothing." Greg raised his head and stared at the small circle of teens. "Sometimes not all problems can be solved."

Cambrie cleared her throat and stood. "Okay. Well, since our time is up for today, I wanted to take a moment and thank all of you for the fantastic fundraising efforts you've made for the pen pal program. Keep up the good work and I'll see you next week." She walked to Greg as he put his coat on. "Greg, how did you get that bruise on your cheek?"

His eyes had shadows in them. "Just solved a problem."

"I see. Have you written Lt. Daly? I've seen you on the computer."

He shrugged. "Yeah. Haven't heard from him. No big deal."

She sighed. "I know, he hasn't replied to me either. But I keep writing because I know he gets them. He'll write when he can. But keep sending the emails. He's a really good listener I've learned. And strong as an ox." Enough to kick your dad's sorry ass.

"Will do. Bye, Miss Brasher."

"Mrs. Ginnity," Cambrie called, passing the front desk. "Do you know who I'd call to report suspected child abuse? The sheriff or child protective services?"

"If you're talking about Greg's bruised cheek, I heard the school nurse already called the authorities, but without Greg's cooperation they couldn't prove his father hit him. The kid said he fell off his bike or something."

Cambrie shook her head, anger consuming her. "Maybe I'll talk with his mother then."

The other woman let out a sarcastic laugh. "Are you kidding? What's she going to do against that bear of a man? He throws her around too, but no one can ever convince her to press charges. The sheriff's talked to Greg senior and told him to lay off his wife and, for the most part, he has, but the woman's still scared stiff and no help to her son. And don't you go getting any ideas about confronting that man yourself. Aunt Annabelle needs you."

Cambrie had a better idea. She happened to have an ox of her own in her corner. When Miller came to visit next, she'd ask him for advice. In the mean time, she'd keep the elder Greg distracted.

"Mrs. Ginnity, would you mind getting a group of ladies together to visit Greg's mom? I'm thinking the more outside contact she has, the more she'll open up."

"Oh, I like how you think. I'll even have the women include her in our bridge games."

"Thank you. If she's that abused, she may be afraid to join you at first but let's keep trying. It'll let her husband know people are watching. Now, I was also hoping to enlist your help in organizing a Harvest Fair to raise money to mail the care packages to the shelter. Would you be interested?"

Mrs. Ginnity jumped out of her seat. "Would

I? Oh, that sounds magnificent. Give me all the details you have so far."

****

Miller's head throbbed and his ribs hurt like hell. But he had won the fistfight and captured the suspected terrorist with his bare hands after his gun jammed—thanks to the goddamn sand.

"Sit down and shut the fuck up," Miller said between clenched teeth, pushing the filthy man into a chair in the middle of an empty room. "If you don't understand English, then I'll have it translated for you, asshole."

"You dirty Americans. My brothers come for me. You see."

Miller leaned back against the wall while Cade stood on the other side of the small interrogation room. "Great. The more the fucking merrier. Keeps me from having to chase their asses through this friggin' sand," Miller said. "Now, let's save us both some time. Tell me where the American weapons are that you and your slime ball friends stole."

"Kiss ass mine," the man said and spit on the ground.

Miller laughed. "When you learn to speak English correctly then we'll talk. Until then, you can rot in here for all I care. Cuff him."

Cade locked the man's hands and ankles to the chair and left the room with Miller.

"Leave him in there. Isolation works wonders on loosening the tongue. I'll check back in a few hours," Miller said, wiping sweat from his brow.

"Yes, sir," Cade replied.

Miller had stepped in as Team Leader for

Chance while he patrolled the southern border. Miller had some time to kill while he waited, hoping the terrorist would crack under the pressure. Probably wouldn't be that easy, but sometimes the good guys caught a break.

Miller found a free laptop in the office and logged into his email. He hadn't been able to reply to Cambrie because he was afraid it'd shake his concentration, but he did like to read each new email and re-read her old ones as often as he could.

When he read her latest email listing all of her accomplishments, he had to reply.

Hello, Cambrie baby. I'm well. I miss you like I hadn't expected. Please keep writing. I read them when I can, even if I can't respond. It makes my day to hear from you and knowing that you're out there thinking of me. I think of you too.

I sleep with a little bit of peace as I dream of your beautiful body. I'm so proud of all that you're doing at work and with Aunt Annabelle. I promise to check with you before I bust her out of the nursing home prison. LOL.

I don't have long, but maybe when I can secure some privacy you can put that web cam to use and have cyber sex with me. You have no idea how crazy it makes me to imagine your sexy body naked on my computer screen while you play with yourself and imagine it's me there.

Christ, my cock is throbbing now just thinking of it. If I were still there, I'd wake you up with my mouth on your breast. Would you wake me up with your mouth on my cock?

God, the thoughts that go through my mind about you. Get the sexy lingerie and heels ready for when we can have some cyber alone time. Until then, baby girl, I miss the hell out of you and will see you as soon as I can.

Oh, and please do me a favor since it's hard for me to send emails where I am. Tell Greg that I've received his emails and want him to email me as often as needed. Tell him that I understand and will gladly do him a favor on my next visit. Sweet dreams, Cambrie. MWAH! Miller

Miller logged off and returned to Cade. The sooner the team recovered the stolen arsenal of weapons, the safer the world would be and the sooner he could get back to Cambrie.

****

Cambrie's living room had turned into a second office, but she didn't mind the extra workload associated with the veterans grant. It kept her busy and gave her something to focus on other than Miller.

It had been such a pleasant surprise to receive his email yesterday after work. She hated not being able to pick up her cell phone and call him. In this modern day, having the technology to keep in touch, yet not being able to do so, blew her mind.

If she allowed her thoughts to wander, then she would conjure up awful images of where Miller could be deployed. His lack of communication probably meant he was in a remote area of the world where technology was scarce or non-existent. Just the thought of not having such amenities made Cambrie appreciate the comforts she had.

After visiting Aunt Annabelle earlier in the evening, Cambrie felt confident that she had convinced the old woman to abandon her ideas of escaping the nursing home. Of course, the barrage of questions she had to deal with from Aunt Annabelle had given her a headache by the time she left. Cambrie couldn't tell her aunt when Miller would be back if she didn't know herself.

Ding!

Cambrie ignored the alarm on her computer since she had been getting so many emails about the pen pal program and needed time to complete her other projects. Emails would have to wait and she didn't expect Miller to write again so soon, so whoever it was would have to wait. She continued to organize more military photos since the first honor board had been so successful and already filled up.

Ding!

Ding!

It took Cambrie a moment to realize that wasn't an alert for an incoming email but an IM notification. She moved the poster board holding a dozen photos and captions to her kitchen table and hurried to sit on the couch. With a quick glance at the computer screen, Cambrie gasped.

An IM text box with Miller's name blinked *"Hey sexy lady."*

"Oh, my God. Yay!" she shouted and typed.

"Hey Miller! What a great surprise this is."

"Don't know how long I've got. We've been on the move for 20 hrs & I'm beat."

"Oh. Well it's still good 2 hear from U."

"I hate 2 be rushed but I only have a few mins & need 2 see U naked. Will U play on web cam 4 me, Cam?"

Desire soaked her panties as her pussy throbbed and pulsed. How could he turn her on with such a simple request? *"U mean cyber sex?"*

"Yes, ma'am. I'm so fucking horny. I need 2 see U, Cam. You don't have 2 touch yourself. Just give me a glimpse of UR naked body. I'll beg but it won't be a pretty sight. LOL."

She laughed, feeling wild and alluring. There was nothing wrong with playing over the Internet with the man who had fucked her to the best orgasms of her life. It was just them, alone, separated by cyber space and thousands of miles. She clicked on her web cam to invite him to view it. *"Oh, I think I'd rather U beg 4 mercy, Miller."*

"Now there's my naughty girl. Show me how naughty U can be, baby." He sent her a link to his web cam.

When they had connected, she wasn't quite prepared for what she saw on her screen. The image was fuzzy and showed Miller dressed in fatigues with a mean looking gun lying on the bed beside him. She swallowed hard and tried not to concentrate on his surroundings.

"Can you see me, Miller? U R fuzzy."

"Yes, baby. I see U. So beautiful & hot. So U think U can make me beg 4 mercy?"

"Do U have privacy?"

"Yes, ma'am. Anyone steps in here gets shot."

"Miller!"

"Jokin'."

"Then if U want me 2 touch myself then U have 2 as well. Mutual masturbation." She thought that was a fair deal. Cyber sex required two people.

"Hmmm, someone's been doing her research. I like that. Ok. Now strip. I can't but will take my cock out 4 U."

His words heated her skin and had her pussy

clenching, wishing his mouth were laying tender kisses on the moist flesh. Looking around the cramped room, she knew she had to keep the laptop on the coffee table and adjust it as needed.

Miller's web cam showed him unzip his pants, pull out his cock through the narrow opening, and stroke up and down. God, she wished she could hear his voice. She made a mental note to join one of the online sites she'd heard about that allowed people to web cam each other for free and talk too.

"Nice cock. I miss how it feels thrusting inside my tight pussy." She stood and quickly removed her clothes, knowing they didn't have a lot of time for her to give him a strip show.

"I get rock hard with every thought of U. Look at UR gorgeous breasts. Wish my mouth was sucking on them right now."

She wiggled out of her pants until she was sitting on her couch completely naked and feeling sexier than ever. Staring at the small image of Miller on the screen, she smiled and typed.

"If I rub my clit will U stroke that cock so I can see U come?"

"Fuck, baby. Just the sight of UR hot naked body has me ready 2 explode. Rub UR clit & pinch UR nipples. Think of my mouth on both."

Oh, God. She could almost hear him saying those words. Leaning back on her couch, she got comfortable to see the laptop screen while she masturbated. Running her hands along her belly to her clit. She stroked the hard nub, not surprised to find her pussy soaked with her juices. She dipped a finger into her wetness to spread the slickness over her clit and rubbed small circles.

On the screen Miller stroked his cock while it

looked like he still typed.

Ding!

Damn the man was talented, masturbating while typing. The background appeared to be getting lighter. Maybe it was morning where he was.

"UR so fucking hot, Cambrie. Now when U come U have to scream my name."

She couldn't possibly type while lying in the position she was in so she offered a thumb's up. Her womb awakened with greedy little spasms flowing over every inch of her vagina. An ache formed over her swelling pussy lips.

Hadn't she been in a constant state of arousal since he'd left? With each circular motion over her clit, her hips bucked more and more. Using her other hand to squeeze her nipples, Cambrie soon found herself crying out, thoughts of Miller's cock pummeling into her, fucking her to orgasm, consumed her until she thought of nothing else but the glorious pleasure encompassing her entire body.

"Miller! Oh, yes! Miller. Yes."

The orgasm ripped through her pussy with lightning fast speed leaving no tender nerve untouched. With spasms and aches overwhelming her, Cambrie's hands fell to her side unable to pleasure herself any more. The intensity of the orgasm made her clit too tender to touch.

Rolling her head to the side, she was just in time to catch Miller jerking off on the web cam, his face set in a determined stare, his jaw clenched. When he jerked forward then back and a stream of cum shot in the air, Cambrie smiled.

She had done that to Miller. She had taken a tough military man and, with no sounds or touches, gotten him to explode. The only thing that would make it better would be if Miller were here with her.

He stood and wiped a cloth over his hands and cock before slipping his softening erection back into his pants. When he sat and started typing, she stood and wrapped a blanket around her and settled back in front of the screen. She hadn't realized that she had been breathing heavy until she tried to relax and had to fan her cheeks where they blushed.

"Baby, that felt so damn good. I just wish I could kiss U right now. Everywhere."

"Mmmm. Me 2. Sounds nice."

"Once again U surpassed my expectations."

"And U mine. But U could be awakening my naughty girl 2 much."

"Never could be 2 much."

"It can if I tie U 2 my bed & keep U there until I have my way with U."

"Ah, careful. You'll tease my naughty boy side 2 much."

"Never could be 2 much." She threw his words back with a smile.

"Damn, what the hell did I ever do 2 deserve U, baby?"

"U answered my email. LOL."

"Smart ass. There had 2 be some force behind U being sent 2 me."

"Yeah, it was called Emma and Finn Coleman. Hahaha."

"Remind me 2 spank U when I get back."

"Oh, not 2 worry, honey. I have a whole list of reminders 4 U."

"Keep those thoughts, baby. I hate 2 end this but I really do have 2 get going."

"I still had a great time tonight, Miller. I love learning 2 do new things."

"Christ, U R getting me hard again. Not a good thing when I can't fuck that sweet pussy & hot ass any time soon. Behave, Cambrie. I'll be in touch when I can OK?"

"OK."

"Sweet dreams, baby girl."

"You 2, Miller. Hugz!"

When the picture of him left the screen, Cambrie sat for a moment just staring at their chat session. She re-read it and was amazed how horny she got all over again. She really needed to figure out why Miller could affect her with just a couple sexy words.

Logging off the computer, Cambrie looked around the apartment and rubbed her arms. Shrugging out of the blanket, she got dressed again, her body still humming from the brief but sweet masturbation session, her swollen pussy spasmed with tiny waves of lingering pleasure. It was probably the result of re-reading Miller's hot conversation that made her horny again.

She feared with a man like Miller in her life that she'd always be a horny mess. One look from his eyes would always set her skin on fire. One stolen kiss would always leave her wanting more. Yeah, she was pretty much screwed when it came to Miller Daly…and not in a good way.

Chapter Sixteen

Miller had only himself to blame for torturing his dick with that hot masturbation session with Cambrie the other day. He should've known it would fuck with his mind and keep Cambrie constantly in his head instead of easing the need for her like he had hoped.

His plan had backfired. Now he couldn't even walk past a computer without his cock stiffening and images of Cambrie's naked body kept him awake at night.

The military transport plane carrying Miller and fellow team members Cade, Chance, Logan, and Killian rumbled out of Kuwait. Miller swore the team spent more time flying to their destinations than they did fighting the enemy. He rested his head back against the plane's fuselage. Aw, hell, he was in a sour mood because he needed to feel Cambrie's naked, wiggling body under his touch and that wouldn't happen today.

No conversation could be had over the roar of the engines, so the men kept to themselves, reading, sleeping, or day dreaming, which was exactly what Miller did. He had worked out the timing of his next assignment. If all went according to plan, he'd be a very happy man in about two days.

He searched his gear for gum and found the pack of envelopes that Cambrie had handed him the night he'd left. *Leave her.* He hated those words.

Opening the letters, he quickly read them with some amusement. The kids had written about everything from school to sports to Cambrie. Now he understood why so many boys were at the library instead of outside wreaking havoc around town. They were infatuated with the hot librarian.

Even with the crushes, it was nice that Cambrie had found a way to include the teens in the pen pal program. The kids should learn to support their troops. Too many were fuck-ups roaming the street and looking for trouble. But this group that Cambrie had writing to Miller appeared to have great heads on their shoulders.

The next letter caught Miller's attention as soon as he spotted the kid's name—Greg Welchum.

Miller now had two reasons to get back to Maddyville. First, for Cambrie. Second, to kick this kid's father's ass for using his kid as a punching bag. Oh, Miller didn't need the boy to spell it out, he knew that's what was happening to him.

Miller was trained to figure out people fast. And Greg was a traumatized youngster, no doubt in his mind. It was evident in the sad tone of Greg's emails. How he talked about wanting to leave home, but couldn't because his mother would never leave his dad. And Greg could never leave the mother.

Miller opened the letter.

Dear Lt. Daly,

It's Greg, the one who Miss Brasher is going to have email you from the library. First, she needs to set me up an email account. She also wanted the Teen Readers Group to write letters because she said troops like to get real mail too.

I think email's better and faster, but Miss Brasher is nice so I don't mind helping her. I don't know what to write because I don't know you. Maybe you can tell me how I can enlist in the military. I can't stay here. My dad's a jerk and, well, we don't get along. He won't send me to college so I need to find a way to go. The military can teach a person to defend themselves, right? I saw a recruitment ad. We can talk about it maybe.

Greg Welchum

Miller folded the letter and shoved it back into the envelope. He swore under his breath, the words chewed up by the noise from the plane's engines. Shoving the stack of envelopes back into his gear bag, Miller sat back grinding his teeth.

He hated fucking bullies and Greg's dad was a bully and a pussy. Wonder how the bastard would do in a fair fight with someone his own size?

Miller smirked. Not very fucking well if he could help it.

****

Cambrie's eyes fought to stay open. Staring at her computer screen, she finished the last column of the monthly newsletter that went out via email to the library's supporters. It was hard to write about Miller as just a pen pal when all she wanted to do was feel his strong arms around her again.

She let out a long breath and shut down the program. She'd have to proofread it tomorrow when hopefully her brain functioned better than today. But the day hadn't been a total waste. It surprised her how much work she had gotten done when her determination not to dwell on Miller kicked into high gear. Looking around her office, she smiled, proud of the clean desk, the neat piles on her wall unit, and organized file cabinet.

A knock on the door won a silent curse from her. All she had was another hour and had hoped to spend it quietly in her office, sulking over Miller. Now she had to deal with either Mr. Hackler or Mrs. Ginnity, and she didn't have any interest in their demanding tones right now.

"Come in." Cambrie spoke sharply, hoping her tone didn't sound too unwelcoming, even if she wasn't in the mood for company.

The door creaked open, inch-by-inch, and she was ready to scream with the aggravation until a handsome face peeked around the door.

"Now aren't you as pretty as I left you?" The strong male voice filled her small office like a booming cannon.

Her eyes flew open wide, blinking three times, before she'd believe the sight before her. "Miller! Holy shit!" Cambrie couldn't contain her excitement. Jumping out of her seat, she launched herself into Miller's open arms and slammed her lips onto his.

His mouth opened to allow her tongue entry. With swift movements to taste all of him, her tongue battled his for domination. Heat from the kiss sizzled between them. Her hands clawed at his head, his hair so short it barely covered his scalp. Lust consumed her, giving her a strength that made her feel like she could compete with this man's potent sexual abilities. So many ideas on how they could make love raced through her mind.

Breaking the connection, Cambrie stared at Miller, her eyes glancing all over him. He was really here back with her. "You came back," she whispered, afraid to speak louder and have her voice crack with the emotions swelling her heart.

"I said I would, baby girl. Now, where were we before my job interrupted us?"

Before he could kiss her again, she placed her hand on his chest and stopped him. "Hold on a minute, Miller. Are you going to run off again?"

His expression showed hesitancy, conflicting emotions etched across his tired, bruised face. "That's the nature of my job, Cam."

Bruised face? What the fuck? "Your face. Oh, no. How could I not notice your face and," she said, turning his head with her fingers, "your neck. You're hurt."

His hands grabbed hers and stopped them from running over his jaw and throat, holding them between their bodies. "Not hurt at all. Just some scrapes."

"Just some—" she stopped. "You're right. You have a job that requires you to dodge bullets and bombs. What's a few fucking bruises, right?"

He smirked. "Technically, you can't really dodge a bomb."

She narrowed her eyes and pushed out of his grasp. "You are so not funny, Miller. Christ!"

How could she accept the fact that his job was so dangerous and, yet, be expected to ship him back out the door the minute his phone rang? There was more to military life than she ever knew. She definitely didn't like it.

"Hey, Cambrie, a man doesn't have to be in the military to get bruises you know."

"Yeah, well, you seem to have gotten your

fair share since I last saw you."

"Correction. The one on the jaw is fresh. I'd say about an hour old. The rest happened last week, courtesy of a terrorist who didn't like the fact that my team and I interrupted his plans. I will never regret those kinds of bruises, baby."

"And the one on your jaw? Why's it fresh?" A sneaky suspicion grew within her.

Miller shrugged those wide shoulders like it took no effort at all. "Just had to stop and pay a visit to Greg's father. Thought he should know what a great son he had."

Her eyes widened. "And did you tell him?"

"Sure did. And I think he heard me loud and clear. Again, I'd take a bruise for that any day."

She clenched her fists at her side. "Oh, Miller. Poor Greg. His father is a mean son-of-a-bitch. What happens when you leave and aren't here to address the situation?"

"First, I would never jeopardize a child's safety. Second, Greg senior and I came to an agreement."

"An agreement?" She raised a brow. "Which was?"

"Simple. He doesn't pound on his son and I don't pound on him."

Snapping her fingers, she spoke calmer than she felt. "Just like that, you think he'll listen."

"You haven't seen *his* face yet, sweetheart. He'll listen. Guys like him are only as tough as their competition is weak. He's nothing but a bully. I gave him a dose of his own medicine. He didn't like it, so he agreed to do things my way."

With her arms crossed, she watched him. "Sounds pretty cocky of you."

"Not at all cocky. Confident. Greg wrote me.

Wasn't hard to see the pain hidden in his words. I couldn't sit back, Cam, and not show the kid that there are still people left in this crazy ass world that will stick up for someone because it's the right thing to do. Besides, I had a better chance of winning against *the ox* than you did."

She gasped. "Mrs. Ginnity!"

"I won't disclose my source, but I better never hear of you wanting to put yourself in danger again."

Laughter bubbled from her throat. "This coming from the man who bleeds regularly for his job."

"Smart ass." He smiled. "Can I convince you to leave a little early?"

"I'd love to, but I have to wait until closing to lock up," Cambrie said, unable to hide her disappointment.

"All taken care of. Mrs. Ginnity said she'd be more than happy to stay for you. Ran into her out front," he said, hitching a thumb toward the half-open door.

"Of course you did," she said, thrilled that he was a man of action. "Let's go then."

Walking out to the main lobby, Cambrie froze when she saw the sheriff speaking with Mrs. Ginnity at the checkout counter. She was sure he wasn't checking out any library books.

"Cambrie, dear. How are you?" Sheriff Haskell said, tipping his hat.

"Fine, sheriff. What brings you here?" Her knees started to shake, threatening to let her fall to the floor.

"Oh, that would probably be me," Miller said calmly with one elbow leaning on the counter.

"And you'd be a wise man, Lt. Daly." The

sheriff extended a hand to shake Miller's. "Sheriff Haskell. It's a pleasure to meet you. Your service to our country is much appreciated."

"As is yours to this community, sir," Miller responded. "I like knowing Cambrie has people around to watch her back. Whatever you need to ask me, go ahead, sir. I respect the law and will answer truthfully. Have nothing to hide."

The sheriff chuckled and Cambrie held her breath. "No questions at all. Just stopped by to meet you after I heard you were in town. Got a call about a military man making house calls. Wanted to thank you for addressing a pesky problem I've had no luck taking care of. I've always wanted to do it, but the badge stopped me. Now you've done it for me."

"Just trying to look out for those that couldn't do it for themselves, sheriff."

"Well, son, sometimes the best medicine is a taste of our own treacherous ways. Appreciate your assistance even if I have to state that Maddyville is a law-abiding town. Just don't want street justice to get out of line."

"Of course not, sir. I understand."

Cambrie stopped holding her breath and sucked in a deep drag of air. Her heart pounded, expecting the sheriff to blast Miller for the fight with Greg Sr., or worse, arrest him.

The sheriff said his goodbyes and Mrs. Ginnity shoed Cambrie and Miller out of the library.

"I've got my truck this time," Miller said, stopping in front of a massive, shiny black pick-up truck. "Too cold for the motorcycle. I'll follow you home."

With a quick smack of lips, Cambrie

abandoned Miller only for the time it took to drive to her apartment.

Once inside, butterflies swarmed in Cambrie's belly. The feeling so welcome after all the misery she'd been having since Miller had left.

"How long do we have this time?" she dared to ask.

He stood in front of her, his hands gripping her waist. "Only until tomorrow. I couldn't stay away so, when the team got back to the States, I headed straight here."

"Only until tomorrow?" she repeated, saddened that their time would be so short, but she had to be grateful for him coming at all. She didn't want to interpret what those actions from this wonderful man could mean. It was too much to think about right now when all she could do was envision him naked and sweaty.

His fingers tucked a lock of hair behind her ear. His gaze held hers. "Yes, I'm sorry, baby. I have to leave with the team tomorrow evening for another assignment in Jordan. Should take about two weeks, maybe more, maybe less. We never know."

"You told me where you were heading this time," she said, wondering if it was better to know or not.

"Yes. This is just a training mission not combat, so it's not so secretive. Just wanted to see you before I had to leave."

Somewhere from deep inside, she pulled on strength that she never knew existed. This man had sacrificed his time and sleep to come see her again. They would make the best of it until they were blessed with more time together. He had a job to protect the country. She had a job to make him forget everything for the hours he was with her.

Her knuckles skimmed his cheek roughened by day old beard growth and fading bruises. "I have never been more proud of someone than I am of you right now, Lt. Miller Daly. Your dedication to your job is inspiring. And for you to come all this way just to spend a special night with me, well, I can only ask for you to have patience with me. I'm not used to how you live, but I want to learn all about it. It's hard for me to say goodbye when all I want is to be in your arms, but I support your military service, Miller, one hundred percent. It's what you do and what you're about. I could never be anything but proud to be a part of your life…no matter where you are. Just want you to know that."

His hard stare couldn't hide the emotions and lust swirling within the depths of those brown eyes as they studied her. "My, God, Cambrie. Just when I think I know you, just when I think I know what you're thinking, you astonish the hell out of me again. I love your honesty. Aunt Annabelle should be very proud of her awesome niece. I don't know what I did to deserve you, but I'm so grateful to be here with."

"Then I think it's about time you show me how grateful you are." Her teasing awakened the naughty girl in her and she stepped backward, hooking her finger for him to follow. "I've been naughty. Think I deserve a spanking."

He growled and leapt after her. She dodged his grasp and ran for the bedroom, shrieking and laughing. When his forearm caught her around the middle and flipped her over his shoulder, she felt like the sexiest woman alive. Miller was all hers for the next few hours. All hers.

Smack! His hand landed on her ass.

"Ow!" she yelled, the heat of the imprint left on her ass cheek arousing her instantly.

She wiggled, but it was a futile effort with his strength as he sat on the bed tugging her up beside him.

"I've been dying to spank this pretty little ass." He flipped her across his knees, holding her with his arm, not even giving her a chance to change from her work clothes. With his free hand, he dragged her skirt up over her bottom. "Very sexy thong, baby. Think I'll leave that in place while I give you your spanking."

"Gonna keep talking about it or you gonna show me what you got?" She swallowed hard, wondering how wise it was to tease the man who had her ass at his mercy.

"Okay, darling. Remember you said that." Was he laughing?

Uh-oh.

With no further warning, his hand rained down on her ass like lightning, fast and hot.

Smack! Smack! Smack!

The fire built rapidly on the cheeks of her ass, spreading quickly to her pussy. The aches taking control of her inner core were impossible to relieve. Attempts to grind her clit against his leg didn't work thanks to the awkward position she lay in.

"Oh, Miller."

After every few slaps, he took a few seconds to massage her tender cheeks with the same hand that had punished them. Lust blinded her and sucked air from her lungs as she rode the pleasure building deep inside her body. Every inch of her needed to feel Miller's touch, his kisses.

"Wish you could see how pink your ass gets when I spank it, Cambrie. The heat drives me insane with the need to fuck you hard and deep."

"Fuck me then. Please. I want to come."

Did he laugh again? Oh, she would choke him when she got up.

"Can't yet. I'm enjoying this. I don't think I spanked you hard enough. I want to feel the fire on your ass when I fuck you and my balls smack against this hot flesh."

Oh. Holy. Hell.

Could she die from not being allowed to come? She really didn't want to find out.

His hand slapped at her bottom once again, but his pace had changed. The tempo had increased to a steady stream of spanks, one after the other. He played a rhythm on her ass, one spank then two, then two then one, each time alternating cheeks.

In no time at all, Cambrie was wiggling like a mad woman over his knees, yelling out, "Miller. Please. Oh. I need to come."

With the steady pace of the spanks, a heat built so deep within her pussy that each new slap across her heated flesh brought her closer and closer to her reward. The orgasm exploded over her pussy lips and clit, with the sheer force of the spasms whipping her body around his lap as if she'd been electrocuted. Holy shit. It amazed her how she could come with only a spanking.

"That's a girl, come for me, baby. I want your juices flowing over those bare pussy lips."

"Oh. My. God. Miller. Miller." She couldn't believe the power of her release, but it did nothing to dim her sexual appetite for the man lifting her off of his lap. She needed to feel his cock possessing her throbbing pussy.

His large hands went to work stripping her of her work clothes. When all he had left was the bra and thong, he surprised her with his next move. Expecting him to rip the lacy materials from her body, his hands instead stilled on her hips, the rough pads of his fingers kneading the skin with gentle motion.

He leaned his head until his forehead rested on the valley where her shoulder and neck met. His warm breath tickled her skin sending goose bumps all the way to her toes. Her hand caressed the back of his head, the short hair so soft under her touch.

When he spoke, his words hung in the air. “Christ, I missed you so goddamn much, Cambrie. I didn’t want to miss you.”

Now what the hell did that mean? “There’d better be an explanation coming about why you didn’t want to miss me.”

His fingers danced on her sides. “I don’t know how it’s happening, Cam, but I’m falling for you hard. Missing you kills me.” He looked up to gaze in her eyes. “I’ve always been able to control my feelings and my emotions. But not with you. There’s something you do to me, Cambrie. Like I’m under a spell or something. I just can’t get enough of you.”

She smiled, needing to lighten the mood, not ready to delve into her own feelings or interpret his. “Those would be my mermaid powers.” Her hand ran over the muscles of his arm to rest over the tattoo he wore with pride.

Just when she thought he wouldn’t respond, he finally spoke. “You are the sexiest smart-ass I’ve ever known. God help me.” His hands worked magic along her waist, softly tickling her heated skin.

Oh, how she wished those strong hands were roaming the curves of her body. “I want to see you naked.” Reaching behind her back, she undid her bra and let it fall from her body before slipping the thong down her thighs to her ankles and kicking out of them. Her ass was tender from the spanking, leaving delightful warmth on her bottom.

Biting her lip, Cambrie worked the T-shirt from the waist of his pants and yanked it over his head to bare his hard chest. Raking her nails over the sharp curves of his pecs, she admired his steel-hard physique.

Allowing her hands to descend to his waist, she watched his face while unbuttoning his pants. He may have controlled his composure so far, but the slight quiver she felt under her fingers when she brushed over his abs was very noticeable. His hands stroked her hair with sharp snaps of his wrists. Pushing the jeans over the cheeks of his ass, she was rewarded with a low growl when she massaged the hard globes.

Taking control, Miller kicked clear of his jeans and boxers and faced her in his naked glory. “Where are our toys, baby?” he asked, looking around.

She had hidden them away from the prying eyes of any friends that stopped by. “Top drawer of the nightstand. Why? What do you have in mind?” Had she always been able to talk in such a husky tone? She felt like layers were peeling away from her with each sexual encounter she shared with Miller.

“Choose one for us to play with. I want to drive you wild.”

“You always do.” She contemplated her

choices. Her ass still tingled from the spanking, so she skipped the paddle. She didn't choose the handcuffs because she needed to be able to touch him. "The chest harness. Let's see how that works."

"Love your mind, baby." Miller strapped the harness to his chest with the lubed dildo sitting in the middle of his breastbone. He lay on his back in the middle of the bed. Offering his hand, he spoke with a lust filled voice. "Come ride the dildo, Cam. I'm going to have a fantastic fucking view."

Her face warmed with the blush that was surely rising over her cheeks. With all the sexual things they've done together, it was silly to feel any shyness around him but trying something new in bed was too thrilling not to raise her blood pressure. She wanted their loving to always be perfect, to always be open to new ideas.

"Hope you enjoy this too."

"Baby, this is so friggin' hot. I'd have to be dead not to enjoy any kind of sex with you."

Climbing onto the bed, she took his hand to help get into place. She straddled his thighs and sat facing his feet. Leaning forward to allow him to slide the dildo into her, she gasped at the cool plastic sliding against her pussy lips.

"Lean back, Cam. Sit on the dildo. That's it. Take it all the way into that sweet pussy."

She followed his instructions until the dildo was seated fully in her vagina. The thick toy stretched her muscles and fought against her tightness. Miller's hands gripped her hips and his torso pressed against her ass and then retreated. The dildo fucked her with slight slurping sounds.

"Holy shit, Cam. This is so fucking hot. I wish you could see how your bare pussy lips spread open to fuck the dildo. Does it feel good?"

"Mmmm. Yes. But I'm afraid your cock would feel much better. This is definitely…different."

To allow him to share in her pleasure, she stretched until her hand could wrap around his cock. Stroking the engorged thickness, earning her a moan from deep in his throat.

Riding his chest proved an awkward position but when the familiar pleasure stirred deep inside her pussy walls, Cambrie only thought of the building tension.

Sliding his hand between them, he manipulated her swollen clit, strumming it like a guitar. "Love the red color of your ass, baby." His breathing was slowly increasing. "Seeing my hand print outlined across your ass in red and pink makes me want to stop fucking your pussy and bury my cock into your tight ass."

The delicious attention of Miller's fingers over her clit and his dirty talk, sent her soaring to the heavens but not quite over the edge. She hovered in a place of pain and pleasure, desiring the release, needing it, but not wanting to lose this amazing feeling wrapping around her body.

His fingers rubbed her clit harder, faster. "Come for me, baby. I know you want to. Scream my name. God, I love to hear you say my name."

"So close. Oh. Wow. Please." Her hands gripped his legs holding herself in position to take the dildo completely into the depths of her pussy. Aches and tingles passed over the sensitive vaginal muscles that prepared to explode. They lay in wait with greedy little nerves spasming and teasing of the pleasure about to happen.

"Come, Cambrie. Explode with the dildo

deep inside your pussy so I can watch these pretty bare lips quiver with your orgasm."

When his thumb brushed over the swollen pussy lips before returning to her clit, she moaned with pleasure, unable to form a word.

His words pushed her over the edge with one powerful thrust of the dildo. His fingers were relentless on her clit, rubbing sharp, tight circles over and over as wave after wave of spasms engulfed her pussy. Her vagina gripped the dildo and stroked it while pleasure tore through her system.

"Yes. Miller! Oh, Miller. Oh." Grateful to find her voice again, she rode his thrusts, totally at his mercy in this position.

With her body still quivering, Cambrie sank onto his legs to rest her head and catch her breath once the dildo slipped from her pussy and Miller lifted her hips the few inches to remove it. She managed to crawl off of his body and lay on her back staring at her ceiling wondering why it had taken her until the age of twenty-seven to discover all the wonderful things sex could offer.

Turning to find the source of the crinkling noise, Cambrie caught Miller sheathing his long erection with a condom. With unbelievable speed, her body responded to the sight of him preparing his cock to fuck her. Her pussy lips swelled more with the ache of anticipation.

Returning to the bed, he turned her onto her side and crawled in behind her. The head of his cock pressed against the entrance to her pussy, her wetness easing him inside. With a determined thrust, he maneuvered his cock into her pulsing pussy and the hard loving began.

The words he whispered into her ear she

couldn't decipher. She only concentrated on the deep sound of his voice and the way his warm breath tickled her ear with every word.

His hand slid around to capture her breast. His gentleness was replaced with a fury of lust so intense she never wanted the feeling to end. He gripped her breasts in a frenzied possession, squeezing one then the other, showing his power and heightening her arousal.

How did she ever capture this vibrant man's attention? God, she yearned for his touch even when she had it. If that wasn't turning into an addiction then she didn't know how else to explain the emotions racing through her.

Under his weight, it was difficult to move in the sideways position, but she did her best to push her ass back to encourage him to take her harder and faster. "Yes, fuck me, Miller. Mmmm. Love that cock and how you use it. Harder."

His hips responded with an instant ferocity that should've scared her but only managed to turn her on more. Every vaginal muscle hummed with life, waiting for that power to overtake them and offer the release they required to stop aching. Never had she achieved orgasms so regularly…or so powerfully.

"Cambrie. Oh, fuck, I wish you could feel how hot your pussy is as it milks my cock. Can you feel my cock so deep inside of you?"

"Yes. I want more."

"Such a nymph, aren't you?" he teased, but his hips continued slapping into hers, the heat on her ass cheeks still noticeable and adding to her enjoyment.

The thick head of his cock reached her G-spot and stroked the same tender muscles the dildo had.

Oh, God, how her pussy ached to explode again, to feel the vibrations of pleasure race through her womb.

Miller was a wild man, his hand crushing her breast in his palm, tweaking the nipple between his thumb and finger and causing her to cry out with the mix of pain and pleasure. His heavy leg lay over hers so she couldn't move, she lay pinned by his body weight and at the mercy of his cock to stroke her to orgasm.

If only she could touch him or touch herself. With her hands stretched to the side above her head, it was impossible to reach her clit or his balls. The need to come grew by the second, and the surge of ecstasy exploded within her taking him for the journey.

"Cambrie! Uhh. Cambrie," he yelled, his body bucking behind her like a wild horse.

"Miller," she whimpered. "I'm coming!"

Helpless against the onslaught of spasms and explosions, Cambrie held Miller's arm when it latched onto her breast. Her pussy exploded with a million tremors, each colliding with another until she thought her pussy would never stop quivering. The vaginal muscles tightened to grasp his cock in a death grip.

His thrusting slowed when her pussy wouldn't allow much movement within its tightness. Her heart pounded and her mind remained sluggish.

"I love you, Miller." Cambrie thought she heard the words come out of her mouth, but couldn't be sure they weren't just in her head. With her throat dry and her breathing ragged, there's no way she could've spoken. Where did that come from?

Was she really in love with Miller? When he inched off the bed to clean up the condom, she dared to turn and look at him. His face showed no sign of shock at her spontaneous profession of love.

Phew! She hadn't said it out loud.

No need to start throwing "love you" around when her emotions were so mixed up she couldn't develop a clear thought. That horrible night so long ago had taught her to bury emotions. Now she wished she knew how to face them because the pain in her chest was either a heart attack coming on or…love.

Chapter Seventeen

Miller held the woman of his dreams in his arms and didn't know how to keep her there. He was an educated man, trained to figure out problems that rarely had solutions. Then why the fuck couldn't he think of one plausible way to keep Cambrie in his life for more than a few stolen hours? Maybe exhaustion played a role in all the dead end ideas he'd had so far.

The alarm on his phone rang with an ear piercing shrill to cut the early morning air.

"What's that?" Cambrie asked, not moving from where she slept on his chest.

"My alarm. I've got to get ready to go, babe." And fast. He was starting to hate these goodbyes more than anything. "Cambrie? I've got to get up."

"Five more minutes."

He couldn't help but chuckle. She wasn't even awake, the poor thing. He'd exhausted her with their rough loving, but, oh God, how he had enjoyed her delightful body and willingness to experiment sexually. "I wish we could spend the entire day in bed."

"Tell them you got lost." Her sleepy whisper was too damn sexy and enticing.

"If my training didn't counter that claim then I'd be tempted."

She rolled off of him and sat up in bed. "Doesn't the military do anything at a normal hour?"

Her complaining and sarcasm was music to

his ears. As long as it wasn't tears, he was good. If he saw a single tear streak down her cheek, he'd give serious thought to going AWOL if it prevented her a second of pain.

He jumped from bed not wanting to think about the crazy ideas running though his head. Go AWOL? Was he fucking insane? He dressed quickly. Never in his career had he ever considered leaving the military. But with this gorgeous, naked woman stretching in bed and staring back at him with sleepy brown eyes and long tangled hair, he ruled out nothing.

Had she really said she loved him last night? The surprised look on her face when she stared at him after the words spilled from her pretty lips had spoken volumes. Thank God he was an expert at masking his emotions.

Cambrie climbed from bed and wrapped a robe around her slender body. Her hair wild and her eyes still droopy with sleep, she looked as sexy as ever. "So this is goodbye again, I guess." Her soft voice was laced with pain.

"For now," he said, as he finished dressing in the clothes he had laid out the night before. "I'll see you as soon as my schedule permits." He kissed her lips, lingering just to feel her next to him. "Believe me, okay?"

She nodded her head.

"I should be able to email and call this time. I'm just training, so it's not as restrictive as when I'm in the field."

She offered a yawn. "It's okay. I've got plenty of toys to keep me company."

Her attempt at humor touched his heart. She tried to make his departure easy for him. God, the woman was always thinking of everyone else but herself. Simply amazing.

"Keep that web cam handy, baby girl. I'll want to watch."

"Mmmm. Then I better practice."

The pink color forming on her cheeks only made her look all the more adorable. Time to leave before he couldn't. "Okay. Bye for now, Cambrie."

She wrapped her body into his arms and clung. When she stepped back, leaned up on her toes, and kissed his lips, he had to give her credit for masking her own emotions, at least trying to. Her eyes avoided his, but he had already seen the sadness within them. He decided it was best to look away as well or maybe she'd see his sadness, too.

They walked to the front door. "I had a fabulous night with you, Cambrie. Nights like that help get me through the loneliness when I can't be here with you. We'll talk soon." One last kiss to her forehead and he stepped through the door and into the dawn, so many regrets weighing heavily on his heart.

****

The days without talking to Miller dragged by, but Cambrie kept herself busy with the grant project and Aunt Annabelle.

Today the Teen Readers Group accompanied Cambrie to Aunt Annabelle's nursing home to read to the residents while Cambrie spent some alone time with her aunt outside in the fading autumn garden. The chilly air was refreshing.

"You're in love, Cambrie." Aunt Annabelle's statement was a loaded one.

"What? Where did that come from?" Cambrie

had never felt uneasy talking to her aunt until now.

"It came from a very wise old woman. Honey, I know you better than anyone. You try not to wear your heart on your sleeve, but I can see the pain written all over your face. You go ahead and deny that you love that boy. I dare you."

Cambrie smiled, her heart aching. "I don't deny it, Auntie. Just nothing I can do about it is all." Admitting it out loud, that she couldn't have a life with Miller any time soon, was a crushing moment and tears licked at her eyes.

"What do you mean?"

"Auntie, we live in two different states. He can't move to Maddyville because he's stationed in Virginia."

"Then you can move there."

Cambrie gasped. "What? I'd never leave you alone, Auntie. You know that."

"I was afraid of that. And how would I be alone? I live in a nursing facility with staff surrounding me twenty-four seven."

"Yeah, one that you think is a prison that you need to be busted out of."

Aunt Annabelle waved her hand in the air. "True, but I'm not talking about that. I'm taken care of and would hardly be alone with all my friends."

"As tempting as it is, I'm not moving anywhere so there's no need to continue this conversation," Cambrie said firmly.

Who was the old woman kidding? She didn't have many friends left who were able to visit her and she absolutely hated the nursing home. Cambrie would never leave her alone for the last years of her life. Never. Not after everthing the dear woman had sacrificed to give Cambrie a decent life.

"You know, Cambrie, sweetie. I'd hate to see you move away, but I'd also hate to be the reason you didn't find happiness."

Cambrie caressed her hand. "Maddyville is my home. Besides, Miller and I aren't even officially dating, so I think long term plans are premature."

"That boy has it just as bad for you as you do for him. You'd be a fool not to realize that. It may not be your typical kind of dating, but any man that runs to a woman the second he has the chance, well, there's a commitment hidden in there somewhere.

"I can't believe that in this day and age when you young people do things so half-assed that you would be blind to the fact that the man spends more time on the road coming to visit you than he actually spends here when he arrives. If that ain't some sort of dating ritual for today's world then I don't know what would be."

Cambrie laughed, part of her knowing Aunt Annabelle was right. But Cambrie and Miller came from two different worlds that were impossible to merge, so no sense in dreaming only to suffer a broken heart when the dream couldn't come true.

"Let's head back inside. It's chilly," Cambrie said, and began pushing the wheelchair.

"How about a game of cards?" Aunt Annabelle suggested.

"Wonderful."

****

Cambrie stared at the email flashing on her laptop.

Hey Cambrie, baby, Internet connection is sporadic at best. Sorry haven't been able to keep in touch. Can't write much. Not secure connection so can't guarantee privacy. Thinking of you! Miller

The email was a bittersweet read. At least she had heard from him and didn't have to wonder if he was alive or dead. But she had half hoped that he'd close it with "love Miller."

She sighed. All this stupid talk of love and romance had her setting her heart up to break. Miller didn't love her. Sure, he cared about her, desired her. But love? Nah.

He wouldn't allow himself to fall in love with his busy lifestyle. He had too much control over his emotions. Maybe he could teach her some of that control.

But she did at least owe him a reply.

Hi Miller, I understand about the Internet. I know you'll write when you can. I've been busy planning a costume party for Halloween at the library this Saturday night. That gives me only five days to finish the planning and decorating.

The proceeds will go to support the library's military program and pay to ship the care packages we've been sending to the homeless veteran's shelter in Virginia that you suggested. The shelter manager has been thrilled with the donations.

I'm so proud of the residents of Maddyville. Donations continue to pour in. I'll text you a picture of me in my costume. Bet you can't guess what I'll be. LOL.

Well, I should get some more work done

before bed...or maybe I'll go play with my toys-hahaha. Miss you! Cambrie

The tone of the email may have been lighthearted, but it was far from how she felt.

With each passing day, the end of the military pen pal program got closer. Would there come a day when Miller was no longer her pen pal...or lover?

She didn't expect Miller to stop talking to her when the program ended in a few weeks, but that would have to happen some day. They couldn't possibly exist on short visits and sporadic Internet communication.

She pushed all negative thoughts from her mind and concentrated on finishing the details for the costume party.

Glancing up at her costume hanging from the coat rack in her living room, Cambrie wished Miller could see her in it. But she'd be sure to give him a private showing once he got to visit again.

****

Saturday evening buzzed with excitement. The costume party turned out to be a major hit and the talk of Maddyville. Cambrie couldn't remember a time when the library held so many people as it did tonight.

There had to be a hundred guests mingling, dancing to party music, sipping warm apple cider, and eating a variety of tasty dishes disguised as brains, severed fingers, worms, and other creepy things.

Everyone was dressed in costume, some very extravagant and all in the spirit of the party.

Cambrie forced a smile on her face even if the happiness didn't reach her heart. She missed Miller too much to put into words. The lack of communication sucked for this training exercise. Besides his email, she had only received a quick text saying "hi."

"Greg? Do me a favor?" she asked, when Greg walked up with a smile on his face for the first time since she'd known him. "I need you to take a picture of me using my phone."

"Sure thing." He snapped the pic and handed her back the cell phone.

"Glad you could make it tonight, Greg," Cambrie said, pleased that he looked like a real teenager for once instead of a scared kid.

"I'd like you to meet my mom, Miss Brasher. Mom," he yelled to a woman behind him. "Mom, this is Miss Brasher, the librarian I told you about."

"She doesn't look like a librarian tonight, dear. I love your costume, Miss Brasher. It's so nice to finally meet the woman who inspired my Greg to read so much."

Or rather, escape his father's wrath. "It's a pleasure to meet you as well," Cambrie began, but a man in a pirate costume caught her eye before disappearing into the crowd. Jeesh, she missed Miller so much now she was having hallucinations of him. "You have a great son. He's been a fantastic help to me not only with the military program, but also with anything I need assistance with here at the library. He definitely takes after his mom."

The woman beamed like the sun shown on her. "I'm having a great time. So many faces I haven't seen in ages. You enjoy your night, Miss Brasher." She wandered off toward the dessert table and a small group of ladies from the bridge group.

"You too." Where did that pirate go? She just wanted another glimpse to prove to herself that it wasn't Miller. And to prove she was finally losing her mind. "Greg, you keep having fun."

The boy went back to his friends. Cambrie texted the pic Greg took to Miller and shoved the phone back into the pocket of her shorts.

Many people stopped Cambrie and lifted her spirits with their compliments of the party and her efforts to support the troops.

A tap on her shoulder had her turning to face the mystery man. Thank God she wasn't holding any punch or it would've fallen from her hands.

"Miller? Is it really you?" she asked, her heart pounding as she studied the man behind the bandana and mask.

"You tell me," he said, gripped her waist and hauled her into his tight embrace. His lips landed on hers, the kiss demanding. Without caring that she was at a party surrounded by the folks of Maddyville, Cambrie sank into the kiss, opening her mouth to allow his tongue to sweep in and steal her heat, her fingers raking through his short hair.

When he broke the connection, but held her close, she stared at him. "Yes, it's really you, Miller. I'd recognize those lips anywhere," she said, running her finger along his jaw and over his lips.

His smile matched hers as she leaped into his arms and clung to his neck, reveling in his strong embrace. "God, you feel so fucking good, baby." He placed her down after a few minutes. "And you look sexy as all hell, my little mermaid."

Cambrie modeled her emerald green costume,

twirling in the shiny shorts that flared at the edges like a mermaid's tail and still allowed her to walk. Her silky top was sexy but conservative enough for the library, a short sleeved sequined blouse that resembled scales. "You like it? I thought it was a no-brainer to dress as a mermaid for a costume party."

"Like it? Baby, I'm blown away by the image of you as a mermaid. One look from across the room when I arrived and I couldn't breathe. It was like seeing you in my dreams again."

"I thought that was you. I just lost you in the crowd." Her heart thudded hard against her breasts.

"I promise you're not losing me tonight, baby."

"Will you dance with me, Miller? I've been jealous all night of the couples on the dance floor. The offers I had weren't appealing."

"Lead the way," he said, and they found a cozy spot on the edge of the make-shift dance floor and rocked slowly in each other's arms. "Good thing you turned the bastards down, I would've hurt someone if I'd walked in and found you dancing in another man's arms."

"Stop it." She slapped at his chest.

"Dead I'm telling you. They'd be dead," he said, but without a lot of heat. The spark of jealousy made her feel even sexier.

The heat emanating from his body warmed her in every private place she possessed. Her body wishing his was naked and making love to her.

"You must have paid attention when I emailed you about the party because you're here."

"Always," he said, pressing his body into hers. "Even if it doesn't seem like I'm listening, believe me…I hear everything."

"This is the best surprise ever," Cambrie said, shaking her butt to the music while holding his hands. "You should've told me you were coming."

"I like surprises. I can stay until tomorrow early afternoon, baby. Sorry. Wish it could be longer but there's a lot of shit going on at work that needs taking care of. But I should be in the States for a bit. Who knows? At least we'll be able to talk."

She didn't want to think of him leaving when he just got here. Again! "Then shake what your mama gave you and let's tear up the dance floor."

He laughed. "Darling, you keep shaking that hot ass of yours and the only tearing I'll be doing is at our clothes to get us naked."

"Now, wouldn't that make this a party to remember?" she teased, her heart overflowing with joy.

"Smart ass," he said, and leaned closer to her ear. "Remind me to spank you later for that."

"I plan to."

****

Being the hostess meant Cambrie had to stay until the last guest left. The Teen Readers Group promised to come in the next day and clean up any remnants of the party but, for the most part, people were careful to keep the library clean. Cambrie didn't want the night to end now that she had partied for hours with Miller.

"Who would've guessed that a bad ass Navy SEAL could dance up a storm? You looked pretty darn sexy out there on the dance floor, Miller. I think quite a few ladies had to fan themselves, and it's fifty degrees out!"

Miller shut the library's heavy wooden front doors and inserted the key that Cambrie handed him. Once he shook them to double check that they were locked, he grabbed Cambrie's hand and walked her down the front steps to his truck.

"I learned a thing of two about dancing after being stationed in Rio years ago. Very wild city." He opened the truck door and she stepped up into the cab. "We'll come back for your car tomorrow, Cam."

Without waiting for a reply, he shut her door and took giant steps to his side and climbed in.

"Wow, you're getting to know your way around these parts pretty good," Cambrie complimented, as he sped off toward her house without any prompting or directions.

"All part of my training, my dear. I've been taught to navigate third world countries with nothing more than a compass and a map. Getting around a quaint town like Maddyville ain't no problem. Hell, y'all have signs marked so well it's impossible not to know where you're going." He dragged her hand to his mouth where his lips smooched over her knuckles. "Besides, I don't want to waste any time getting home. If I had to watch you wiggle that ass one more time tonight without being able to bury my cock in you then I'd probably kidnap you for some privacy."

His sexy talk drenched her in goose bumps. How could she not squirm when he hinted at how he wanted her? "I've missed you, Miller."

If she could chew her tongue off she would. Why the hell did she blurt that out now? The mood was light and fun. Why layer it with heavy and deep emotions? Ugh!

"Ditto. I only broke two laptops, though,

while waiting to get back to you."

"What? How?"

He shrugged as he turned the corner to park in her driveway. "Got tired of the fucking Internet bouncing me off every time I needed to talk to you."

Needed to talk to you. Could he have missed her as much as she did him?

"Cade, one of my buddies on my team, said I didn't know my own strength and then busted my balls when my best friend, Chance, ratted me out that it was over a woman."

Oh, man this was getting heavy. Hot sex first then heavy emotional talking.

"I hope you don't mind that I played with my toys while you were gone. I tried to web cam you, but it failed to connect. Oh, it was so kinky to sit in front of my laptop hoping you'd get a connection and see me manipulating my pussy with the vibrator." She squeezed her legs together as best she could in the sitting position but still a heavy ache developed deep within the muscles of her pussy.

Miller killed the ignition and practically growled. "Stop or I warn you, you'll be naked before you reach the porch, baby. And I don't give a damn who watches."

She quickly exited the truck while he waited for her to come around to his side where he took her hand and walked side by side.

"God, I'm blistering your ass for this hard-on," he complained and adjusted the front of his jeans. "Can't even walk."

She stifled a laugh and walked to her front door, keys in hand. "Don't worry, Miller, sweetie. I plan to show you in person what you missed."

Her feet felt like they floated on air.

Inside, he tossed his jacket aside and had barely shut the door when he had lifted her to straddle her legs around his waist. His mouth landed hard on hers, branding her with a fiery tongue whipping inside her mouth. She matched his power, unable to fight the growing need within her to devour every inch of him. His fingers dug into her sides as she felt the room moving. When a soft cushion hit her back, she broke the kiss to find he had laid her on the couch.

"Beautiful. Fucking beautiful," he said, his desire plain even in the dimly lit room. Only the small desktop lamp illuminated their bodies. "Just want to remember you in this costume forever. My mermaid," he whispered, the corners of his mouth lifting in a smile.

Her hand slid under his shirtsleeve on his upper arm and captured his tattoo beneath her palm and caressed the decorated skin. "I was with you, Miller."

"Absolutely, baby. And not just on my arm."

The reality that sprang forward with his admission had her trembling, not out of fear but out of concern. The last thing she wanted was to be a distraction while he worked. If he ever took a bullet, or worse, because he had been preoccupied with thoughts of her then she'd never forgive herself.

She stared at the sharp angles of his handsome face and smiled. No, Miller would never let a distraction keep him from performing his best on the job. He was too good a SEAL to do that. It was evident in how organized he was with his time, how controlled he was with his emotions and temperament, and how dedicated he was with any endeavor he took on.

Bracing her wrists above her head with one hand, Miller unbuttoned her blouse, sliding his hand under the silky fabric to melt over her breasts. Oh, God how she had yearned for his touch all of these lonely nights. Now that she had it, she didn't want it to stop. She prayed for time to stand still.

"Touch me everywhere. Miller, I need to feel your touch." She didn't care if she whimpered. All she cared about was Miller's closeness.

With devastating slowness, he undressed her until she lay naked on her couch. He had only pulled his shirt off and straddled his half naked body over hers.

"I had a dream of you while I was away, Cambrie," he whispered into her ear, his hot breath tickling the sensitive skin along her neck.

"Dreaming of mermaids again, were you?"

"No. Only of you." He hovered nose to nose with her, his gaze glued to hers. The closeness shared a glimmer of heat deep in those brown depths, but it was the vulnerability she saw shadowed in the depths that stunned her. "Let me show you how my dream was, Cambrie. I promise wild and crazy for later. But first let me show you how I dreamt of us making love on this couch with the moonlight streaming through the windows."

"Miller." Her strangled voice came out in a hushed tone.

"Sshh. I'm right here, Cambrie, baby. Give yourself to me. Let me love you like you deserve." He kissed her lips. "Let." Kissed her jaw. "Me." Kissed her cheek. "Love." He kissed her ear lobe. "You."

A shiver so strong ran through her, that his hand holding her wrists above her head tightened its grip.

"I broke speeding laws to get to this moment, Cam." The admission weighed heavily with emotion so raw she felt like she had been elevated on a pedestal, cherished beyond measure.

God, was that the most romantic thing she had ever heard? The man was all about upholding laws and here he went and broke them to get to her. She never wanted tonight to end. Living in this moment forever would be just fine with her.

The hand on her breast squeezed, caressing the heated flesh. With his fingers, he tweaked the nipple, rubbing his thumb over it until flames shot down to her pussy. He worked her body into a frenzy of fire, sparks igniting under her skin where the roughness of his fingers roamed.

"Miller. I love to feel your strength."

"Ah, but baby, you're my strength. I love how I feel when I'm with you."

And she believed him. There was no need to fluff his words with her. Honesty had been his most attractive quality. Well, that and the amazing cock that he was grinding against her thigh as he trailed wet kisses along her neck to her shoulder. His hand released hers above her head.

Without hesitation, she latched onto his shoulders, her fingertips dredging along the hard outline of muscles. The bare skin under her touch radiated heat and power. A shiver raked along his long body before he arched his head back.

"My, God, Cambrie. Fucking goose bumps now? What are you doing to me?" he asked, lowering his gaze to hers, a crooked a smile adorning his parted lips.

Needing no further prompting and reveling in the power she had over this strong man, she raked her nails along his back. Up and down over taut skin, she memorized every outline of muscles. "You have the most incredible body, Miller. But it looks a lot better naked. Strip. Now."

He cocked an eyebrow and laughed. "Yes, ma'am."

His words may have been compliant but the cocky smile he offered as he eased off of the couch and kicked out of his boots, pants, and boxers until he stood gloriously naked, warned of his friskiness. Slipping a condom over his erection, confidence poured from him.

Without further conversation, he lay over her again, the sheer weight of his body pressing hers into the cushions until they were molded as one. Her legs straddled his hips, the thick head of his cock nestled over her pussy lips. She rocked her hips, barely able to move an inch under his weight, hoping to encourage him to enter her and fuck her like mad.

"Uh-uh, Cam. This is my dream re-enactment. Remember? I promise fast later. But, first…slow."

Her whimper came from sheer frustration of needing his cock filling her up and failing to convince him to do it now. "Tease."

"Hardly. Just a very patient man who wants—no, *needs*—to show you how amazing you are. I crave you, Cambrie. Now I want to hear you scream my name."

His mouth landed on her breast, dragging the areola into his warmth. His tongue darted over the stiff nipple, licking and lapping before switching to the other breast and displaying the same treatment.

"Oh, Miller. Yes. Suck harder. Oh, yes."

The pull from his mouth was so exquisite,

beams of heat radiated from her breasts to her belly where nerves jumped with expectation of the building pleasure. Harder and harder he sucked, tugging at each nipple, alternating back and forth until she was mindless with the slight pain in her nipples increasing the awareness in her pussy. Her pussy lips swelled with her arousal, the wetness preparing her for his cock.

"Miller!"

She couldn't help herself. The need within her rose too sharply to keep her thoughts focused.

Inching slowly down her body, his large hand splayed over her belly. "You have the softest skin, Cambrie." Laying soft kisses in his path, he continued his descent. "And the sweetest pussy. Even with your juices on my tongue, I can never get my fill of you. I think I'm addicted to you."

Raising her legs, he placed them over his shoulders while he settled in front of her throbbing pussy. Just him lying that close to her femininity awakened a greedy need within her core for his touch.

"Let me look at you, baby. Let me look at this beautiful pussy."

Oh. Dear. God. She'd combust soon if he didn't make her come.

"Miller. This is too much. I need you inside me now. Fuck me now."

With the most delicate touch she had ever felt from him, he spread her pussy lips apart and trailed a long finger up and down the moist folds. "Ahh. Soon."

Keeping her ass on the couch while his finger toyed with her wetness was a test of her willpower. How she wished she had the strength to throw him onto his back, straddle that magnificent cock, and ride him until she made them both come hard.

"So pretty. These soft, bare pussy lips were made for my tongue."

She whimpered but was rewarded with his mouth on her mound. That long tongue licked lazy strokes up and down her parted flesh, dipping inside her heat to lap at her juices before returning to do it all over again.

The steady rhythm of his mouth on her pussy had her climbing a wall of pleasure, but each time she thought she'd topple over the top to claim her relief, he eased off his attentions. The jerk! Tormenting her like this when she was on fire and barely able to form words.

"Miller."

She was prepared to beg, plead. Anything to get him to let her finish. But when two fingers sank into her wetness and fucked her pussy with long, fast jabs, she lost it.

Gone was the proper librarian. Gone was the well-mannered southern woman. In her place was a mad woman blinded by lust and an orgasm so powerful it convulsed her entire body like her limbs would be torn off as she thrashed over the cushions.

"Yes. Miller. Yes. Yes."

Thank God she at least remembered his name because she couldn't her own. It didn't matter. The sensations rocking through her body were well worth the amnesia. Wave after wave poured from her womb, blasting her with heavy aches and long spasms so wonderful, so fulfilling that a lone tear trickled from her closed eyes.

When the heavy head of his cock slipped into her pussy, the spasms caressed it, welcoming him. His thrust seated him fully into her tightness.

"Damn, Cambrie. I love how your tender muscles milk my cock."

Not wasting a moment's time, Miller began a steady thrusting motion, in and out, holding when all the way in, then in and out, holding. Over and over he kept the tempo, suspending most of his weight off of her with his strong arms anchored beside her head.

She enjoyed the swaying of his body into hers and ran her hands over his arms, back, shoulders, anywhere she could keep a connection with him, to feel his heat, his strength. "Oh, Miller. Please. Don't stop. It feels too good."

He didn't reply. He didn't have to. One look into those brown eyes provided her with insight into the heart he wouldn't share.

She had always seen lust and desire raging within the brown orbs, but now, now it was all replaced with a glorious flame, like she was all he saw, all he needed.

Could it be love that she saw? Her heart swelled with the knowledge. It had to be because it was the only emotion strong enough to shatter his usual control.

Sometimes words weren't necessary to be loved. But they sure as hell would be nice to hear. Conceding to whatever stubbornness kept his feelings locked up, Cambrie lost herself in the moment, too aroused to delve any deeper into her own emotions.

Miller's pace increased with his breathing. Hovering above her with his naked body illuminated in the soft light, he dragged deep breaths into his lungs.

Her body reacted with his, her breathing hitched, her vaginal muscles tingled in anticipation of the orgasm that lingered on the horizon. He pounded his hips into hers, his cock stroking her pussy in a merciless wave of bliss.

"Rub your clit for me, baby. I want to feel you explode around my cock."

She did as commanded, inching her hand between their bodies and over her belly until her fingers touched the hard nub. Each thrust he gave pushed her hand harder onto her clit, making the sensations that much more powerful. The way his thick cock stroked along the inside of her pussy, elevated her to hover between pure ecstasy and the need to surrender to the pleasure assailing her.

With her slippery fingers, she pressed hard circles over her clit. Her limited movement not a factor because his cock filling her pussy only increased her arousal. Stimulated beyond reason, her womb lashed out with a flood of spasms that crammed into her tight pussy, flexing against his pulsing cock. His body tightened as he held his hips into hers, keeping his cock buried entirely within her warmth.

"Miller! Yes, oh God. Miller!"

"Cambrie," he growled through gritted teeth, the sound such a compliment. She loved the way she could make him lose control.

With her heart pounding and her lungs in desperate need of air, Cambrie clung to Miller's neck while he buried his face into the crook of her shoulder as they rode out the final spasms of her orgasm together.

When his cock slid from her slickness, he stood to clean himself. Returning to the couch, he lifted her into his arms and carried her toward the bedroom.

"Can't give you too much time to recover,

babe. I'm wanting my fill of you and, somehow, I'm scared I'll never get it," he said, storming through her bedroom door and laying with her on the bed.

"That makes two of us."

Chapter Eighteen

Cambrie sighed with complete contentment. If she never got out of bed again, she'd be a happy woman as long as Miller remained with her.

"I can only give you a few minutes to regain your energy, Cambrie, because lying in this bed with your naked body cuddled to mine is just too much for me to handle. Fair warning. I already want to flip you onto your back and bury my cock deep inside your sweet pussy."

She purred and stretched with a laziness she hadn't allowed herself in a long time. The clock beside the bed read one in the morning, but she was too aroused to be sleepy. Being close to Miller was an automatic turn on. His voice stirred visions of lovemaking each time he spoke of his desires.

"I'm trying to decide which sex toy I want to use with you," she said, contemplating more loving.

A growl escaped his throat as his arm slid under her to haul her on top of his chest with hardly any effort. "I swear, baby, talk like that will get you kidnapped."

She laughed and toyed with the soft chest hairs sprinkled over his muscles. "No need to kidnap me, hun. I'll be right here always." Her words did something to the jovial expression he had worn all night.

A seriousness etched into the faint lines around his eyes. "You've never thought of living somewhere other than Maddyville, Cambrie?"

Well, wasn't that a mood killer. "No, not since I returned from Nashville after Aunt Annabelle's illness. I could never leave her again."

"Understood."

The air hung with unspoken words. Maybe it'd be best to not broach such a tough subject, one that had no real answers or solutions. But the conversation had already been started, leaving it in the middle wouldn't serve a purpose either. "It's like you, Miller, not being able to imagine leaving the military."

He sighed and twirled a strand of her hair in his fingers, keeping eye contact. "I've never had to think of settling down outside of military life. My career has always taken precedence over all other things. Until now. Until you. But the military is in my blood. I could quit, sure, but then I'd be miserable. I just can't think of a way to make us work in the long run when we have such obstacles separating us."

A knot formed in her throat. Avoiding this topic would've been so much better than facing the reality of their limitations.

"I've already told you that I'd never ask you to leave the military or choose between me and your career, Miller. No matter how much I enjoy our time together and wish it could be more."

"And I'd never ask you to leave your aunt. So we're fucked and not in a good way." His tone filled with a sadness she had never heard from him before.

With her heart ready to shatter into pieces at the bleak outlook, she spoke quietly. "Even if you were to retire or something, Maddyville just doesn't have opportunities for someone like you. And a career change is a decision you'd need to make on your own. I wouldn't want you to do something you know you will eventually regret and maybe end up resenting me for your decision."

"So what do we do?" His eyes held the same concern she felt. "Long distance relationships rarely work out."

Never had a question held so much angst. "I don't know. You can't keep coming here for a day and leaving to return to work. It's not fair to you. You'll exhaust yourself."

"Always worrying about everyone but yourself, Cam. I'm fine. I wouldn't travel if I couldn't do it. But the need to see you again overwhelms me and it's all I can think about after a mission is complete."

"And us not being together in a more realistic fashion doesn't bother you?"

"Well, of course it does, but I'm not willing to give up on us just yet, baby. No one knows what the future will hold, but at least we can work with the present, right?"

"Who knew you were so philosophical?" she teased, enjoying his insight, letting it ease her anxiety.

"Just stating the truth, my dear. We can take it day by day."

"Winter's coming soon. Quick visits will be even more difficult."

"Then we have to wait for me to have time for longer stays. After this visit, I can't get back for a few months anyways due to the team's schedule. But we shouldn't dwell on the future. Let's enjoy this time and we'll figure out something. Sometimes impossible problems have a way of working themselves out." He kissed her forehead, the simple endearment comforting.

"Can I tell you something that might make you mad?" she asked, needing to explain part of her feelings while they lingered in the awkward moment.

His eyebrows creased, adding sternness to his hard features. "Sure. But I won't promise not to get mad."

Fair enough. "Um, I have to admit that it's hard to send you off on missions. I get to thinking it may be the last time I see you." She blinked quickly to ward off tears. "It reminds me of how my parents left that night and never came back."

"Aww, honey," he said, his lips reaching hers for a brief touch. "Never think like that. I don't ever want to be the reason for your pain. I swear, I'm extremely careful on missions. I believe in my training and in my team. We have each other's backs always. *Always.* I happen to like living. I'd never go down without a fight, especially knowing you're here waiting, thinking of me."

"I have complete confidence in your ability to do your job, Miller. But your missions sound so dangerous and the lack of communication is scary. Not being able to reach you is nerve-wracking, not knowing if you're alive or dead."

"Yeah, I know that part does suck. I'm sorry."

"Then sometimes I'd say to myself that I should just walk away from you and not go through the pain of worrying how you're doing and not finding out until you can get in touch."

His eyes widened. "You'd walk away from me, Cambrie? Walk away from us before giving us a chance to work out?"

"Yes, I would." By the pained expression on his face, her honesty shocked him. His eyes narrowed and his jaw stiffened. "But I'd like to think I'm learning not to run from life any more. But it's taking me some time to learn how not to since I've been doing it since I was seven."

"And you should know I wouldn't let you run. That wouldn't be fair to either of us. I'm here for you, Cambrie. Maybe not always in person but know that there's nothing I wouldn't do for you."

"And you know, Miller, that not having you at all would hurt more than losing you for a little time here and there. But I guess what I'm thinking is that I wouldn't be cut out for military life anyway."

He rolled his eyes. "You're so spanked, baby girl."

"What? Why's that?"

"For putting yourself down."

"How the hell am I doing that?"

He flicked her hair over her shoulder and toyed with the long strands. "By thinking you're not cut out for military life. Honey, you're already living military life in a way. Just because you don't reside on base doesn't mean shit. You're still a part of my life, you support my military service, you spend days worrying about what I'm up to, you keep the passion alive with your emails, texts, calls, and most of all by welcoming me back into your arms after I've been gone. So, hate to break the news to you, babe, but you've been doing a damn fucking great job. And you don't even know it."

She laughed. "I love your mouth, Miller. Never know what's going to come out of it. The fact that you speak your mind is an admirable quality. Very sexy."

The corner of his mouth lifted to form a

smirk. "That so?"

"Very so." Falling in love hadn't been part of the deal when she first emailed Miller. Looking back, she couldn't say exactly when it happened, but she couldn't imagine loving anyone else. "And I do believe you told me to remind you to spank me."

"That's right, you've been a naughty girl, tempting me with this hot body all night, grinding this beautiful ass into my cock while dancing. All these curves showcased in that fucking hot mermaid costume. My God, I love every surprise you give me, Cambrie."

But do you love me? The words stayed on her tongue without being spoken. She couldn't bear knowing if he didn't love her like she did him.

There was still a very good chance his feelings for her, while serious, weren't true love. Even if he loved her, it changed nothing. She wouldn't leave Maddyville and he wouldn't leave the military.

Being together would have to mean stolen moments like this. Still, she didn't regret falling in love with Miller. How could she ever regret this wonderful feeling bubbling inside her heart for this bad ass Navy SEAL currently staring at her like she was a delicate dessert?

"You also promised me wild and hot sex. Or did you forget?" she teased, thankful the mood had turned back to playful. No sense wasting their remaining hours together debating issues out of their control.

A low growl emanated from his throat as he rolled her onto her back. "Just remember you said that, sweetheart." With a quick smack of his lips against hers, he jumped from the bed and strutted to the pile of sex toys in her nightstand.

Returning to the bed, he dropped the toys on the sheets. Cambrie leaned up on her elbows and crawled onto all fours. The urge to taste him overwhelmed her. “Bring that magnificent cock over here. I owe you the pleasure you’ve shown me.”

His grin widened as he stepped closer to the bed, his long, muscular body standing before her. “Baby, anything for you.” His cock jutted out from his body, saluting her. The thick purplish head already glistened with drops of pearly white cum.

Taking hold of his cock, she stroked her fingers up and down the length, thrilled how the erection filled her grip. “When you were licking my pussy, I wanted your cock in my mouth.”

He shook his head, standing with his hands on his hips. “Christ, Cambrie. Are you trying to make me come before your pretty mouth even sucks my cock?”

A smile formed on her lips as she leaned forward and licked at the beckoning cum. Salty and hot, a combination she couldn’t get enough of as she slid her mouth over the steel length of his engorged cock.

A moan echoed in the room and encouraged her to continue her attentions. With her jaw opened as far as it would go, she barely accommodated his thickness. Taking the solid size of him to the back of her throat earned more moans and groans. His hips rocked back and forth to fuck her mouth slowly. God, had she always had this power within her to drive a man wild?

When his hand fisted in her hair and held her in position to keep his cock in her mouth, a wave of lust hit her, increasing her rhythm until slurping sounds filled the room with his moans.

"Oh, Christ. Baby. Don't. Stop." Miller's voice trembled like his body.

Cambrie couldn't stop. Addicted to the power she wielded against this hulk of a man, Cambrie continued on, sucking his cock with an urgency she felt deep within her womb, how she had to taste him, had to give him the same pleasure he always gave her.

She ran her tongue along the thick vein that covered the length of his cock, reading somewhere of the intensity it held when stroked.

"I'm. Gonna. Come." The strangled words blurted from him. "Swallow me, baby. Oh, God. Please."

She wouldn't have it any other way as she prepared for his explosion, his cock flexing within her mouth. The first spurts of hot cum hit her tongue before she took him to the back of her throat. Hot bursts of the salty liquid ran down her throat while she greedily took her fill until each drop had been expelled and his cock empty of its seed.

His hand released her head and she felt him shudder. With slow movements, she eased his erection from her mouth, lapping over the length of him before looking up. The contentment she witnessed in the depths of the dancing eyes staring down at her filled her with pride. But she didn't have long to rejoice.

Miller settled her onto her belly in the middle of the bed. Raising her hands above her head, he slapped the handcuffs over her wrists. Lying stretched out with no way to move her arms, she was as vulnerable as ever but still had complete trust in Miller to keep her safe.

A beefy hand landed across her ass with a loud smack.

"Ow." She hadn't been prepared for the slap but was when the next one followed. Her body reacted to the sting on her exposed ass. Between her legs, her juices ran over her pussy lips, the coolness against her throbbing flesh very noticeable.

"You have the best ass to spank, Cam," he said, running a finger around the curve of her bottom. "Love the pink color where my hand left its print."

Oh, his words unglued her and she allowed the naughty girl within her to awaken. "I've been naughty. Spank me harder, Miller. Let me feel it."

It amazed her when the words fell from her lips, but she couldn't deny the urges deep inside her body or how she wished to be at Miller's mercy to experience the greatest pleasures only he could offer her.

"Not to worry, baby. When I'm done spanking you, you'll be lucky to sit down for a week. This hot ass is about to get even hotter."

Her pussy convulsed with his declaration. Oh, how she wished she could rub her clit, touch herself. But the binds at her wrists prevented such. The restraints only served to increase her arousal, drive her desire beyond measure.

From behind her, Miller's hand rained down over the cheeks of her ass, one side then the other side, back and forth, keeping a steady stream of spanks cascading over her fiery butt. The heat created by his hand penetrated to her pussy where the greedy muscles spasmed in anticipation of the orgasm building within the depths of her womb.

"Oh, Miller. Ow."

"Remember, if you want me to stop, if it gets to be too much, use your safe word. Otherwise, I'll decide when this naughty ass has had enough punishment."

Breathe. The reminder whooshed air into her oxygen-starved lungs as she hovered somewhere between pleasure and torment. "Make me come, Miller. I. Need. To Come. Oh, please. Ow. Oh."

"Maybe I won't let you come. Maybe I like to hear you beg and beg."

She whimpered, wanting to strangle him. "Be careful, Miller. Two can play that game," she warned, fighting the binds.

His laugh sounded menacing while he continued spanking her. "Maybe so, but right now you're at my mercy. Beg me to let you come and I just might."

Oh, he wanted to torture her tonight. She moaned unable to fight the rising needs within her body. "Please let me come."

"I think you can do much better than that. I need to know how badly you want to come."

She could plot his death or beg to come. Good thing for him the latter appealed more. "Miller! Make me come. Please. Oh, God, please. I need to come. Make. Me. Come."

Her body hummed in new places each time they made love. Deep inside her pussy, muscles quivered, came alive, roaring through her womb on a mission.

"Miller! Miller! Yes. Oh, Miller!"

The orgasm hit full force, unleashing a fury of trembles and shivers. With her arms stretched above her head and still held in place by the cuffs, Cambrie convulsed as Miller's hand landed one more spank to her sore bottom before he began gentle massaging of the stinging flesh.

She was lost in the euphoria of her release, floating somewhere between pleasure and pain as her ass smarted from the spanking and her pussy throbbed with the power of the orgasm.

"I swear, baby. I'll never get tired of hearing you scream my name."

Sinking into the mattress, her limbs weighing more than they should, Cambrie sucked in deep breaths. "You almost heard it yelled in frustration holding off orgasm for me. That was suicidal for you, Lt. Daly. I advise you not to try that again."

Rolls of laughter echoed as he undid her hands, gently rubbing the wrists. "I'll remember that, baby. Don't get any ideas about moving from this bed. I've had to stare at this hot ass for too long now. I want to bury my cock in its tightness."

Not wasting any time, Miller ran a lubed finger along the puckered entrance of her ass and slid inside. Her anal muscles offered some resistance, but his clever finger worked them quickly into submission and soon he fingerfucked her ass with ease.

Keeping her body in a constant state of arousal was his specialty, one that she was ever grateful for.

When his finger pulled out, disappointment filled her. But it was short lived as he inserted the lubed butt plug into her ass. The pinch lasted only seconds, replaced by a fullness that made her crave his cock to replace the toy.

"I need your cock in my ass, Miller. I want to feel your heat."

With the butt plug secured in her ass, Miller's hands rubbed her tender ass cheeks and the rest of her body with slow gentle caresses. The fire between her legs ignited once again with the tender nerves lining her pussy awakening from their spent passion.

Now a hunger consumed her again. Miller's hand slid under her body to pinch her nipples until she writhed with desire.

"Miller, I don't want to wait any longer. Fuck my ass like you fuck my pussy. I need you."

He waited for no more pleas, removing the butt plug. A slurping sound caught her curiosity and she turned to see him slathering his cock with the lube. His erection sported its usual thickness and length. Just watching his hand jerk over the engorged cock aroused her beyond explanation. Wiping his hands on a towel, he moved toward the bed again.

The mattress dipped with his weight. His arm glided under her belly to haul her onto her knees. With his hips against her ass, he pushed his cock into her tight rosette with patient strokes until he was seated fully inside of her. The tightness subsided as her body adjusted to the intrusion. The intimacy they shared never failed to thrill her, making each time better than the last.

"My God, Cambrie," he said, the words rushed, his hands gripping her upper thighs hard enough to hold himself against her. "Fucking your ass is too damn intense. You make me want to come with the first stroke." A rush of air left his lungs before he started pumping his hips again.

Moaning with the ripples of pleasures racing through her pussy that lingered from her last explosion, Cambrie reflected on the orgasm that teased her, hovering within reach yet unwilling to show itself yet. How could this man give her so much pleasure, take her body to places that stole her breath and mind?

Long strokes pounded her ass as his grip tightened. Her pussy lips, moist with her juices, ached to be touched, caressed. Her clit pulsed with a life of its own, begging for a finger to flick it or skim it. Miller fucked her ass harder and deeper than the last time, edging her toward the bliss she craved.

"Cambrie! Fuck! Oh, Cambrie!" Miller yelled, holding his cock deep within her ass. His explosion sending hot cum into her tight ass.

Rocked by his loving, Cambrie joined him with a release as powerful as the one preceding it. This orgasm had smaller but numerous tremors radiating through her womb.

"Miller. Don't. Stop."

And he didn't until they both collapsed on the bed, gulping air and murmuring words. When he climbed off of her, she didn't have the energy to move. He applied a warm washcloth to her ass, cleaning away their loving. She adored how he pampered her, always attentive to her needs.

Miller crawled back into bed and hauled her on top of him to cover them both with the blankets. He scooted her to his side and cradled her head against his chest. She draped a lazy leg over his.

"Tell me not to leave, Cambrie, and I won't." His tone was soft, but there was no mistaking the seriousness within.

Did she just hear him right?

She took a moment to let the statement sink in. She believed he would stay if she asked him to. He'd give her anything she wanted. Even if he hadn't said the words…he loved her. There was no doubt in her heart. So she did the only thing she could do.

"I won't, Miller, and never ask me to do that again," she said, leaning up on her elbow. "You're the only one who can make that choice."

Staring at the ceiling, pain etched in his expression. "I know. But there's nothing I wouldn't do for you."

"I believe that. Really I do. But you had a life before me and that life needs you, too. You make a difference in this world, Miller. I could never ask you to stop doing that. No matter how much I love you." Her words hung between them as his head slowly turned to face her.

"Why do you love me, Cambrie?"

"Because you never tried to change who I am. Only helped me discover the real me." She sighed but kept eye contact. "I like who I am when I'm with you. I'm relaxed, energized, happy. I love you, Miller, because you gave me a chance when you didn't have to. Because you have one of the biggest hearts I've ever seen."

"God, Cambrie. Just what the hell am I going to do with you?"

"Well, you'd have to give me some time to rest, but I think we can come up with some ideas."

He flashed a killer smile that made butterflies dance in her belly. "That's not what I meant."

"I know," she whispered, unable to smile. "But let's not do this to ourselves. Our lives are what they are. End of story. Dwelling on it or wracking our brains for a solution is a waste of time and energy. We just need to accept that there's no real future for us."

"My team has a saying we all believe in. Never say never."

She snuggled close, resting her cheek on the soft mat of chest hair. "Those are just words,

Miller. Reality sucks is all."

****

Cambrie loved him. Holy fucking shit in hell. When the fuck did that happen? Aw, hell. He knew she had fallen in love with him. It was easier to deny because facing reality sucked big time.

The warm body snuggled in his arms while she slept kept his cock hard and his mind wandering to all sorts of possibilities. With sleep evading him, he stared at the dark ceiling, his thoughts jumbled.

The military had been good to him throughout the years just like he had proven his worth and did a damn good job with every new challenge. He could retire, seek other employment, move near Cambrie. If he quit the military then he'd be free to move anywhere he chose.

Miller loved Cambrie. He had gone and fallen in love with this amazing woman. When? Oh, he knew exactly when it had happened even if he couldn't admit it to himself until now.

When he awoke to find her staring at him sitting on her porch, the very second they had first met. He had fallen in love first with her beauty and then with everything about her.

Closing his eyes, he prayed for sleep to come because no matter how hard he wracked his brain, there was only one solution that would work.

With a heavy heart, Miller squeezed Cambrie tighter, needing her warmth when he felt so damn cold.

Chapter Nineteen

Cambrie should really be used to this by now, but each time Miller packed up to return home, something in her heart broke, another piece shredded with pain.

"I'll miss the hell out of you, Cambrie. I don't think I can come back for a few months."

She faced him, her palms flat against his chest. "I understand. Just be safe." She didn't feel like talking, fearing she may give in to selfishness and beg him to stay.

He leaned down and kissed her lips, the heat from his body warming her. Her hands roamed his body, the last touch they'd have for months maybe. She opened her mouth, allowed his tongue to whip inside, needing his kiss to linger when he left. At her sides, his fingers kneaded her skin like they couldn't let go.

Stay. Please stay.

She took her last taste of his warmth, his power. If she didn't break the connection now, she feared she never would. Stepping back, she licked her lips. Trembling, she stood and watched him lift his duffle bag. With one last kiss to her forehead, he opened the door.

"Don't worry, baby girl. I could never stay away from you."

When the door shut, Cambrie remained where she stood. It wasn't until she heard Miller's truck speed off that she allowed herself to sink to her knees onto the floor, bury her head in her hands, and cry.

Why hadn't she begged him to stay when she knew he would've? Damn!

Deep down inside her breaking heart, she knew that wouldn't have been the right thing to do. It wouldn't have been fair to force Miller to choose between her and a career he loved. He would never ask her to choose between him and Aunt Annabelle, so she could never ask something of him that she wasn't willing to do herself.

After she was all cried out, she got back to the one thing she knew how to do. Work.

****

Waiting for the results of the grant program added to Cambrie's anxiety. She hadn't heard from Miller in four days and their hectic schedules interfered with any real communication in the three weeks since he had left. Hating her job for its constant reminder of Miller, she knew she was screwed and stuck with no options.

"Cambrie, is it true that the Veterans Affairs Department is sending a committee here today because we're a finalist for the grant?" Mrs. Ginnity asked, rushing in from outside.

"Yes, ma'am, it is. Although they were expected by now," she said, glancing at the clock on the wall by the front desk before returning to the work she had been doing. "Must be something keeping them."

"Oh, I'm sure they'll be here any minute." The woman was very giddy but Cambrie dismissed it as one of her usual quirks. "Mr. Hackler is outside waiting to greet them."

Cambrie would've replied but the front door

swung open and a highly decorated military man stepped inside with Mr. Hackler and a contingent of military personnel. Cambrie swallowed hard and stepped from behind the desk.

"Miss Brasher," Mr. Hackler began. "General Sherwald from Veterans Affairs."

She shook his hand alarmed by the number of people still streaming in through the doors. "It's a pleasure to meet you, sir."

"Ah, the pleasure is all mine, Miss Brasher. I assure you. I can't tell you how glad I am to finally meet you. I wanted to come here personally." The general's tone was confident and professional.

Cambrie caught sight of familiar faces in the crowd surrounding the general now that he had stepped forward. "Emma? Finn? Oh, my God!" she yelled and jumped into Emma's arms for a big hug before doing the same to Finn.

"God, I love when I can make Miller jealous," Finn whispered to Cambrie.

"He'd have to be here to be jealous," Cambrie said, her heart aching for the man she loved.

"Young lady, when did you lose your eyesight?" Aunt Annabelle hollered from a wheelchair behind Emma and Finn.

"Auntie? What are you doing here?" Cambrie gasped and looked around at the crowd. What was going on? Why were all these people here? Did they win the grant?

When Cambrie went to speak to the general, she froze and stared at five impeccably dressed military men standing behind their leader. "Miller?"

"About time you opened your eyes, girl," Aunt Annabelle quipped, but Cambrie ignored her.

Cambrie covered her heart with her hand and stared at Miller. "Oh, my God." She faced the general. "What is this about?"

"Like I said, Miss Brasher, I wanted to come to see you personally. You have been an example for our nation with your support of Lt. Miller Daly's military service. I have come to offer you a job with my national office in Washington, DC."

The crowd gasped and some clapped while Cambrie stood stunned, her eyes flashing between the general and Miller who hadn't made a move toward her, just remained standing with the other men in a serious stance, feet together, arms at his side.

"I've made arrangements for your aunt to move with you as well. Her doctors agree that the medical facilities in the area are superb," the general continued.

"You what?" Cambrie asked before turning to her aunt. "You'd move, Auntie? But why? Maddyville has always been your home."

Aunt Annabelle waved her hand in the air. "Oh, sweetie. There's nothing left for me in Maddyville. My home is gone. Most of my friends are dead. I feel terrible that you won't leave here because of me, so I'll come with you. We can always come back for a visit. And the general here has promised to help me learn the Internet thingy so I can, what's it called, go onboard?"

"Online," General Sherwald corrected, clearing his throat and flashing a bright smile. "Or the job can be set up in Maddyville for your aunt's convenience."

"Nonsense, general," Aunt Annabelle scolded. "We've already discussed this and I'm all for breaking out of that prison and looking forward to a change of scenery."

Miller stepped forward when the general signaled to him. "Cambrie, listen to your aunt. You have the right to want your own life. You've done a great job taking care of her and repaying her kindness. That's what family is all about." He looked back at his men then back to Cambrie. "You don't have to be alone anymore, Cam. You can be with me and together we can take care of Aunt Annabelle, with her permission of course," he said toward Aunt Annabelle.

Aunt Annabelle spoke up. "Well, I don't need much taking care of and the general has been too kind to offer to visit me in Virginia. So what's a lady have to complain about with those prospects? You youngins need to take care of each other."

Miller returned his attention to Cambrie who all but forgot the crowd around them. Her heart pounded being this close to Miller again. "I've got to tell you, Cambrie. It's either me or no one because I won't allow another guy taking my place. There's no way in holy hell I'll stand for that."

"Smooth, jackass, real smooth," one of his team scolded when her hands went to her hips and she frowned. "Name's Chance and please pardon his mouth, ma'am, but he's not used to being gentle."

"And right now his words are coming out of his ass. Name's Cade," another man said, before nodding at Miller. "Smarten up, man. Where's your romantic side?"

Miller rolled his eyes. "Ignore them, Cambrie. They're just jealous."

"Can say that again," Chance said. "Screw this one up, Miller, and you ain't ever living it down. Ever."

Miller smirked. "They're half right, Cam. I'm not good at sharing feelings and emotions. But I know what I want and plan to get it." He sighed. "What I'm trying to say is…I love you. I loved you from the moment I woke up on your porch and found you watching me. That day my life changed forever and for the best. I always knew that serving in the military was my calling. It's what I was meant to do. But, honey, it's not all I'm meant to be. I can be your husband, too. I can do both, I promise. My job keeps civilians like you safe and I wouldn't choose any other career until I'm forced to retire from this one. But through it all, I will love you and give you the best life I can."

"That better include keeping yourself safe, Miller," Cambrie said, tears pricking at her eyes.

He looked stunned. "Does that mean you'll marry me?"

"That depends."

He scowled. "What the hell do you mean? Depends on what?"

"On whether or not you'll ask me. I didn't hear you propose. Did anyone else?"

The crowd chanted "no" while shaking their heads.

Miller smirked and got down on his knee, pulling a ring from his coat pocket. Holding it up, he stared at it then at her. "Cambrie Brasher, would you do me the honor of walking down the aisle, taking my name, and keeping me in line for the rest of my life? I love you and promise that love will be as strong when we're together as it'll be when we're apart. Marry me, Cambrie, and love me forever."

"Will I still be in your dreams nightly?" she

whispered.

"Oh God, baby. You *are* my dream."

"Then yes, I'll marry you, Lt. Miller Daly, because I love you more than I could've ever imagined possible. You were never just my pen pal. You are my other half, the part that completes my soul. I love you." Tears welled in her eyes. Happy, long-awaited tears.

Miller slipped the ring on her finger and stood. He lifted her into his arms and kissed her. The crowd erupted around them with cheers and applause. His men slapped at his back once he placed her back on her feet.

The general yelled out. "Does anyone want to know who won the library grant?"

"Yes!" the crowd screamed and then fell silent.

The general faced Cambrie. "Miss Brasher, on behalf of the Veterans Affairs Department, I am pleased to award the one hundred thousand library grant to Highland Library for its fine example of how to support our troops and proving that patriotism still exists today. There were selfless acts of kindness documented by Lt. Daly that were not only orchestrated by Miss Brasher but supported by the entire community, young and old alike. Together you have made a difference in the lives of countless veterans with your donations. Congratulations."

The crowd cheered. Pride swelled within Cambrie. At her side, Miller squeezed her hand.

The general continued speaking. "I have also included Miss Brasher's signed petition in a letter to Congress about supporting bills to increase all veterans' benefits instead of trying to decrease them with budget cuts. The overwhelming support in that petition will hopefully open the eyes of lawmakers who choose to cut funding for the very people securing their freedom to run for office and freely express their opinions.

"Miss Brasher, your new job will focus on the efforts you've begun in that petition. I believe that, while you will have your work cut out for you, there is no one better to defend our soldiers' benefits."

"Thank you, general. And I look forward to the hard work," Cambrie said, hoping it was not all a dream.

Once again the crowd erupted.

Miller and Cambrie stepped over to her aunt. "Aunt Annabelle, thank you, ma'am, for your permission to marry your niece. I'll make her happy. I promise."

Cambrie's jaw dropped. "You knew about this, Auntie?"

"Yes I did. This young man came to me on his own asking permission. Why, I had to keep my tongue in my mouth for far too long before he could get here to do the official deed. But I must say you proved me wrong, Miller."

"How so?" he asked.

"I once told my niece that today's young people didn't know anything about romance. You certainly do, Miller. That's why you got my blessing and because you make my Cambrie smile like I've never seen before. Now excuse me while I go speak with the general. He's single you know." She winked and wheeled herself off.

Cambrie gasped. "Did you hear her? That's not my aunt in that wheelchair. She would never openly flirt with a man."

"Maybe you just never noticed that side of

her," Miller said, holding his arm at her waist.

"Maybe. And now we're moving to Virginia. Wow." Cambrie was still in shock.

"Thank you, Cambrie," Miller said. "The general tore up my retirement paperwork."

"You were leaving the military? For me?"

"Yes, even if it's the job I love, I would've found another. As long as I'm with you, baby girl, that's the only thing that matters. You were stuck here because of your commitment to your aunt, which couldn't be changed. I had a contract with the Government that, while also a commitment, had more flexibility to change so I could be with you. But your aunt had spoken to the general about trying to keep us together once she learned of my plans."

"She what?" Cambrie would never under estimate her aunt again.

"Yeah, it's not every day a general gets involved in matchmaking, but my exemplary service record caught his attention and between your aunt's phone call, my request for retirement, and your library winning the grant, well, he said it was a no-brainer. He gets you as a great employee while keeping me and making the acquaintance of your aunt. He told me on the ride here that he's been widowed for three years, so he knows something about loneliness. And Aunt Annabelle said seeing you happy has given her a new breath of life."

She clutched his shoulders. "Wow. I never knew any of this was happening. I missed you so much, Miller. I regretted not begging you to stay."

"You won't have any reason to miss me, at least for a while. Not with us getting married and the babies."

"What babies?"

"The ones we're going to have. I plan on enjoying your sexy body every chance I get. We'll make us lots of babies."

"Kiss, kiss, kiss," his men chanted behind them.

"Oh God. Is this what the wedding will be like?" Cambrie asked, thrilled with the turn of events.

"I'm afraid so. From what they've told me, they didn't let Emma and Finn come up for air."

Cambrie laughed as Miller leaned in close to her ear. "But all you need to think about is how fantastic the honeymoon will be, Mrs. Daly."

Wrapping her arms around his neck, she never planned to let go. "I can honestly say I have no worries about that. Now kiss me before the crowd gets too wild and Mr. Hackler has a heart attack."

"I love you, Cambrie Brasher."

"I love you more, Miller Daly."

Her lips met his and the rest of her life began.

The End

Make a Wish and Blow

Christina James

Chapter One

Turning another year older wasn't the highlight of Cassandra Wright's day. Being a horny single woman just added to her misery. She sat at her kitchen table sipping the glass of wine she'd poured as soon as she arrived home from work. She ignored the four voice mail messages from various friends wanting to get together to celebrate her birthday. Oh sure, she enjoyed partying, dancing, and having a great time as much as the next person, but none of that mattered as she held a private pity party in her tiny kitchen. The man she desperately loved had apparently forgotten her birthday.

When her doorbell rang, she cringed, knowing one of her friends had decided to come by and haul her out on the town. If she believed they'd go away, she'd ignore the ding-dong sound. But she knew better. With her car in the driveway during a humid Connecticut summer evening, it was obvious she was home and, unless she wanted to continue to listen to the shrill ringing, she'd better answer the door. She prayed they wouldn't sing a pathetic rendition of Happy Birthday. She gently placed the wine glass on her counter before walking to the front door.

When she peeked through the view hole, she immediately perked up, recognizing Daren Hughes, her best friend since sixth grade. So he hadn't forgotten her birthday after all! Daren was also, to her utter disappointment and constant torture, her *platonic* friend.

Cassandra opened the door and quickly ran her gaze over the hard male body leaning against the doorframe. At twenty-nine, Daren was six-feet-two with chocolate brown eyes and thick wavy hair the color of caramel. His body was toned and lean, without an ounce of fat anywhere, thanks to his relentless daily workout regimen. The solid muscles of his thighs strained against the light blue material of his jeans. Broad arms and flat abs were covered by a tight short sleeve black T-shirt. Daren made her mouth water and her pussy clench every time she set eyes on him. What she wouldn't give to nibble on him for one damn night. She could easily picture her teeth nibbling along that hard skin inch by inch, tasting the saltiness of flesh that was firm and muscular. She'd start her feasting along the curve of his thick neck and head down to…well…anywhere on his body would be fine with her.

Cassandra spoke softly, squashing the urge to fan herself. "If you start singing to me, I'll slam the door and not talk to you for a week."

"You'd break my heart, babe," Daren replied easily, his deep voice lulling her into a hornier state. He held a lovely bouquet of red roses and a small ice cream cake. "Besides, the only singing I do is in the shower. You'd have to join me, if you're interested in how well I carry a tune. I promise you won't be disappointed."

His smile was devastating as it widened to show perfect teeth, the kind also made for nibbling heated skin. Her body heated a few degrees at the thought of his teeth grazing lazily over her hot flesh. God, how she wanted to take that shower. If only he was serious and not teasing her like he usually enjoyed doing, she'd strip now and haul him into the bathroom. Just the thought made her panties dampen with arousal. Her legs shifted in response and her pussy heated up. If she could only clench her thighs together hard enough, then maybe her cunt wouldn't be so aware of Daren's body inches from hers. She hated how easily he could arouse her with just one look, one word, one touch.

She leaned her shoulder on the open door for support. "Tell me, Daren, did you stop by to flirt or did you have something else on your mind?"

Shrugging, he kept his eyes on her. "Wanted to wish you a happy birthday."

She sighed. "It's just another day."

"No, it's your special day. You should be celebrating, especially since it's Friday."

She leaned her head against the door. "Only kids celebrate birthdays. Adults really have no right. It only signifies another year of leaving youth behind."

He frowned. "Ah, I can see the Cynical Cass is here tonight. Pity, since I much prefer the Playful Cass."

If only she could tell him about all the games she'd like to play with him between her 1200-thread count soft-as-heaven bed sheets. Oh, the hell with that. She'd play games with him on the cold hard floor if it meant that magnificent body was pressing hers into the gleaming wood planks. But his friendship was more important than a few orgasms—no matter how glorious they'd be.

"Not cynical. Just worn out. That's all." *I'm exhausted from facing the fact I can't have you.*

"Uh-huh." He sounded doubtful. Of course he

wouldn't believe her. She'd never been able to lie to him.

She prayed he wouldn't interrogate her now. If he did, there was a good chance she'd jump into his arms and spill her heart.

"You gonna invite me in?"

"Oh God, yes. I'm sorry. Told you I was tired." She stepped aside and let him move past before shutting the door.

He placed the cake on the foyer table in her front hall and faced her. His massive body hovered over her, making her feel shorter than her five-foot-four stature, and then pinned her against the closed door.

"No problem," he said, leaning on his elbow and pushing into her personal space. Now he looked straight down into her eyes as she tilted her head back to keep eye contact.

"In answer to your question, I came over to spend the night with my favorite girl. Well, that is unless she has other plans." His finger skimmed her cheek. She sucked in her breath.

She laughed hoping it didn't sound nervous. "Favorite girl, my ass. You have more girls than you can keep straight."

His face remained serious. "Hey, that may be true, sweetie, but none of them compare to you. You're my favorite. So what do you say? You going to let me make the night memorable for you?"

She raised her eyebrow. "Memorable, huh? Now you've got my attention."

He smiled. "I bet I do. And you've got mine. The night is yours. What do you want to do?"

Fuck you, then fuck you again.

She looked past his body to where he left the

ice cream cake. "Looks like we should start with dessert first, before it melts, then get something for dinner."

His thigh brushed hers as he turned to glance at the cake then faced her again. The firm touch of his muscle against the bare skin under her skirt heated her flesh. A slow, warm tingle traveled up her thigh to pool in her belly. The warmth was like the slow stroking of a flame, every cell in her body aware of his closeness. Every cell longed for his touch. Even her brain wasn't immune as she struggled to keep focused on the connection. Just a slight shift of his feet and they no longer touched. With the connection lost, disappointment filled her.

"Sounds good," he said, simply.

She blew out an aggravated breath. She was practically humping his friggin' leg. What the hell had gotten into her tonight? Why was she acting like a schoolgirl instead of a grown woman? She rationalized that any breathing woman would react to such a sexy male body. It was all just a normal female-male reaction and nothing to do with the fact that each night she dreamt of his hot, sweaty body gliding over hers in every position imaginable. And now the subject of those dreams was standing oh so close to her.

She quickly snapped back to reality. "Thank you for the roses, Daren. I can smell them all the way over here."

"Mmmmm. I can only smell you, Cass." His head bent, his nose lightly resting behind her ear. When he inhaled, his warm breath teased her ear. She expected her legs to drop from under her. "Of course, you always smell great. Makes a man want to lay you down and kiss you from head to toe. You're intoxicating, Cass." His whispered words created goosebumps over her entire body.

Her mouth opened in shock. It took her a minute to find her voice. “Daren?”

He slowly pulled his head back, but remained nose to nose with her. She swallowed hard, her mouth suddenly so dry. He said nothing. His gaze scanned her face before fixating on her eyes. Was that lust in the brown depths staring back at her?

“Daren? Do you have a head injury or something?”

“No, babe. Why?”

This close, Cassandra could see the creases around his eyes when he frowned.

“Because it sounds like you’re hitting on me. That thing you just did to my ear…”

“Thing?” he asked, his lips forming a sexy smirk.

“Oh, shut up. You know what I mean.” She shoved against him, but he didn’t budge. “You practically stuck your tongue in my ear.”

“Mmmmm. Now that sounds like fun.”

What? Oh God, Daren had obviously encountered extraterrestrials, because she was not his type and yet he was clearly hitting on her. Hadn’t she dreamt of this moment? But now that it was happening, it seemed so surreal.

“What’s gotten into you?” she demanded, her back against the door and her eyes mesmerized by his.

He smiled again, his eyes offering a challenge. “Tell me to stop and I will.”

Stop? Was he fucking crazy? This was the closest he’d been to her other than on a dance floor, and he’d never pulled these moves on her there. Oh, hell no, she didn’t want it to stop.

She smiled, her heart did a slow drum roll.

"So is this why you came over? To tease me? Doesn't sound like a very nice thing to do to your best friend."

"It's not a very nice thing to do to myself either."

"What are you talking about?"

His gaze flicked down to his waist then back to hers. "I think if you lowered those gorgeous eyes of yours south of my belt, you'd see that you've given me a hard-on with no relief in sight."

Okay, she'd just *look*, but only to satisfy her curiosity. And she didn't care about any damn superstitions about curiosity and cats. She was a woman. Her eyes widened at the obvious erection straining against the front of his jeans. The thickness grew longer as she watched and she swore it flexed. Well, now she knew what curiosity did to her *pussy*…it flooded instantly with desire.

"*I* gave *you* that? You're the one who has me pinned against the damn door, practically sucking on my neck."

"I hardly have you pinned, Cass. You could move away at any time." He leaned in again, his lips against her ear. "But make it soon before I change my mind about letting you get away. Maybe I like to have you pinned as you call it."

She took a long steadying breath, closing her eyes briefly, then opening them to see that he was still there. "So this is what you came here for? To play games?"

"Do you really want to know why I came here tonight, Cass?"

"I've only asked like five times."

A long finger brushed a curly strand of hair behind her ear. "I wanted to see you. Wanted to make your birthday special." His voice dropped to barely louder than a whisper. “And, of course, you need your birthday spanking.”

For a long moment, Cassandra could only stare at her handsome best friend, the vision of him spanking her the only thought in her mind. His words, his stare, entranced her.

“Promises, promises,” she muttered, not really meaning to say it out loud, but it was too late. The words had slipped passed her lips.

The gleam of Daren’s eyes told Cassandra he wasn’t kidding.

“Are you serious?” she asked, her voice giving away her shock followed by a nervous giggle.

He continued looking down at her. “Absolutely. You know better than anyone that once I set my mind to something, I finish it.”

She swallowed hard and told herself to breathe. She wanted to speak, but her voice was mute. When she opened her mouth to take a deep breath, words slowly formed. “And you know better than anyone that I don’t play games, Daren. So stop. We’d better eat that ice cream cake before it melts everywhere.”

She pushed easily past, his muscular body giving way. She walked the few feet to the table and picked up the box and flowers. Daren’s hard body pressed against her, his chest to her back.

His voice whispered into her ear. “I’m not into playing games either, Cass, unless, of course, they include sex toys and paddles. You take life too serious. I’m here to show you how to have a little fun.”

She turned to face him, her bundles getting squished between their bodies when he didn’t move back even an inch. “I know how to have fun,

Daren. Let's start with this cake, then you're taking me dancing."

He followed her into the kitchen and leaned against the counter while she busied herself with plates, forks, and a knife.

His hand clasped over hers when she went to slice the cake. "Uh-huh, Cass. Not so fast."

"It's melting. If we wait any longer it'll be soup."

He stood behind her. His arms circled her until his hands covered hers as she held the knife over the cake. His mouth rested on her ear. Every cell in her body was alive with the awareness that he was hard, muscular, and potent. Her pussy wept with little waves of pleasure, pleading for his attention. She did everything she could not to lean her head back onto his chest and offer her throat up for his exploration.

"You need to make a wish, baby. Make it one I can help come true."

The promise in his voice was all she needed to tremble. She swallowed hard, closed her eyes, and formed a thought. There was only one wish she wanted—Daren to be hers, forever. No fling would do. No one-night stand would satisfy. That would leave her aching more than she was now. One taste of Daren would make her want him forever. She knew that as much as she knew she needed air to live.

"Make a wish, Cass. Make a wish," Daren whispered into her ear.

Cassandra silently made her wish, allowing herself a moment to envision it coming true and waking up to Daren every day for the rest of her life. But the Roaming Romeo was not the settling down type. Daren preferred a different woman in his bed every night. He liked to play and enjoyed variety. To him, the thrill was in the chase. Once he got a woman in his bed he tired of her quickly and set his sights on the next target. Cassandra couldn't ever remember when Daren had a steady girlfriend. She had managed to stay in his life all these years simply because she'd never fucked him. Aw hell, didn't he just think of her like he would a sister? She could hear her dreams slowly shatter. If only birthday wishes could become reality.

Cassandra sighed and opened her eyes.

"Gonna tell me what the wish was, Cass?" Daren cooed, still close to her ear.

"No. You know if I tell you then it won't come true."

He laughed and raised his head, but remained with his arms around her. "Or maybe I could make it come true. There's nothing I wouldn't do for you, sweetheart. You know all you have to do is ask."

Would you be mine? Cassandra smiled at the cliché and immediately thought of the little Valentine cards kids traded at school. Daren could never be hers.

But at least she had his friendship. Adding sex to the mix would destroy the one relationship that had remained a constant in her life. Even the best orgasm in the world wasn't worth that, unless there could be future orgasms. Her only future with Daren was as his *platonic* best friend.

"You've brought me cake. That's a start." She avoided eye contact, feeling too vulnerable about her silly wishes.

Daren helped her slice into a cake that was now very creamy. She scooped two pieces onto plates, handed him one, and walked to the kitchen table. He sat next to her, his knee brushing her leg. Why was she so aware of his touch tonight?

She welcomed the coldness from the ice cream. Her body felt as if she'd laid out in the sunshine all day. She prayed her cheeks weren't flushed, although the warmth indicated they were. So she kept her head lowered, hoping the ice cream would cool her down.

"This is delicious. Very creamy," Daren said, his voice hinting of charm she didn't believe was just for silly ice cream. Could it be for her?

Cassandra risked a glance up and wished she hadn't. Daren was licking his spoon, front to back, in slow strokes. Visions of him doing that to her pussy danced in her head.

She spoke softly, her eyes still mesmerized by his tongue. "This was a very nice surprise, Daren. Thank you."

"Pleasure's all mine."

She laughed when a drop of vanilla ice cream smeared onto the corner of his mouth when he took another spoonful. "Eat much? You're wearing it," she teased, placing her spoon carefully on her plate.

She leaned over, a gesture too automatic to think about, and wiped her fingertip across the corner of his mouth to remove the ice cream drop. As fast as a lightening, he captured her hand. She sat in stunned fascination as he raised her finger to his mouth, his firm lips closing over it and taking it into the wet, warmth of his mouth. She gasped when he sucked on her finger with a slow pull so erotic that her pussy spasmed in greedy awareness. Oh my God, his mouth was like heaven—full of promises of out-of-this-world pleasures.

Her eyes shot to his, the chocolate brown color glazed over with lust. His mouth moved slowly over her finger, licking it up then down. His stare was intense, her body reacting in more ways than she could imagine from such a simple touch. Her skin was feverish. Her mind was blank. The smell of vanilla from the cake made her drunk with desire. All she could focus on, all she could see, was Daren's mouth holding her finger prisoner. All she could feel was the heat of his mouth, the pressure of his tongue.

With deliberate slowness, he withdrew her finger from his mouth, kissing the tip before releasing it. He smiled wickedly, the devilish grin acknowledging that he'd turned her on.

"My, with lips like those, it's no wonder you can have any woman you want," Cassandra said, trying to make light of the situation. The last thing she wanted was to confirm the affect he had on her.

"Not true. I don't always get every woman I want."

She laughed and stood to bring her plate to the sink. "Yeah, right. There isn't a woman in this state that hasn't fallen into your bed."

"You haven't," he said matter-of-factly as he brought his plate to the sink and stood beside her.

"Ah, true. But we're best friends, so I don't count."

"On the contrary, my dear, I believe you count a lot."

She stared at him before speaking. She didn't want to be teased right now. "I need to change. You're taking me dancing. So go home, change, and pick me up in an hour."

He smiled, wide and bright. "Aren't you the

bossy little thing, huh? But you forget that I like to be in charge."

"Your Dominant side doesn't count with me. I'm your friend not your lover, so dominating me won't happen."

He smiled dangerously, as if she'd just challenged a tiger to a wrestling match. Expecting a smart-ass comeback from him, she was shocked when he said nothing but continued to watch her intensely.

"It's my birthday. I get to call the shots," she continued and walked him by the hand to the door. "One hour."

His hand squeezed hers before letting go. Once in the hall, Daren turned to face her, his eyes dancing with heat. "One hour, Cass, and I'll be back. If you're not ready then we go out the way you are when I get here. Dressed or not. And I choose the place we dance."

His smile was soft but he left no room for argument as he swiftly turned and walked out into the night. Cassandra looked at her watch, noted the time, and smiled. If he thought he could boss her around, he'd better think twice. After all these years, didn't the man know any better? Oh, she would sorely test Daren's Dominant side if he thought of using it on her.

Daren Hughes would be eating out of her hand by the end of the night not just sucking on her finger.

About the Author…

Award winning, multi-published author Christina James lives in a Massachusetts suburb with her two children. When penning stories, she enjoys writing of romance and heartache and of characters who overcome the odds. Passion is at the heart of every tale, and she strives to create realistic characters, so the reader can fall in love with them as much as she does. A sucker for a good love story, Christina writes hot, sensual romances with a little sarcastic wit and some humor in a contemporary setting. Look for her naughty Operation Series to continue featuring the other Navy SEALs. For naughty and wicked romance with no strings attached…read a Christina James novel.

Other titles by Christina James:
A Place to Call Home
For the Love of a Woman
Make A Wish and Blow
Operation: Spank Me
Saving Christmas
Web of Lies

www.christinajamesauthor.com/
Join Christina on Facebook
www.facebook.com/#!/profile.php?id=100003019022368&sk=wall

Here's what reviewers are saying about Christina James' books:

"In *Operation: Spank Me*, the interplay between Emma and Finn is not only scorching hot but touching as well (pun intended). *Operation: Spank Me* is not just a kinky sexual exploration…but the journey of two lonely people finding that they need someone else in their life, and that special person is a friend they already have. *Operation: Spank Me* surpassed my expectations with both its emotional story and wicked scenes between Emma and Finn. This one is a keeper!"
Five Hearts From Vicky at Sizzling Hot Books

"The more I read, *Web of Lies*, the more I couldn't stop reading it. This book had it all, drama, romance with a hint of mystery. With all of these elements, this book is recommended to those who need to be reminded that even though life has its downs, it has ups as well."
4 Stars from M. Whelehan at Night Owl Reviews

"*Make a Wish and Blow* is a spicy erotica novel, that will have you breathing heavy, because of the heat between Daren and Cassandra…"
Four Hearts from Marissa D. at Sizzling Hot Books

"*Operation: Spank Me* is my kind of military mission. Both sweet and full of heat, *Operation: Spank Me* is one successful mission. For those who enjoy the fire hot and for it to dominate the story, this is one you must check out."
Four Stars from Michelle R. at The Romance Reviews

"*Operation: Spank Me* is an interesting study of personalities, Emma's, Finn's and their family relationships, which guide their adult lives and determine how they react to situations and to each other. The sex is scorching and my e-reader has the burn marks to prove it…it is non-stop fun and games, in the bedroom, the garden…You will enjoy it."
Four Stars from Patrizia Murray at Manic Readers

www.ingramcontent.com/pod-product-compliance
Lightning Source LLC
Chambersburg PA
CBHW070656180626
46817CB00006B/2394

* 9 7 8 1 9 3 8 7 9 9 0 1 3 *